TOO MANY YESTERDAYS

TOO MANY
YESTERDAYS

Sara Hylton

This first world edition published 2009
in Great Britain and in the USA by
SEVERN HOUSE PUBLISHERS LTD of
9–15 High Street, Sutton, Surrey, England, SM1 1DF.
Trade paperback edition published
in Great Britain and the USA 2009 by
SEVERN HOUSE PUBLISHERS LTD

British Library Cataloguing in Publication Data

Hylton, Sara.
  Too Many Yesterdays.
  1. Birthday parties–Fiction. 2. Family reunions–Fiction.
  3. Family secrets–Fiction. 4. Great Britain–Social
  conditions–1945- –Fiction. 5. Domestic fiction.
  I. Title
  823.9'14–dc22

ISBN-13: 978-0-7278-6793-3   (cased)
ISBN-13: 978-1-84751-163-8   (trade paper)

All Severn House titles are printed on acid-free paper.

Typeset by Palimpsest Book Production Ltd.,
Grangemouth, Stirlingshire, Scotland.
Printed and bound in Great Britain by
MPG Books Ltd., Bodmin, Cornwall.

To my friend Marg in recognition of her continuing confidence and encouragement.

You may give them your love but not your thoughts,
For they have their own thoughts,
You may house their bodies but not their souls,
For their souls dwell in the house of tomorrow,
You may strive to be like them,
But seek not to make them like you,
For life goes not backward nor tarries with yesterday.

A THIRD–CENTURY PERSIAN POET

One

It couldn't have been anything else but a perfect day for the eightieth birthday of Charlotte Chaytor, the lady of the manor. And although it was only just after eight o'clock large white vehicles were already trundling along the narrow country road towards the large house set in its acres of gardens and lush green lawns. A spacious marquee had been in place since the day before and now the vans were being used to bring caterers, waiters and crates of china, indeed everything to ensure that the day would be perfect.

In one of the cottage gardens on the road leading up to the manor Annie O'Connor was already busy looking for non-existent weeds and erring branches that didn't need trimming. There was a look of annoyance on her face as she beheld a small plump woman plodding up the road and obviously heading in her direction.

She could cheerfully do without Molly Woods' company this morning of all mornings. She'd promised to meet a group of her friends for coffee around lunchtime with the express purpose of giving them a full report on the comings and goings further up the road; now Molly Woods would make every excuse under the sun to hang around. Showing that she was not welcome would not deter her; she'd known Molly Woods too long not to know what she was capable of, even when she came through the gate with a huge smile seemingly unaware of Annie's less than polite welcome.

'What have you come for?' she snapped.

'Well, I thought you'd be on your own, we could keep each other company,' she replied.

'Well, I'm busy in the garden right now,' Annie answered sharply.

'I thought you had a gardener,' Molly snapped.

'Well, they don't do everything do they, there's always something for me to do.'

'Your garden looks all right to me.'

Annie proceeded to push and poke in the shrubbery, and Molly said, 'Why don't we go inside and have a cup of tea? Nothing's going to happen along this road for hours yet, the family won't be arriving until much later on.'

There was no getting out of it so the two women went inside the cottage and Annie could do nothing but ask her visitor to sit down and wait for the kettle to boil.

Molly's sister Rose had worked for the Chaytor family for years as a kitchen maid before she retired and Molly was quick to bring her into the conversation.

'My sister Rose used to talk about the family all the time,' she began. 'She saw the girls growin' up and Mrs Chaytor was allus nice to the staff, very kind she was. I suppose they'll all be comin' to the do.'

'Well, I'm not so sure about Miss Gloria, doesn't she live in Austria?'

'It's not the earth away.'

'Maybe not, but it's hardly on the doorstep, and when does she ever come.'

'Today could be an exception.'

'And there's that daughter of hers, Elvira wasn't she called? My but she was a little madam, allus in mischief. It's ten years since she left here, will she be comin' do you suppose?'

'They all used to come here in the summer,' Annie recalled. 'The girls were so pretty. I used to hear them in the gardens, and that youngest one Elvira was into horses, riding past the cottage and allus smiling she was. She used to ride with the boys mostly, particularly that boy Master Alex brought home.'

'Oh, I remember him all right. Roland Bannister. My but he was a handsome lad, all the girls fancied him, but then that girl Joyce liked him, and they were pushed together.'

'Why for heaven's sake?'

'Well, she was such a nice girl, beautiful, gentle, very nice and you could never say that about Elvira.'

'Why Elvira?'

'Because she fancied Roland Bannister too, and I used to see 'em going off together. I don't think Joyce Mansell was into horses.'

'How do you know all this?'

'Because I live near the market, don't I — and nothing that goes on in this part of the road escapes me seein' it. My husband used to sit in the garden keepin' his eye on things. After his stroke he didn't have much else to do and the youngsters used to wave to him all the time.'

'Ay, well, he was only an onlooker. My sister Rose lived in the house so she knew more about what was goin' on. She told me Miss Joyce was destined for the Bannister lad.'

'Wasn't her father somethin' in the church?'

'Deacon at the cathedral, or somethin' bigger. Could have been a bishop no less.'

'And what was goin' for him?'

'Came from a rich family, his father was a lawyer or somethin'. Isn't that what he is now?'

'I've no idea.'

'It's very quiet on the road now, it seems to me all the vans 'ave arrived. Did you make that cake?'

'Yes. I makes the same one every week, favourite it is with the WI.'

Annie handed over the cake stand for Molly to take another slice and after a few seconds Molly said, 'The old lady's been a good soul for the village, allus givin' her time for the schools, the functions and the things goin' on – the dog shows and the agricultural shows, the art exhibitions and the singin' concerts. She was a magistrate till she retired and after her husband died there was really no call for her to do all that but she did.

'My sister Rose still had that vase she gave her when she retired. It was worth a bob or two but she gave it her daughter when she got married.'

They both leapt up with alacrity at the sight of a long black car driving past the cottage and Annie said feelingly, 'That's not one of the caterers. It could be family.'

'Well, we couldn't 'ave seen who was in the car even if we'd been in the garden,' Molly said. 'I still say it's too early for family.'

'Won't they be comin' early to help out?'

'Why should they? They have servants and Mrs Martin Shand has been here all week.'

'Which daughter is that?'

'Glenda, the eldest one. My sister Rose allus said she was the nicest one, Miss Georgia was stuck up and Miss Gloria won't be in evidence.'

'We don't know that for sure.'

'What? Three marriages, this last one to a foreigner – and when has she ever been around, either her or her daughter?'

'There's another car,' Annie said quickly.

'Well it can't be anybody important. Time for another cup of tea don't ye think.'

Annie felt exasperated. She already knew the outcome of the morning. Molly would accompany her to the cafe and hog the conversation, and there wouldn't be much to tell. At the rate they were going on 'my sister Rose's memoirs' would be the sole topic of conversation.

'It's only half past nine,' Molly said. 'Mark my words there'll be nothin' going on up there for a while yet.'

'It's not an evening thing,' Annie said. 'The old lady's eighty, she'll not be wantin' the party to go on all day.'

'Why ever not? She's attendin' things at the school here that take place at night, surely for her own party she'll be up for it.'

It did no good to argue and, resigned to how their morning was progressing, Annie offered her guest more tea.

Charlotte Chaytor hadn't slept well. She'd been aware of the activity going on outside her window for some time, the comings and goings of traffic and hurrying footsteps, muffled conversation, and she greeted the housemaid's smiling face with a shake of her head.

'Oh, ma'am, it's a beautiful mornin',' Milly said, 'it's goin' to be a wonderful day.'

'How old are you, Milly?' Charlotte asked gently.

'I'm seventeen, ma'am.'

'Seventeen, now that's something to celebrate. Not an eightieth, don't you think?'

'Oh no, ma'am, my grandmother's only seventy but she doesn't look as good as you. I hopes I live to be eighty.'

Charlotte didn't continue the conversation, a seventeen-year-old would never understand.

She drank her tea, ignored the toast and, reaching for her walking stick, she eased herself out of the bed. She looked at her reflection in the mirror and asked herself for the third time that morning, 'Why eighty, what is so wonderful about being eighty?'

The mirror showed a face that was still comely. Good bone structure and eyes as blue and beautiful as they'd been throughout her life.

Silver hair where once it had been golden hadn't detracted from her once acclaimed beauty, but another wrinkle, another brown spot. No, eighty was not a reason to celebrate but her daughter had put so much into this affair she had to be appreciative or she'd upset everybody.

The door opened and her eldest daughter Glenda came in, smiling, embracing her, saying gently, 'Happy birthday, darling, there's loads of mail for you and so many presents it'll take you all morning to look at them.'

'Why do people bother? I don't need anything, they should be spending their money on their things,' Charlotte answered her.

'Oh, Mother, they want to do this for you, and please don't tell any of them that. How do you feel this morning?'

'I feel the same every morning, Glenda, my arthritis isn't good and it's going to be a long day.'

'It'll be a wonderful day. Everybody happy to see you – you have so many friends.'

Friends: oh, yes, she had friends in plenty; she had a family too, but there were doubts about them that raised too many problems. Looking at her mother's expression Glenda said, 'Mother, stop worrying about the family. Georgia and her brood are coming, don't even think about Gloria, she's always been unpredictable.'

'Well, she isn't coming is she?'

'No, but Elvira's coming, that's something of a surprise.'

'What sort of an excuse did Gloria give?'

'Darling, she lives in Austria, it's a long way away.'

'I know where Austria is, I've been there many times when I was young and travel was harder in those days. Why isn't she coming?'

'She's sent you presents, Mother, and she and her husband are attending some function in Vienna that they couldn't possibly get out of. Really, Mother, we don't know anything about their commitments so we can only believe what she tells us.'

'And Elvira, is she living in Austria too – where did you send her invitation?'

'To her, Mother, in Vienna.'

'And did she reply from Vienna?'

'I'm not sure, how can I possibly remember where all the replies came from. She's coming, Mother, shouldn't that be enough?'

'She had the makings of a tearaway, Glenda. I hope she's changed.'

'That was ten years ago, Mother.'

'I know, but why do we never hear from her, why doesn't she write or come to see me?'

Glenda didn't answer, but she was remembering Elvira with her shining auburn hair and green eyes, her temper and her often unruly behaviour. Her penchant for boys, particularly the boys her sisters and cousins favoured, particularly Roland Bannister who Joyce Mansell had adored.

'She could be married,' her mother was saying.

'Well, she's coming alone to your party.'

'That doesn't tell us anything.'

'Mother, let's leave it until tomorrow. We'll all look back on today and tell ourselves how perfect it's been.'

'I don't know which dress to wear,' Charlotte said. 'What do you think?'

'Oh, the blue one, darling. You bought it specially, and you always look your best in blue.'

'I did once. Now I'm not so sure. I thought something a little more subdued.'

Glenda laughed. 'Subdued, Mother? It's not flamboyant, it's a beautiful dress and just right for the day. Do wear that and I'll look for that wrap that will be just perfect.'

'Will I need a wrap? It's June, and warm. We're not sitting outside.'

'I know, but it might get draughty and I don't want you catching cold. Do you want any help or shall I ask Mrs Johnson to help you?'

'No, she fusses too much. I'm better on my own.'

Charlotte knew she was being fractious but she was wishing the day was over. Georgia would be irritating Glenda with talk about her children's prowess, always attempting one-upmanship, and she'd never really liked Peter Georgia's husband. He was vain and cynical, and he and Glenda's husband Martin had never hit it off. Then there was Elvira, always Elvira. What had the last ten years done to her youngest grandchild?

She was remembering her three daughters as children: two pretty ones and one gloriously beautiful one – the one who had had the pick of boys and who had elected to marry Dennis Lester, the playboy of the group. Too much money; too much swank; and too much bravado, which had ended his life on the hunting field ten months after his marriage.

Then there had been James Stanhope: older, richer and a barrister. James had been a decent man but Gloria had never really loved him even though she had presented him with their only child, Elvira.

Throughout their marriage Gloria had had affairs with several different men, including the husbands of some of their friends. Gloria Stanhope had been very well known for behaviour, inappropriate for her circumstances and what was expected of her.

When James died at fifty-five he left a beautiful wife and a ten-year-old daughter. Gloria was rich, independent and determined to live her life to the full without any interference from anybody, and so she'd gone off in search of the sort of life she'd yearned for and thought she was entitled to. She'd left Elvira with her grandmother, making the excuse that she'd be better educated and cared for than if she'd stayed with her mother.

Charlotte had never met her husband. Gloria had simply written to say that he was handsome, rich and titled – a count no less, although, since Austria was rotten with counts, they should not be phased by that.

His name was Count Ludvig von Heichell. None of them had ever met him although she had from time to time sent them photographs of their life together in Austria. Skiing in the winter snows, resplendent at some ball or other, even on Safari in Africa. When Elvira was sixteen her mother decided she should be with her in Austria. It had originally been meant only as a holiday, but she had never returned and both of them had suddenly been two people consigned to infinity.

The sound of a car outside the window sent her to see who was arriving so early and in the courtyard beyond she saw a long grey car with several people alighting from it. She recognized her brother Nigel and his family immediately, and she smiled.

Nigel was sanity; he was funny, with a dry sense of humour she understood, and she liked his wife. Isabel was down to earth, normal she called it, and their children too were nice. Three decent grandchildren with a sense of humour and no pretensions, as different from Georgia's brood as chalk and cheese.

She didn't blame the children entirely, it was the way they'd been brought up: to think they were the best, the brightest, and everybody else inferior.

That was how Georgia had considered herself to be, and Peter had fostered the illusion.

She was looking forward to seeing Nigel and was glad they had come early. He was her younger brother by six years but they had always been good friends and she'd see what he had to say about what she considered a quite unnecessary event.

Nigel and his wife entered the hall and stared aghast at the sight that confronted them. The hall was filled with flowers, huge baskets of them, bunches everywhere and plants in ornate tubs and vases and Glenda stood with the housekeeper and two other servants staring in dismay at the tasks that awaited them.

'Gracious me,' Nigel said. 'The place looks like a garden centre, what are you going to do with all this lot?'

'You tell me,' she answered him.

'They've been arriving since yesterday morning and we simply haven't the vases for all of them. I love flowers, but even the hospitals are not finding room for them now.'

'Don't worry, love, we'll sort something out,' he answered and his wife said, 'Thank goodness we decided against flowers, we felt sure it would be like this. Can't we make use of the urns in the garden?'

'Most of them are already filled with geraniums,' Glenda said.

'I'll look around for more,' Nigel said, 'there's sure to be some. Now how about my having a word with Charlotte before it gets too crowded. I suppose she's still in her room.'

'And fractious,' Glenda said feelingly.

'Well of course. She'll love every minute of it.'

'Have you had any help in doing all this?' Isabel asked.

'The servants have been wonderful, but we have caterers in, because the weather is so wonderful it will mostly be outside.'

'And what about Georgia in all this?' Nigel asked.

'Oh, I'm better off without her, she'd have taken over and nothing would have been right. Do go and have a word with Mother, Uncle Nigel, cheer her up.'

Nigel found his sister standing at the window, elegant in her new gown, the sister who had always been happiest in her pretty dresses and looking forward to some function or other.

'I'm so glad you're early,' she greeted him. 'Are you the first?'

'It would appear so. You're looking very well, old girl.'

'The *old* girl is right, Nigel. Why on earth am I having this party? All this terrible amount of money, it would have done so much for the children's education.'

'You won't be eighty again, Charlotte.'

'I'm not exactly thrilled to be eighty this time.'

'Shame on you, woman. Everybody's looking forward to it, and what about Glenda, all she's put into it.'

'I know, I'm an ungrateful brat.'

'Then cheer up. Think about all your friends, think about your family around you, think about what you've done for this village and the people who respect you.'

'You often asked me why I stayed on here after Donald died. I should have moved away, made a new life.'

'I know, and you answered that your life was here, that you loved the house and the village. Are you telling me you wish you'd changed your mind?'

'No. But when I've gone, who will want to move in here?'

'Steven?'

'I really don't know.'

'Then we're not going to talk about it today. Let me escort you downstairs, you can sit in some regal state to have your picture taken, then you can receive your guests in some style.'

She laughed as she took his arm. Nigel had always had the power to make her feel better, but underneath it all she wished she could have confided in him her more worrying thoughts.

Perhaps the party would be good, perhaps her disjointed family would bury their differences for one day, and perhaps all her anxieties would be proved to have been ridiculous.

She stared with dismay at the flowers in the hall but Nigel was quick to reassure her that everything would soon be in order.

'But where have they come from?' she asked. 'Surely they can't all be for me.'

'Of course they are, Charlie, they can't be for anybody else. Now come into the drawing room and put your feet up, then let me go and give the girls a hand to get them sorted.'

'But I want to help, Nigel.'

'No you don't. I'll send Isabel in to join you with a glass of wine or coffee, no more arguments, Charlie.'

Two

Isabel found her sister-in-law sitting with a worried look on her face and Charlotte was quick to say, 'I feel so useless, Isabel, and there's so much to be done. Why isn't Georgia here?'

'She'll be here,' Isabel was quick to reassure her. 'The servants are very helpful and Nigel's doing his share. Too many cooks spoil the broth.'

'I suppose so. You know, Isabel, I would much rather have had a small family party, I can't help worrying that this affair is going to be too much.'

'How?'

'Too many people who haven't seen each other for years have completely lost touch and I don't like being eighty.'

'You're a very pristine eighty, dear.'

'So everybody tells me, but it doesn't alter the fact that I don't think I can cope with all this.'

'You don't have to cope with anything, it's all been done.'

'I'm an ungrateful wretch I'm sure you're thinking that.'

Isobel laughed. 'Why are you really so worried?'

'I don't honestly know. It's just a feeling I have. Donald always said I saw problems where they didn't exist – he was right.'

'It's a beautiful day, Charlotte, isn't that a good sign?'

'It should be.'

'Then let's enjoy it, look on the bright side, welcome all your guests with a smile and not a care in the world. Surely you can do that?'

'I'll try. Isabel . . . Elvira's coming. I don't know where she's coming from – who is she living with, is she married or what?'

'You'll soon know.'

She wished she could confide in Isabel but she was too close to family, she knew them all so well and she would be tempted to tell Nigel.

It was easy to make out her worries were centred around Elvira

but it wasn't altogether true. Glenda was worried about something so that could only mean family, and Georgia's children,
however perfect she made them out to be, were rather less so in
Charlotte's eyes.

She felt that all their problems were concerned with money
and this stupid party was costing a great deal of it. Would she
really be able to look in her son's eyes and see his suddenly shift
away as they always did these days.

A hundred and fifty thousand pounds he had asked her for,
with a multitude of reasons for needing it. She had given it to
him reluctantly and that had been ten months ago. Today would
be the first time she had met him since and she was dreading
the questions she needed to ask him. How many more hidden
secrets would lie buried beneath the smiles and embraces, how
readily could people lie?

There came the sound of children's voices from the gardens
below and Isabel went to the window to peer out.

She waved. 'It's the grandchildren, Charlie. They wanted to
travel with us, I rather think that suited their parents just fine.'

'They'll be happy in the gardens,' Charlotte said. 'I don't expect
they've managed all the flowers yet. Shouldn't the guests be
arriving?'

'There's heaps of time, dear. How many are you expecting?'

'Ask Glenda, she's done all the arranging. She's been so good,
Isabel. I hope it's taken her mind off other problems.'

Isabel stared at her uncertainly. Nigel had said only recently
that his sister had things on her mind but Isabel had merely
answered that he was imagining things. What had Charlotte to
worry about? She was rich, nice family, good friends, but Nigel
hadn't been convinced. Today Charlotte was a long way from
being the party girl.

Seeing Isabel's sudden concern Charlotte decided now was not
the time to air her problems. Maybe they didn't really exist,
perhaps Steven would smile cheerfully and present her with the
money he'd borrowed. Perhaps the girls would keep their doubts
hidden behind their smiles and perhaps Elvira would arrive beautiful and smiling as she was meant to do.

Glenda and Nigel came in the room together and Glenda was
quick to say, 'The flowers have been arranged beautifully, Mother,

Uncle Nigel's been such a help I think we've time for coffee then perhaps we should all make our way to the marquee.'

'Hasn't anybody else arrived?' Charlotte asked.

'No, Mother, I said definitely not before twelve noon so there's pleny of time. The vicar will be the first to arrive, he always is. Joyce and Roland are always early, she was always like that, and she'll be looking beautiful and elegant as always. You remember how perfect she was, Mother?'

'Yes, dear. Your girls tried so hard to emulate her; Elvira never took the trouble.'

'Well, today we might have the surprise of our lives, let's hope so.'

Nigel moved over to join his wife at the window. 'How is she?' he asked her.

'Worried I think, but I don't know what about.'

'Well, it's understandable. She's eighty and this is going to be quite a party. I don't want anything like it when I'm eighty, I intend to be out of the country.'

Isabel laughed. 'You'll be at home wanting loads of attention and all the presents that go with it.'

'Oh well, it's six years away, much can happen before then.'

'Glenda looks tired, Nigel, she's had too much to do and largely on her own I think.'

'Yes, well, she's probably been better left alone to get on with things. Georgia can be a bit overpowering.'

Charlotte too thought her daughter was looking tired, but she complimented her on her dress and Glenda replied, 'It isn't new, Mother, I had it for Shelagh Osborne's wedding.'

'You look pretty in green, dear. I didn't need anything new either.'

'Well, Georgia won't be wearing the same dress she had for the wedding. She's got something from Jenettes and we all know how expensive she is.'

Such rancour, Charlotte thought. Why did it always have to be like this?

'We've got the hall to rights now, Mother, we'll go in there and you can look at the flowers and some of the presents. Lots more will be coming I've no doubts; finding room for them all is going to be the problem.'

They moved into the hall together and set about duly admiring the flowers and Charlotte looked with some trepidation at the mountain of gaily wrapped presents.

'I don't need them,' she moaned. 'I have everything I need at my age, what am I going to do with them all?'

'Well, you haven't had a good look at them yet, Mother. Perhaps you'd like to open this one, it's from Gloria.'

'Why did she send me something? Elvira is coming, couldn't she have brought it?'

'Apparently not.'

The parcel was long and narrow, exquisitely wrapped, and Charlotte took it reluctantly as if in some way she feared what was inside. She stared uncertainly at the dark-blue velvet box. Her first thoughts were that it could only contain jewellery and her first instinct was that she didn't want it. She stared at her daughter before putting it back on the table saying, 'I'll open it later, Glenda, it's probably something quite silly.'

'Open it now, Mother – if you don't you'll be wondering all afternoon why she sent it and what it is.'

Charlotte turned away and, impatiently, Glenda said, 'I'll open it, it's not going to bite you, Mother.'

She snapped the lid open and revealed a necklace, a long gold chain from which suspended a single exquisite pearl drop.

It was beautiful and strangely simple, and yet it was extravagant. It reminded Charlotte of the daughter she hadn't seen for so many years, beautiful mercurial Gloria who had waltzed through life and given little regard to the other people in it.

Exasperated, Charlotte said, 'I have so many necklaces, Glenda, I suppose it was kind of her but where do I go these days to wear my jewellery?'

Glenda was thinking of the cashmere shawl they had bought her mother. It had been very expensive, too expensive, and that was why her dress had had to take second place.

Charlotte was quickly rewrapping the velvet box and, putting it back with the others, she said, 'I'll look at them all later. Why don't we all go out into the garden? The day is lovely, too nice to stay indoors.'

Her brother's grandchildren ran across the garden to meet them and they strolled through the rose garden towards the lawns at the side of the house.

Charlotte was wishing her birthday could have been a simple family affair. It would have been so wonderful simply to have sat in the garden looking at the flowers, listening to the birds, enjoying a simple repast then waving them farewell.

She looked in amazement at the vast marquee and Nigel said, 'That's set you back a bit, Charlie, given the village something to talk about I'm sure.'

'Yes, I expect it has.'

'Wildly extravagant would you say?'

'Yes, I would. Some of the villagers have been going through a pretty bad time since the war was over, I'll make sure that they all benefit from the catering.'

'You've done plenty for the village, Charlie.'

'I know, and they appreciate it. I intend to do more.'

'You are eighty, old girl.'

'I'm aware of it, who wouldn't be.'

They sat together on the chairs laid out on the lawn and Charlotte looked down the gardens towards the winding country lane and the square tower of the village church beyond.

She had been married in that church and all the village had been there. Donald had looked so handsome in his army uniform and it had seemed then that he had brought them glamour and excitement, the young man they'd watched grow up and who had brought home to them his beautiful young bride.

So many years, so much happiness and sadness.

'The street will be busy with cars in a little while,' Glenda said. 'I've told them all to be here around twelve, we don't want to cause problems for the waiters.'

'Well, unless I'm mistaken,' Nigel said, 'that's the vicar's car on its way here now.'

'Oh gracious, he's always the first,' Glenda said.

'Well, he can join us here, he's always good company – what about a drink?'

'His wife doesn't drink,' Glenda said hurriedly.

'Well, he does, in moderation I'm sure. A glass of sherry wouldn't come amiss.'

In spite of his wife's doubtful expression he said, 'I'll rustle up one of the waiters, surely they'll look after us out here.'

The vicar and his wife arrived happy and smiling, bringing

with them a huge basket of carnations and all Glenda could think of was more flowers to add to the rest. How many more would there be before the afternoon was over?

The vicar greeted his hostess with smiles and great affection. She'd been responsible for so many generosities to the church – where would they have been without her? Even now he was hoping there'd be an occasion when he could talk to her about the leaking roof in the vestry and the church fete in July.

His wife had admonished him to say nothing on her birthday but time was important in such matters and Charlotte would understand.

The Chaytor family had been benefactors in the village for years, but idly he wondered who would take over when the old lady was no more. He had little faith that Steven would.

It was almost twelve o'clock when Annie and Molly let themselves out of the gate and already the lane was crowded with cars. They were having to drive slowly giving them every chance to see the occupants of the vehicles and Molly said quickly, 'Did you recognize any of the family?'

'Miss Georgia and her daughter, not the children though.'

'Well, they have their own cars, they'll be comin' separate.'

'I thought Miss Glenda's eldest girl was in one of the cars, I've never seen her husband.'

'We don't need to walk so fast, they'll be drivin' very slow, there's a lot to come.'

'Did ye see the Bannisters?'

'No, I don't know what sort o' car he'll be drivin', they don't often come here now.'

'I suppose you're meetin' your friends,' Molly said.

'Yes, around twelve.'

'I might just join ye, I've nothin particular to go home for and they does a nice little meal at the cafe.'

Annie had known exactly what would happen – there was no shakin' Molly Woods off once she had made up her mind.

Their friends had already gathered in the cafe agog for news but Annie was wary.

Molly was quick to entertain them with her sister Rose's memories and after all they had little to report. It was true they had recognized some of the people sitting in their cars, but that was nothing important, maybe if she'd stayed in her garden she'd have seen more, after all she could see the marquee from her vegetable plot.

The vicar had waved to them in passing; she'd known what he was thinking.

Two nosey old women trying hard not to miss a thing.

The courtyard was rapidly filling up with cars and now they were parking down the lane and droves of people were walking up to the house and into the gardens.

Who were they all? Charlotte wondered. She couldn't think where Glenda had conjured them up from. Did she really have so many friends?

There were more flowers and she was thanking people she couldn't remember, then an elderly man stood in front of her elegantly dressed and wearing a white panama hat.

He didn't seem even vaguely familiar but he was smiling, his eyes twinkling as he said, 'You still look wonderful, Charlotte, but you don't remember me do you?'

'No, I'm sorry. There are so many people here and my memory is not what it was.'

'Not even when I was the best man at your wedding.'

'David Henshall. You're David, after all these years?'

'I am. More changed than you I think.'

'But we only saw you briefly after the wedding.'

'I know. I went out to India with the regiment, I got married and we settled in Australia eventually . . .'

'Your wife is here, David?'

'Alas no. I'm a widower these past twelve years, visiting my son and his wife here. How long since you lost Donald?'

'Fourteen years.'

'We have a lot to talk about, Charlotte.'

'Yes, it would seem so. I think we're moving into the marquee now, David, will you help an old lady out of her chair?'

He laughed. 'We'll talk again, dear. I want to hear all about your family, what the years have done to you, and hopefully meet them. Ah, here's your daughter come to your rescue.'

Glenda, harrassed, saying quickly, 'I'm not sure how many have yet to come, Mother, but perhaps we should go in there, the waiters are expecting us.'

'Is Georgia here?' Charlotte asked.

'Yes, but Kate hasn't arrived yet. My girls are here somewhere but Steven hasn't arrived. It's probably her, she's always unpunctual and I did ask them both to be on time.'

'Has Elvira arrived?'

'I don't suppose I'd know her if I saw her but she's not made herself known if she is here.'

'Glenda, don't worry, you've done so well to arrange all this. This, by the way, is David Henshall, dear, he was our best man when we were married.'

Glenda took his oustretched hand and he said, 'I'll catch up with your mother later on, my dear, I'm sure you've a lot to do.'

Charlotte took her seat at the top table and by this time the room was rapidly filling up with people. Her one thought was how huge the place was, and why had it been necessary to find people who had moved out of her life years before.

She must be careful not to hurt Glenda's feelings. She should be excited, grateful, thankful that a caring daughter had taken the trouble, but the problems that had worried her the last few months had surfaced and they refused to go away . . .

She could see Georgia talking to her son and some other people now and, excusing herself, Georgia moved along the table to talk to her.

'I'm sorry, I couldn't get here earlier, Mother, but Kate had to see a client this morning so she had to go into town.'

'On Saturday, Georgia?'

'Well, yes, Mother. Kate's work quite often means that she keeps unsociable hours. She doesn't mind, you know how very ambitious she is. Steven and his family haven't arrived yet. They're always late for everything.'

'Well, I'm sure they're coming.'

'And what about Elvira? We're all wondering what she's like these days. Have you heard from Gloria?'

'Yes. The dress looks very nice dear.'

'Oh, do you like it. It was expensive but we all have to do you proud today, Mother.'

'I can't think it was bought purely for my benefit, dear.'

Georgia laughed, 'Well, yours and some function Kate and I are having to go to. I haven't seen Joyce and Roland Bannister, I suppose they have been invited.'

'Yes, of course.'

'Well, you know Joyce, always pristine, not many to touch her.'

'She was a nice girl I thought, and you liked her.'

'Oh yes, of course. She always got what she wanted didn't she, Mother: money, the house, the man, the boy Elvira wanted?'

'Elvira was only a child, Georgia.'

'Elvira was never a child, Mother, not with Aunt Gloria to contend with.'

'Shouldn't we be taking our places, dear, other people seem to be sorting themselves out.'

'Yes, I suppose so. Ah, here's Kate. She's such a caring girl, Mother, in spite of her business in town she's not really late.'

The seats on the top table were almost all occupied and Charlotte asked, 'Where are the children eating?'

'The small marquee in the garden, Mother. Children can be so disruptive when they get bored and they can always go out into the gardens after they've eaten.'

'Two marquees?' Charlotte murmured.

'Only a very small one, Mother, and there are several children.'

Looking down the table she could see that two places remained empty next to Glenda and her husband, and another place further down which she assumed was waiting for Elvira. She was wishing the day was over.

Three

Steven Chaytor slouched in his favourite chair in front of the window with the morning's racing pages spread out in front of him. It was half past eleven and they had well over half an hour's drive to his mother's birthday celebration.

It didn't worry him unduly. He and his wife had a reputation for unpunctuality and his wife was still chopping and changing her attire.

The idea of the party was ridiculous. There was racing at Chepstow and he was entirely resentful of the money being spent to celebrate an eightieth birthday party, when it could have been better spent.

He didn't want to see his mother, he owed her money he was not in a position to repay. He knew she wouldn't ask him for it, but even so her expression would say it all.

His sister had spent weeks organizing the affair and the money was being spent on people who probably hadn't seen his mother for years.

He scanned the pages looking for what they had to say about the horse Harvey Neal had insisted he should bet on. Harvey was pretty reliable, but he'd had some disastrous gambles recently and he couldn't keep on losing money the way he had been doing.

The door opened and he looked up to see his wife standing there, and his first thoughts were that she looked overdressed and altogether ridiculous.

She was wearing a white lace dress and a large bright-red hat adorned with black poppies, and she was posing for his attention and smiling that confident smile that belied her appearance.

'Well,' she demanded.

'Why the hat? This isn't Ascot we're going to.'

'There'll be hats. You know what your family are like, particularly Georgia.'

'It's simply a family party in the gardens, hats like that will be silly.'

'Well, it was expensive so I intend to wear it.'

The entire rigout had been expensive. Julie spent money as though there was no tomorrow and she invariably looked overdressed.

She wasn't a popular member of the family. His sisters and their children thought she was odd and outside their class. A bookmaker's daughter with plenty of money and little breeding. His mother had always tried to be nice to her but Julie had responded somewhat too arrogantly over the years.

Barry, their one son, had elected to go climbing in Austria instead of attending his grandmother's birthday party and that had not gone down well with the rest of them. In all he was not looking forward to the day ahead of them.

Julie eyed their waiting car with some hostility. 'I thought you intended changing that car,' she said sharply.

'I will when I can afford to.'

'Well, it looks shabby. Every time we see your family one or another of them has a new car.'

'Well, with you spending money like water I have to think twice about such things.'

That was the trouble with Julie, her father had brought her up to expect everything when she wanted it.

'Aren't they having a marquee?' she asked.

'I believe so.'

'How terribly posh,' she responded as she stepped into the car.

The journey was taken largely in silence until they became aware of the cars parked along the lane and in the courtyard beyond.

It was quickly apparent that most of the guests were already in the marquee and Steven said sharply, 'We'd better get in there – why don't you leave that hat in the car?'

'I've bought it and I'm wearing it,' she retorted.

'Please yourself,' he snapped, 'but you'll soon find out that you're in the minority.'

'Wasn't that the Bannisters' car that passed us on the road?' Julie asked.

'I've no idea, I don't know what kind of car he's driving.'

'Well it'll be better than this one.'

He strode off ahead and Julie said quickly, 'She's wearing beige, it does nothing for her.'

Steven was thinking about what he remembered of Joyce Mansell, a gentle, quiet girl, a girl most people thought well of, a girl who'd been quietly elegant and obviously impressed with Roland Bannister to the exclusion of anybody else.

They took their places on the top table, received his sister's frown of annoyance at their lateness and his mother's distant smile.

'Who's the vacant seat for?' he asked Glenda.

'Elvira, when she decides to turn up.'

'So, she's coming then. And Gloria?'

'No. She's too busy. She's sent an excuse and an extravagant present.'

He noticed that the Bannisters were taking their seats at one of the side tables, a handsome smart couple being greeted by those around them.

The waiters were serving the wine and the meal and, looking down the table, Charlotte thought, still no Elvira, perhaps she wouldn't come after all.

Glenda was praying that all would go well. From the laughter and the conversation it was evident that people were enjoying themselves. The meal was excellent, the service perfect, and the speeches that followed appropriate.

Her mother was bearing up well, and later when they moved out into the garden no doubt she would enjoy chatting to people she hadn't seen for so long.

It was evident Elvira was not arriving for the meal, but where was she coming from? Her acceptance of the invitation had come from Austria so evidently she had been staying with her mother, but if she lived with her all the time they really didn't know. She could be married, have a family, live anywhere under the sun, but it was after all the speeches had been made and people were drifting away that Joyce Bannister said, 'Hasn't Elvira arrived?'

'No, I'm really rather concerned,' Glenda replied.

'But if she wasn't coming surely she would have let you know.'

'Yes, I'm sure she would. I'm sure she'll come, after all there's the rest of the day.'

Joyce smiled, and Glenda said, 'You're looking very nice, dear. I could never wear beige but it suits you.'

'Yes, Mother always liked me in beige. Roland isn't fond of it.'

'He's looking very well.'

'Yes, we've just come back from the Canaries, I love it there.'

Glenda smiled. Surely everything would always go right for this golden couple.

Elvira pulled her car into the lay-by at the top of the hill and sat for a while gazing down at the village below.

It seemed at that moment that she was living in a time warp. Nothing seemed to have changed, from the stone church with its square tower to the rows of whitewashed cottages surrounding it. In the distance she could see her grandmother's large stone house set in its acres of lawns and gardens but she was sure there would be changes. Nothing stayed the same.

She remembered the street along which she had ridden her horse, exercised her dog, laughed with her schoolfriends. Was it still there, that first primary school she'd attended? Did the stalls set out with their fruit and flowers still exist along Green Lane as she remembered them?

She eased herself out of the car and started to climb the hill. She had loved this hill with its preponderance of heather and thrift and she climbed until she reached the old oak tree where she stopped to look down.

The invitation had said they would be eating lunch at noon but it was well past that time and obviously the meal would be over. It didn't really matter. She would go down to the house and make her excuses. She didn't want anything formal, simply to show them that she hadn't forgotten, that all she had really come for was to see her grandmother and the few people she might remember.

She looked up at the huge tree above her. The bark was covered with moss and ivy and somewhere under it her initials had been carved with those of the boy she had been with. It didn't matter now, it was all too late.

She would have liked to sit on the hill with her memories, remember her grandmother as she had once been and then leave without being forced to see the changes the years had brought.

She had little doubt that outside the village things would be changed, but along the main street the shops seemed the same: the bakery and the post office, the Black Swan Inn where old men were sitting outside in the sunshine, and a new small cafe which she didn't remember but which seemed to be doing quite a trade.

As she climbed the hill towards the manor house she was aware of cars parked nose to bumper long before she reached the gates and she hesitated with the feeling that there might not be a parking space inside the grounds.

It's like a royal garden party, she thought ruefully, there were so many cars, and recklessly she decided to park her car with inches to spare beside a large Bentley.

It was obvious that the guests had left the marquee and were sauntering across the lawns and as she locked her car door two young girls came running towards her. The eldest one looked about twelve, the younger one six or seven, but it was the older girl who adopted a seemingly important manner.

'If you've come to great-grandma's party you're late,' she said sharply.

'I know, I'm sorry, I was sure lunch would be long over.'

'Well, yes it is. We all had to be here for twelve o'clock.'

'I know. What is your name?'

'I'm Josephine Deptford-Smythe, this is my half-cousin Lucy.'

'I'm Elvira Stanhope, your father's cousin. Your mother is one of my cousins too, Lucy, which one?'

Before Lucy could reply the other girl said, 'Her mother is Jessica. She's over there talking to Mrs Bannister.'

Her eyes followed Josephine's pointing finger and the memories came flooding back. Joyce, always neat and serene, not just her expression but everything about her from her tidy, short brown hair to her dainty, well-polished shoes.

Joyce had never needed to be told to be quiet, to sit decorously while her elders spoke, Joyce who the other girls tried to emulate and the boys admired.

Joyce and the cousins would keep until later on, but it was time to greet her grandmother and with a smile she said, 'Perhaps it's time for me to tell grandmother I'm here and make my apologies.'

'She's over there, we'll come with you if you like.'

'I'm sure you've both got better things to do. I'm sure I'll see you later.'

'Are you the Elvira who went to live abroad?'

'My mother lives abroad.'

'Gloria?'

'That's right. I can see you've heard of her.'

'Daddy said she'd married a prince or something.'

Elvira laughed. Trust Alex to boast about her mother's connections even when he was probably being caustic.

Josephine seemed reluctant to leave her, indeed it was the younger girl who scampered off leaving Josephine to chase after her demanding impatiently that she wait.

Relieved, Elvira took her place behind others waiting to speak to her grandmother and it was several minutes before they gazed into each other's eyes and Charlotte said with a smile, 'You must forgive me, my dear, my memory is illusive and I don't remember seeing you over lunch.'

'No, I'm sorry, I must apologize for being late.'

There was no hint of recognition in the older woman's eyes, and after a few moments Elvira said, 'It's been a long time, Grandmother. I always had a terrible reputation for being unpunctual, apparently I haven't improved.'

Charlotte's eyes lit up and with a little cry she held out her arms and Elvira rushed into them.

'Oh, my dear,' she said, 'I really thought you'd decided not to come, why are you so late?'

'It doesn't matter, darling, I'm here, and you're looking wonderful. This is really quite a party.'

'Yes, too much of one. I'd have preferred to have a small family party so that we'd have had much more time to talk as a family.'

'Surely it's nice to meet old friends again.'

'I've forgotten most of them, that's what old age does to you, my dear.'

'Who arranged all this then? It's surely quite an achievement.'

'Glenda's done it all. She's been so good, I'm an ungrateful wretch.'

'I'll meet them all presently. I've already met two little girls.'

'Oh, which ones are they?'

'Josephine and Lucy.'

'Josephine with too much to say and Lucy with hardly anything.'

'You describe them very well. I wonder how you described me?'

'Different . . . interesting.'

'All the way here I was thinking about what we would have to say to each other, that it would be difficult, but now there doesn't seem to be enough time to make up for all the years we never met.'

'How is your mother, dear? She sent me a very wonderful and costly present.'

'I was sure she would.'

'Would she mind if I gave it to you, after all I have enough baubles for where I go and what I do?'

'I couldn't possibly tell her you gave it to me.'

'She needn't know. I'm not even sure I shall see your mother again, perhaps for my funeral. Then I'll be the one who is missing.'

'And that's ages off I hope. You ask how my mother is, Grandmother, and I can only tell you that she's as I remember her and you remember her. Beautiful, extravagant and completely besotted with Gloria.'

'And what of her husband?'

'I've only seen him rarely. He's handsome, distant and rich. They're a very good pair.'

'And is she happy in Austria?'

'But of course. She loves the winter snows and the balls. They enjoy their travels and she only remembers what she wants to remember.'

'How much time do you spend together?'

'Very little actually. I obey the royal command to visit and I hardly ever agree with her.'

'But your life, Elvira, what is going on in your life?'

'It will take too long, Grandmother. Before I go I'll tell you the interesting bits.'

'But you'll stay, dear, what do you mean "before I go"?'

'Well, I can only stay one night if that's convenient, tomorrow morning I have to go. My life isn't so important that the story needs to take so long.'

Charlotte looked away with a smile as a man and a woman stood smiling down at her, saying quickly, 'Joyce and Roland, this is Elvira, arrived at last.'

Joyce embraced her and Elvira thought quickly that there was always a soft peach-like feel to her skin, and perfume, pale and elusive, the child and the woman were intrinsically the same, delicate and strangely untouchable.

Her hand was taken in a firm grip and she was looking up into eyes she had not seen since that afternoon ten years before when they had said their farewells on the hill in the shade of the oak tree.

He smiled, and his voice too she remembered, low, faintly teasing as he said, 'You could always be relied on to be late, Elvira, but somehow when you did arrive the excuses didn't matter.'

Joyce said, 'We thought perhaps something had happened to prevent your coming, Elvira. It's been so long, nobody seemed to know much about you or what you were doing these days . . .' Her smile was serene, her manner genteel and faultless.

'I expect you keep yourself very busy, Joyce, you always had so many things to do.'

'I still have. I'm a magistrate, I serve on a great deal of committees, I enjoy my work.'

She wanted to ask if they had children, but somehow it was a question she wanted to avoid without quite knowing why. Instead she said, 'Perhaps I should circulate. I'm staying over this evening so Grandma and I can talk then. I'll no doubt see you later.'

'Not in another ten years, Elvira,' Roland said, smiling down at her.

'It's amazing how quickly ten years passes,' she said softly. 'Where do I start?' she added.

'Well, Georgia's family are over there and I'm sure young Josephine won't have wasted any time in telling them you've arrived.'

Josephine took it upon herself to perform the introductions, and she knew immediately that she wouldn't have recognized any one of them if she'd met them in the street.

Alex was handsome and confident. His wife shy, obviously happy to relax in his shadow, and it was Kate who surprised Elvira the most.

Like her brother she was sure of herself, but she seemed totally at variance with most of the other women, preferring unadorned Navy and White. She was good-looking without being considered pretty, and she greeted Elvira with a firm handshake and brisk greeting.

'You have changed, Elvira, you're really quite a fashion plate,' she said.

'I didn't set out to be.'

'And pretty, certainly more beautiful than I remember you.'

'Perhaps I should be pleased about that, I was always a harum-scarum.'

'Well, yes you were.'

'I haven't spoken to Aunt Glenda and her family yet, perhaps I should make my way over there.'

'Just as long as you don't let her bore you with the awful amount of work she's put in,' Georgia said.

Kate called after her, 'We must talk later, Elvira, we're all anxious to know about your mother.'

Four

First came the chastisement on her lateness, then the greeting when she learned about her cousins' marriages, their homes and their children, and considering that she hadn't seen them for ten years, very little interest in her.

It was Uncle Steven who intrigued her the most with his talk of horses and racing, slightly boastful, and she found his wife overpowering and the hat she was wearing slightly unnecessary.

Steven found a like-minded man to talk to and Elvira walked in the gardens with Julie, instantly aware that friction existed between her and her husband's family.

'They've never liked me,' Julie confided. 'I'm not upper crust enough for them. My father's into race meetings and gambling, he's a bookie, made plenty of money so they've no need to be quite so patronizing.'

'Not my grandmother surely.'

'No, she was always nice, but the rest of them I can do without.'

'Oh well, I was always at variance with my cousins, largely because my mother was often absent.'

'Oh, I know all about you, they were jealous of you.'

'Jealous? But how could they be? I was always the odd one out.'

'That was why. You spent time here at the manor, your mother was beautiful and rich, now she lives abroad with some nobleman or other.'

'Oh, Julie, don't you think I always wished my mother was different. I didn't even know my father very well, he was nice but distant and I was only nine when he died. What had they to be jealous of me for?'

'Well, believe me they were.'

'Didn't Uncle Steven go into law?'

'He gave that up years ago, now he's into gambling and only gambling. 'Why didn't you come back in all those years?' Julie asked.

'A great many things happened. My education for one thing, and my mother lived in Austria.'

'I never met your mother.'

'No.'

'But she's not here today either.'

'No, they had something on in Austria they couldn't get out of.'

'But it is her mother's birthday.'

'I know, but I came, didn't I?'

'I'd better go and look for Steven, he wanted to leave pretty early.'

Elvira watched her walking away. A few words was all they had had and the feeling persisted that she knew so little about so many of them. They'd talked briefly about their homes and their husbands and children, and yet they'd asked few questions even when she knew they regarded her as something of an enigma.

She turned towards the formal gardens becoming suddenly aware that she had company and a man's voice said softly, 'Why did you never come back, Elvira, why didn't you write to me?'

She paused to look up into Roland's eyes in a face she remembered more vividly than any other and suddenly she became aware of old anxieties that she'd believed she'd put behind her a long time ago.

'I had nothing to come back for, Roland. I was sixteen, my mother lived abroad, it was a new life.'

'You never wrote.'

'No. What was there to say, that I was never coming back?'

He stood looking down at her, his eyes strangely sad, and impulsively she asked, 'Have you been happy, Roland? You got what you wanted, your career, Joyce.'

'You seem very sure that I got what I wanted. I was nineteen when we last met, does a boy of nineteen really know what he wants?'

'It's what everybody said you wanted.'

'I know. To follow in my father's footsteps in a career he'd excelled in. To marry the girl who was right for me. Isn't that the epitome of perfection?'

'Only you can answer that, Roland.'

He smiled, that sweet, grave smile she remembered so vividly, before he said, 'Tell me about you, Elvira, what has life done to you?'

'I teach painting to children around ten years old. Some of them are good, most of them are inferior, but I enjoy it and I think they do too. In the winter I spend time in Austria skiing and I have a horse I love riding. My life is pretty full.'

'You haven't said if there is a man in your life.'

'Perhaps there is, perhaps there isn't. We'll leave it at that, Roland.'

'But why so diffident? What is there to hide?'

'It would take too long and I think Joyce is coming this way to find you. She's looking very beautiful, Roland, but then she always did.'

'When will you come again, Elvira?'

'I don't know.'

'In another ten years perhaps?'

'Like I said, I really don't know.'

Joyce smiled as she joined them and Roland said quickly, 'Joyce has often spoken about you, Elvira. I'm sure there are many questions she would like to ask you.'

'I've wondered what you were doing with your life,' Joyce said. 'I'm so glad to see you today, you look well and somehow so different from what I expected.'

'Why am I so different?'

'It's difficult to say, gentler perhaps, more beautiful.'

'I never expected to be called beautiful.'

They all smiled and Joyce consulted her watch saying, 'We do have to be leaving soon now, we have another function to attend unfortunately.'

'Two in one day.'

'Yes, Aunt Bessie. I'm sure you remember Aunt Bessie, it's her birthday too.'

She remembered Aunt Bessie vaguely but Roland had taken her hand and Joyce embraced her swiftly before saying, 'If you are staying on for a while, Elvira, do call to see us, we live in that big white house near the bridge in Ashlea, I'm sure you remember it.'

She did remember it, a beautiful old house in a glade of beech trees. She could imagine Joyce in that house, one she had always wanted and managed to get, just as she had always got what she wanted.

They both smiled and walked away and she stood for several moments looking after them. They joined the handful of people waiting to say their farewells to her grandmother and she turned and walked towards the lawns which were suddenly devoid of children.

The old swing was still there and it was obvious that her grandmother had allowed it to remain for the next generation of children.

As she sat gently swinging the memories came flooding back. The screams of laughter and the arguments as to who should sit on it next. The teasing of the boys and sometimes the tears. Today had not been what she had expected of it.

There had not been the curiosity, her cousins had been too wrapped up in themselves, their marriages, their children, their lives. She had merely been the cousin who had gone away, remembered briefly for her frivolity and the memories they had of her mother.

Those few words she had had with Steven's wife had only made her feel that she was back with people she no longer knew, and Joyce had seemed unfamiliar.

She remembered Joyce Mansell at school, pretty and studious, gentle and predictable, and she remembered Roland Bannister because she had loved him with a childish need to possess him like a favourite toy.

The catering vans were leaving now and the men had arrived to take away the marquee. Somehow the house and its grounds were falling back into place and she watched the last of her grandmother's guests slowly walking towards the gates.

She could see both her aunts and a few others still talking to her grandmother but she guessed that they too would soon be making their excuses to leave. Reluctantly she left the swing and strolled towards them.

Her cousin Alex came to meet her, a smile, as teasing as she remembered it, lit up his face and he said with obvious humour, 'Been making the best of the old swing, Elvira, my but I've spent hours pushing you along on that old thing.'

'I remember, Alex, in fact it was while I was out there that I remembered so many things.'

'We're leaving now. I don't know where Kate is, probably with James, she seems to spend most of her time with him.'

'James?'

'James Harrison, Barrister, chap she works with.'

'I haven't met him, in fact I've only met Kate briefly.'

'She's asking for trouble, rumour has it that his wife isn't exactly happy with the arrangement.'

'Don't you think it might be a good idea if you dropped a few words of advice then, Alex?'

'Not me, old girl. I decided long ago that I would never interfere in family matters, particularly Kate's comings and goings.'

'Doesn't that sound like shirking your responsibilities?'

'It sounds like being sensible . . . Elvira, did you manage to speak with my wife?'

'We were introduced, then more people joined us and I haven't seen her since.'

'Oh well, I wouldn't worry about it, you haven't missed much.'

'That's not a very nice thing to say about your wife, Alex.'

'No, it isn't is it, but then if you were staying on longer no doubt you'd have become aware that Marian and I aren't exactly a devoted couple. We tend to go our separate ways.'

'Don't tell me your mother knows about it.'

He laughed. 'No, she doesn't. My mother thinks her children are sweet gentle souls living perfect lives and neither Kate nor I have had the courage to shatter her ideas.'

'I hope Aunt Glenda is having better luck with her family.'

'Indescribably dull my dear. Uncle Steven's a bit of a loose cannon. What did you think of his wife's hat? – she thought she was coming to Ascot.'

'It was probably very expensive.'

'Probably, but can they afford it?'

'You sound very cynical, Alex.'

'Yes, well, perhaps I am.'

'Have you said your farewells to Grandma?'

'I have. How long do you intend to stay here?'

'Just for tonight.'

'Gracious, after ten years. Is that all you can manage?'

'I do have another life, Alex.'

'Yes, it would be interesting to know what it is, where it is and who with. I might just come over here this evening and ask a few questions. It's my bet the old girl will want to go to bed early after the trauma of the day, you'll be glad of some company.'

Elvira smiled. 'I'll see if she's ready to return to the house, Alex, like you say she's probably very tired.'

'Do see that she doesn't stay up too late, Elvira,' Glenda admonished her, 'it's been a long day. Do you have to go back in the morning?'

'Surely after all this long time you could have arranged to stay on for a few days,' Georgia said firmly. 'We haven't had much time for talking and we'd like to hear a little about your mother, what she's doing with herself.'

'She's quite well.'

'But surely there's more. Foreign husband, new life in a new environment, I thought you'd be full of it all.'

'When did you last see her?' Glenda asked.

'About three weeks ago.'

'Oh well, we all know Gloria, she's probably living every minute of what's on offer, didn't she always?' Georgia said. 'We're not being envious, darling, simply curious about our dear sister who never writes, never keeps in touch. You'd think we were no longer family – couldn't she possbly have made an effort for Mother's birthday?'

'Shall we get back to the house, dear,' Charlotte said suddenly.

'We were just discussing Gloria, Mother,' Georgia replied, sharply, 'she should have been here.'

'Are we all going back to the house or have you other plans?'

'Well, I'm going home to get out of these glad rags and put my feet up. It's been a long day,' Georgia said, to which remark Glenda said quickly, 'Well, it's been an even longer one for me I'm afraid. I'll go back to the house with you, Mother, just to make sure I haven't left anything. I suppose there'll be more flowers, heaven knows what we can do with them.'

'We could give them to the church and to people in the village who haven't been well,' her mother said. 'The vicar will be able to tell you who would appreciate them.'

'Well, considering that he brought you some he'll not be very much help in that quarter,' Glenda said sharply.

By the time they reached the terrace Georgia had kissed her mother briefly and was walking quickly away to join her son and his wife. Elvira could see that her grandmother was leaning heavily on her walking stick and looking decidedly weary.

'Mother won't want to stay up late, Elvira, it seems such a pity that you have to leave in the morning. Can't you possibly stay longer?'

Before Elvira could answer Charlotte said, 'Don't fuss, dear, let Elvira decide what she wants to do.'

They stared uncertainly, looking at the vast array of flowers in the hall, smelling their perfume. Already so many of their petals had fallen in the heat of the day.

'Such a waste of money,' Glenda muttered. 'Why does everybody's mind centre on flowers when there are so many other things that you would have preferred.'

'What things?' her mother said. 'I don't need anything, Glenda, and I love flowers – what else does an old lady need?'

'Well, I'm going to get off now, Mother. You'll have Elvira for company but don't stay up too long. You will see to that, Elvira, won't you?'

How her feet had once waltzed through the rooms of this house. She'd known it better than the others because her mother had been away so many times and her grandparents had been young then and energetically living their lives.

She'd been the gypsy child whose cousins had called her the rich kid because her parents had had too much money – money that had brought them independence from their child.

There had been love of a sort, but Elvira had learned to do without love that demanded freedom and distance.

She was remembering the last conversation she had had with her mother, sitting on the terrace of her house overlooking the beautiful Vienna woods.

She'd spent the morning riding her horse through the extensive grounds of the house and when she'd returned she'd found her mother sitting at the breakfast table on the terrace still wearing a long silken robe, still incredibly beautiful, her hair a little less vibrant but still framing a face whose beauty had found her so many lovers and made so many enemies.

Tossing an envelope across the table Gloria had said with a smile, 'Read this, darling, it's a reply to your invitation.'

'You're replying for me, Mother?'

'I think so, after all I can't go and Ludvig has arranged for us to attend this other function, one we can't possibly get out of.'

'Not even for Granny's birthday, Mother?'

'Not even for that, dear. You know what it'll be like, darling, it's been too long and they never really liked me, they were terribly jealous of everything I did.'

'You didn't exactly help them to like you, Mother.'

'Don't be sanctimonious, Elvira, we all had the same chances, I just happened to make more of mine.'

'Doesn't it bother you that they may not like me, Mother – after all this time why would they?'

'Darling, why should you care. Mother'll be so pleased to see how beautiful you are, not the little tearaway who waltzed around in trousers and hated dressing up.'

'Hardly somebody to be proud of, Mother.'

'Oh, I don't know, darling. You were funny, pretty in a tomboy way, and you knew what you wanted out of life.'

'I didn't always get it, Mother.'

'No. Whatever happened to Roland Bannister, and who were the others?'

'What others?'

'Are you telling me that Roland was the only one? I've often wondered.'

'And I'm telling you mother that there were too many others and Roland belonged to Joyce. They are married you know.'

'Such a dull little girl, Elvira.'

'Nobody would agree with you, Mother, she was sweet and gentle, very pretty and very nice.'

'Very dull, my dear. Trying to live up to too many expect-ations and a boy who had been set up for her.'

'I'd like to change this conversation, Mother, let's talk about the birthday party – are you sending a present or am I expected to take it with me?'

'I've already sent something, they'll think it ostentatious and so it is but Mother will possibly be amused. We must shop in Vienna – get you a dress to make everybody there patently envious.'

'I don't think so, Mother, that's the last thing I want.'

Her mother had eyed her mischievously, and at that moment her husband had joined her for breakfast, favouring Elvira with his charming smile before depositing a kiss on his wife's cheek.

She liked Ludvig, he was handsome and charming, all attributes that suited her mother, and he was also very much in love with her.

He would never be a father figure but she didn't mind, after all she barely remembered her own father. He had been an ambitious man, wealthy and proud, seeming happy to let his beautiful flirtatious wife go her own way, and singularly not involving himself in his young daughter's activities.

That he had died when she was still a child had barely registered in Elvira's life. She had her grandparents and a mother who was occasionally there, even when she was adored.

There were odd times when Gloria was curious about her life, but for the main part she was happy to see her occasionally and her questions were put teasingly rather than earnestly.

Looking at the pile of gaily wrapped presents in the hall she looked down at one that had been opened and left beside the others.

Curiously she opened it, even when she suspected it was her mother's gift. She smiled at the necklace. Her mother would have delighted in its extravagance, picturing the cynical, envious looks of her sisters. It would not matter to Gloria if she gave it away.

What was she going to do in this huge house, what could they hope to achieve in another week?

She went into the library and looked at the pile of magazines on the table. The same old country magazines she remembered, filled with hunt balls and county shows, pursuits that were long gone.

The door opened and a young housemaid with a smiling face said, 'There's a telephone call for you, Miss Elvira, in the drawing room.'

Her first thought was that it would be Alex as he'd half threatened to telephone her anyway, but she was surprised to hear a woman's voice saying, 'Elvira, it's your Aunt Georgia, I suppose mother's gone to bed and you won't know what to do with yourself in that huge house.'

'Granny was very tired, Aunt Georgia, it's been a long day for her.'

'Well of course. I'm alone here, Kate's going out so I thought you might like to drive over and we could have a chat. You know the house – Maple Dene at the top of the High Street.'

'Well, if you're sure, Aunt Georgia.'

'Quite sure, Elvira, we got very little chance to talk at the party, too many people and too much going on. What time can I expect you?'

'I'll leave in a few minutes if that's convenient.'

'Of course. Park your car on the drive and I'll leave the side door open for you.'

They had to come sometime, Elvira thought to herself. The questions, the searchings, whether they would be about her or her mother she would soon know. There were questions she wouldn't answer, others she would elaborate on and others they had no right to ask.

As she drove away from the house she received a wave from the elderly lady sitting in the garden of the first cottage in the lane and she waved back without recognizing her.

Annie O'Connor asked herself which one that might be.

Five

Georgia replaced the telephone and looked up to find her daughter standing in the doorway looking at her curiously.

'So you won't be on your own, Mother, after all,' she said.

'No, I've invited Elvira over.'

'Well, that's all right then, she'll no doubt tell you all you need to know.'

'I wouldn't have asked her over if you'd been here to keep me company. I hardly see you these days, Kate, either you're working late or you're off meeting somebody. You didn't come home last night.'

'No, Mother, I worked late at the office and you know what the traffic's like on Friday evening. I stayed with a friend.'

'Which friend?'

'You don't know her, Mother, and I needed to work this morning.'

'Most people showed surprise that you worked Saturday morning; I explained that it was a special case and needed your full attention.'

'Why should you explain anything, Mother? It was nobody's business.'

'Is there something going on between you and Harrison?'

'Mother, James and I work together, he's a senior partner, I really don't know what you're talking about. Who's been spreading rumours anyway?'

'Nobody's actually said anything, but their looks have said enough.'

'Mother, I don't have to listen to this, James and I are colleagues. You were delighted when I was taken into the practice, now all I hear is that there's some sort of scandal.'

'I don't want people talking, it's been simmering all day.'

'Don't tell me they've had the nerve to discuss it with you.'

'Like I said it was the speculation, and it was something Alex said.'

'Alex!'

'Yes, he was sarcastic like he usually is.'

'Well, Alex has no room to talk about anything with people right and left discussing his marriage. Marian spent all afternoon with the vicar and his wife, we know her entire life revolves around church and Alex rarely sets foot in it.'

'He's very busy.'

'I know you'll stick up for him, Mother, but if he starts talking about me he can shut up. There's enough scandal about Alex to fill the church magazine.'

'What scandal? I don't know of any.'

'Never mind, Mother, it's just gossip like it is about me and James.'

She turned away when they heard the sound of a car and Kate said, 'I'll let myself out at the front of the house, Mother, I don't need to meet Elvira right now.'

By the time Elvira had let herself into the house Kate had left and Georgia said quickly, 'I'm sorry Kate isn't here, dear, unfortunately she had to go out and we both thought it would be nice for us to spend the evening together. Was Mother very weary?'

'Yes, and hardly in any mood for chatting.'

'No, well come in the conservatory, dear, it's such a lovely evening it's a shame to sit in here. We'll chat, then I'll ask the girl to bring in some refreshments.'

'This is a nice house, Aunt Georgia. Isn't it rather large now for just you and Kate?'

'Well, yes it is, but I do entertain, and Kate shows no sign of getting married. Now, tell me about your mother . . .'

'What is it that might interest you most?'

'Tell me about her husband, dear, her lifestyle, all her comings and goings that kept the entire village engrossed when she lived here. Gloria and her life kept the entire village alive.'

'I doubt if they would now, Aunt Georgia. They live in a beautiful old house overlooking the Vienna Woods, they go to balls and they ski in the winter, she rides her horse and Ludvig has suddenly taken up golf. They are respected and popular, their lives are pleasant and normal.'

'Normal! Dancing, skiing and horse riding, it doesn't sound too normal to me.'

'For Austria perhaps, Aunt Georgia.'

'I suppose so, dear. Has he been married before?'

'No. They met in Venice where they were both on holiday, perhaps it was love at first sight.'

'I can't begin to tell you how often your mother fell in love at first sight, Elvira. It was sad that her first marriage didn't last long, he died so tragically but they were like each other, frivolous and reckless, when she married your father he couldn't have been more different. He was very serious. Do you remember him, Elvira?'

'Hardly at all. He was kind but somehow remote.'

'Exactly. They went their separate ways, understandable really, he was too dull for her, and she was too flamboyant.'

'But they stayed together, didn't they?'

'They stayed together apart you might say.'

'I saw very little of Kate at the party, I spoke only briefly to Alex.'

'Did you meet Marian, his wife?'

'Briefly.'

'Well, she's a bit dull, not at all like Alex who is so outgoing and amusing. Her father was a vicar you know so she's had a fairly quiet upbringing. She's very well thought of at the church, always helping out there and the vicar's wife thinks very well of her.'

'Their daughter came to meet me when I arrived at the party, she seemed a very lively little girl.'

'Oh goodness yes. Josephine. She's very bright, doing well at school but not at all like her mother.'

'She was with one of her cousins.'

'Yes, probably Lucy. We don't see much of them even though we live in the same village. Glenda is so involved with her family, it sometimes seems as if none of them have left home. If she's not with them she's up at the hall looking after Mother.'

'Isn't that very sweet of her?'

'Cloying, my dear. Mother doesn't need all that attention, she's very well for her age and she gets plenty of visitors and between you and I, I rather think she would like to be left alone sometimes.'

'Is Aunt Glenda in the same house?'

'Oh no, she went into something smaller when Peter died.'

Soon would come the questions about herself and she desperately wanted to avoid most of them. Quickly she said, 'Joyce and
Roland Bannister were going on to another party. They both
look very well.'

'Oh yes, that would be Aunt Bessie's birthday, on the same day
as Mother's. Joyce is so kind to her parents, her aunts and her
friends. She was always like that, very nice, very sincere.'

'Have they been happy, Aunt Georgia?'

'Well of course. He idolizes her. Always did. They were destined
for each other even as children. You liked him, didn't you, Elvira,
but he was always for Joyce wasn't he?'

'Yes, I rather think he was.'

She reached across the small table and picked up Elvira's left
hand. 'No wedding ring or engagement ring then − we know
so little about you. You're twenty-six Elvira, surely there must be
some man in your life?'

Elvira smiled. 'Nobody special, Aunt Georgia. I'm very independent. I like my life . . .'

'But what is your life, dear?'

'I have a class of people who are interested in painting, I ride
my horse and I even go sailing.'

'Sailing!'

'Why yes. I have a small cottage in Cornwall, I also have a
small boat down there, so you see I haven't much time for anything
or anyone else.'

'But surely you intend to get married one day?'

'One day, perhaps, if the right man comes along.'

'I wish Kate would get married but perhaps she's like you, too
independent, but she's awfully ambitious too, so wrapped up in
her work. Did you talk to her today at all?'

'Very little.'

'Outside her job she doesn't seem terribly interested in anything.
She's totally involved with her work as a barrister − and she does
represent one of the leading law firms in the city. She's working
on a very important case at the moment but she doesn't talk
about it much.'

The sound of a car outside sent her hurrying to the window
where she stood peering through the curtains. 'I thought it might
be Kate but I don't think so. It could be Alex.'

At the sudden pounding on the front door she hurried into the hall saying, 'I wonder who it is, definitely not Alex, he has a key.'

Elvira was glad the interruptions had come so soon in the evening because all the way to her aunt's house she had felt unsure about how to answer the questions she was sure her aunt would ask her. Aunt Georgia had always been the domineering one and it was doubtful that she'd changed.

She was suddenly aware that the voices in the hall were raised in anger, strident women's voices, tearful and accusing. The door into the hallway was flung open and a woman stood there glaring at her before her aunt said, 'Dora, I have a guest, my niece Elvira – I've told you Kate isn't in, let's not have a scene now.'

'I know she isn't in, I know where she is.'

'She's gone to see some friends, Dora, she's not been gone long.'

'She's with my husband, she was with him last night, he didn't come home.'

'He wasn't with Kate, Dora, she was here.'

'You're a liar, she was with my husband. I saw them go into the hotel and I waited outside in a taxi for over an hour and they didn't come out – he didn't come home last night.'

'You know they're working on a very important case.'

'In some hotel bedroom all night, don't give me that. It's been going on for months, and her so proper and full of herself. They're not getting away with it, I'm well thought of in this town and I've my children to think about.'

She stood looking down at Elvira menacingly so that Elvira jumped out of her chair and moved quickly away. 'Do you know my husband?' she asked sharply.

'No, I'm sorry.'

'Don't be, who are you anyway?'

'Elvira, Kate's cousin.'

'I've heard about you; they talk about you – and your mother.'

'Perhaps I should leave,' Elvira said anxiously.

'No, Elvira, you're my niece and my guest, if anybody should leave it's Dora with her wild accusations.'

Instead of leaving Dora sat down heavily on the nearest chair, her face vindictive, her voice tearful. 'I wonder what those people at your mother's birthday party would think if they knew about my husband and Kate. There they all were so grateful for their invitations, and there was she most of the time with James. Why he actually came back to the house for me I can't imagine.'

'Dora, why don't we sit down in a civilized manner, have a cup of tea and get to know Elvira? She's been missing from our lives for over ten years, there should be a lot to talk about.'

'It's Kate I came to see, not your niece.'

'Well then, wait until she gets home.'

Dora threw back her head and laughed discordantly. 'She's not coming back, at least not yet awhile. Do you want to know where they go? Bluebell Wood. I've sat in the car waiting for them. They didn't know I was there but that's where they used to meet. Sometimes he got there first, sometimes her, but it was always his car they preferred.

'I wonder what they'd have done if I'd knocked on the windows, but I never did. I went home and lay awake most of the night waiting for him and then when he did come home he slept in the other bedroom at the end of the corridor. When I saw him at breakfast he said he hadn't wanted to disturb me because it was so late, they'd been working late – what a joke!'

Georgia sat down heavily in the nearest chair and Elvira stood uncertainly at the window longing to leave but helpless to do so.

Dora suddenly giggled nervously. 'What an end to a birthday party,' she said. 'I bought a new dress for it and he didn't even notice. She was wearing the things she'd worn the night before.'

'Why aren't you thinking about your children?' Georgia asked. 'Have you left them in the house alone?'

'Mrs Stanley is with them, I never leave my children and Mrs Stanley knows what's going on.'

'This is quite terrible, it'll be all over the village and there's absolutely no truth in it. You should go home, Dora, and come back when you've calmed down. I'll be happy to receive your apologies then.'

'You'll get no apologies from me. I'm not going home until I've seen her; however long it takes, I intend to wait.'

They sat in silence listening to Dora's occasional sobs and then Georgia's face lit up at the sound of the hall door opening.

She rushed to her feet and made for the door, but it was Alex not Kate who stared incredulously at his mother, red-faced and angry, and then at Elvira, pale and bewildered and at Dora's stricken tearful face.

'What's going on here?' he demanded. 'I was driving past the house when I saw the cars. Is something wrong?'

'Nothing that need bother you, Alex,' his mother answered firmly.

'No? Well obviously something is wrong. Where's Kate?'

'Visiting friends,' his mother replied.

'She's with my husband,' Dora snapped. 'That's why I'm here.'

Alex decided to take the nearest chair and, looking at Elvira with a cynical smile, he said, 'I was driving up to Granny's. I thought I might be better company in that big place if Granny decided to retire. Now I can see my entertainment value couldn't possibly have come up to this. I'm new to the argument, what's it all about?'

'It's about James and your sister,' Dora cried.

'Oh that. Storm in a teacup, my dear, on its way out wouldn't you say?'

Glaring at him balefully Dora cried, 'How dare you talk about my marriage as if it didn't matter. It's been going on for months, everybody feeling sorry for me, even the children asking why their father is never at home.'

'But they work together,' Georgia cried.

'Not all night they don't, not every hour that God sends.'

Getting to her feet Elvira said anxiously, 'I really do think I should leave, Aunt Georgia, I feel I'm intruding into something that doesn't concern me.'

'Yes, Mother,' Alex said quickly. 'Even a member of the family can be embarrassed by all this. Are you really leaving tomorrow, Elvira?'

'No, I've decided to stay on for another few days. I didn't get the chance to talk to Granny and I really need to.'

'But not to tell her anything of this I hope. Poor Granny, she really does like to think that her family is functional, scandal-free and thoroughly decent.'

'And so we are,' his mother said sharply. 'There's never been a hint of scandal in our family and you know it.'

'Of course not, darling, glossed over beautifully.'

'What do you mean by that?'

'Oh never you, Mother, or Aunt Glenda, not anybody except poor Aunt Gloria because nobody ever really knew her, just like none of us ever really knew Elvira. What have you got hidden behind the skirting boards, darling?'

'I'm going, Alex. Thank you for having me, Aunt Georgia, and I do hope to see you again during the next few days. I'm sorry we didn't meet in happier circumstances, Dora.'

Sitting with her head in her hands Dora didn't reply and thankfully Elvira let herself out of the house and ran gratefully towards her car.

It was still a beautiful day, the setting sun sinking in a blaze of glory behind the western hills, leaving the sky a delicate pink over the line of beech trees at the end of the lane. It would not be dark for some time and Elvira didn't think she could face the loneliness of her grandmother's house for the rest of the day. Instead she steered her car towards the hills.

There was music coming from the inn in the centre of the High Street and people were still sitting outside to make the most of what remained of a perfect summer's evening.

She met no other drivers as she drove slowly up the hill and there was just one large car parked in the lay-by. She stopped her car. Suppose it was James Harrison's car . . . or some other couple parked there . . . perhaps she could turn round and drive away, but as she restarted and drove slowly towards the other car she could feel its emptiness . . . somehow it did not seem that it was there to accommodate lovers.

She locked her car and walked slowly up the ridge, then before she reached the summit she saw the figure of a solitary man and nervously she turned to retrace her steps. As she reached the stile a man's voice said softly, 'Elvira, is it you?'

She turned to look back and was amazed to see Roland Bannister walking swiftly towards her. He smiled, holding out his hand. 'I couldn't believe it was you, Elvira, what are you doing here all alone? It'll soon be dark.'

'Just cherishing the rest of the day.'

'You've been keeping your grandmother company?'

'Actually no, I've been with Aunt Georgia.'

'What time are you leaving in the morning?'

'I've decided to stay on for a few days.'

'I see.'

'What happened to Aunt Bessie's party, did it finish early?'

'Most of them are still there. I made an excuse that I had work to do that was rather urgent.'

'Weren't you enjoying it?'

'It's always the same thing. Joyce is still there – she'll probably stay the night.'

She stared at him uncertainly. It had been a funny sort of day and she wondered how many more unexpected things she was likely to hear before it was over.

'You seem surprised,' Roland said softly.

'Surprised to be hearing it from you. You went to a party with your wife, she stays on, you leave, unusual to say the least.'

He smiled. 'Well, yes it is, but not so unusual if you'd spent more time here in the last ten or so years.'

'Not another one telling me there are undercurrents I could never have imagined.'

'How did you hear about the other undercurrents?'

'Oh, family. Not my mother, not me . . . how could I ever have thought there might be others.'

'This is a village, Elvira, when you stumble the entire village limps.'

'Even if it's not true?'

'Even then.'

'Well, you're not sitting up here with some other woman whose husband is going mad searching for her, and your wife's at a party.'

'And which member of your family could be accused of doing that?'

'Can you think of one?'

He smiled. 'Every family has its miscreants, Elvira.'

'Don't I know it. It was always my mother, my beautiful mercurial mother who I hardly ever saw; then I'm pretty sure it was me because everybody expected me to grow up like her.'

'And you have . . . beautiful . . . I'm not too sure about the mercurial.'

'Oh, Roland, I'm beginning to wish I hadn't come, it was just going to be Granny's birthday at that beautiful old house in a village I always loved and never forgot. Instead it's been unexpectedly strange.

'It will amuse my mother. While she's waltzing the night away with her very respectable husband I'm here listening to things that at one time were only attributable to her.'

He smiled, and after a few moments she said, 'You don't seem surprised, Roland, you haven't asked me what they were.'

'No. Either I know, or I don't think they're any of my business.'

'You could tell me if they're likely to be true.'

'My dear. Scandal today, forgotten tomorrow . . .'

'But suppose it isn't forgotten tomorrow, suppose it's real and people are going to get hurt, children perhaps.'

He didn't speak, his expression grave as he looked down on the village from the door of her car. Impatiently she said, 'Roland, I'm upset by the things I've heard tonight and I wish I knew if any of it was true. You've not made it any easier by simply being here.'

'When I should be with my wife in a perfect marriage that was preordained years ago. We both know about that don't we? Elvira, we shouldn't ask questions now, it's too late, and in another ten years who knows?'

For a long moment she stared at him, then she got in her car and slammed the door. He stood in the lay-by until she had driven out into the lane, then he got into his car and followed. As the tears rolled slowly down her face she could not have imagined the expression on his: sadness and bitter with regret.

She left her car in the courtyard and walked round to the front of the house, surprised to see another car parked there. The driver was getting out.

Alex greeted her with a smile saying, 'I've been waiting ages out here. Where on earth have you been?'

'I didn't know you were coming. Why are you here?'

'I thought we should talk, we've a fair bit to say to each other.'

'Did Dora go home?'

'Eventually.'

'And did Kate come home?'

'No, but she will, probably in the morning.'

'I don't think it's funny, Alex.'

'Nor do I, my dear, that's why we should talk.'

Six

The journey home had been taken largely in silence and on their arrival at the house Steven had gone immediately to his study and he was still on the telephone.

Julie sat at her dressing table looking morosely in the mirror until she removed her hat. The hat had been a mistake, it had been silly and glamorous but there had only been a handful of women wearing them, mainly older women who wore hats for every occasion, mostly boring and outdated.

The dress too had been a mistake. It was too dramatic, too theatrical and her husband's family had been amused by it rather than impressed.

She was glad to get out of her finery and into something casual. It was evident they would not be going out again. Steven would sit slumped in his chair, his head buried in a newspaper or finding fault with what the television had to offer. As parties went it had been pleasant enough. The food had been good, the atmosphere largely relaxed and if there had been any disparities at all they had been within the family.

Steven was still on the telephone so she went to sit in the living room waiting for him to join her. When he did she saw immediately that his face was dour, which told her that the telephone conversation had hardly been cheering.

After a long silence she said sharply, 'You're in a rotten mood, Steven, who was that on the phone?'

'Nobody you know.'

'You didn't speak to your mother before we left, why was that?'

'She was surrounded with people, I wanted to get away.'

'Why, for heaven's sake, we're not doing anything?'

'I'll talk to my mother when she's on her own, not surrounded by well-wishers.'

'You didn't seem to have much to say to anybody. Did you speak to Elvira?'

'Briefly. I left that to the others, all falling over themselves to hear about Gloria and her elevation into Viennese aristocracy.'

'She's really quite pretty.'

He scowled. He didn't want to talk about his mother's birthday party or any of the people who had turned up for it. The horse he'd placed so much faith in had come in fourth and he'd lost a packet he could ill afford to. Of course he hadn't spoken with his mother, he owed her money and on the few occasions when their eyes had met he had read in hers only doubt and anxiety.

He couldn't afford to pay her back but he didn't know how to tell her. He felt his wife's eyes on him, searching, puzzled, but her next words did nothing to calm his fears.

'What is your mother going to do about the house?' she asked.

'The house?'

'Yes, the manor. It's far too big for her, she should be looking at something smaller, a bungalow perhaps so that we could move in there.'

'Move in there, what are you talking about, woman? I don't want that house.'

'You're her son, Steven, your sisters are both widowed, they won't want it and who else is there? I've always liked it, even when I was a child I used to walk up there and sit in the field pretending I lived there; it was my dream house.'

'Then, Julie, you'd better forget your dream.'

'You mean you never want to live there?'

'Never in a thousand years. For one thing we couldn't afford it and for another it's too big.'

'How can it be too big when your mother lives in it on her own apart from the servants. She'll probably leave it to you, so why don't we think about it now rather than later.'

'I'm not thinking about it at all, so you can forget it.'

'But what's going to happen to it?'

'I neither know nor care.'

'Well, I care. Who else is there for it?'

'Some industrialist with money to burn, perhaps Alex, who never seems short, certainly not me.'

'My father would be interested. He can afford it.'

'Julie, it is my mother's home, so far as I know she's shown no interest in moving so I think she intends to stay there.'

'She *is* eighty.'

'And from the looks of her a fairly robust eighty. She could soldier on til she's into her nineties. Let's have no more talk about the house, Julie. I have another call to make, then I think I'll wander along to the pub. I want to see Jerry Martin, he's usually in there on Saturday evening.'

She stared after him infuriated. He wasn't going to get away with it, tomorrow she'd visit her father – she'd always been his little girl, Julie had to have the best, be the best – and her father was a down-to-earth man with good advice and money to go with it.

She heard the front door close and then the sound of Steven's car. She went immediately into the small study across the hall without quite knowing what she was looking for. There were names on the telephone pad that she hadn't heard of.

Steven had never been methodical and the drawers in his desk were untidy – crumpled chocolate paper screwed up with invoices, and letters from people she'd never heard of and didn't understand anyway.

The middle drawer in the desk was locked. Julie was looking for his bank statements which were evidently in there. She searched for a key but was unable to find it. She wondered if Steven himself knew where it was.

What was so urgent that he needed to see Jerry Martin? She'd mentioned him to her father and he'd said Steven should steer clear of him. Jerry was a gambler, dodgy and not one to be trusted, so why on a Saturday evening was he searching for Jerry leaving her here alone?

She decided to telephone her father only to be answered by her stepmother's voice saying, 'He's out, Julie, not back from the races. I thought you were at a birthday party.'

'It was luncheon.'

'Oh, really. Well I didn't go to the races, I had something else on. Can I ask your father to ring you?'

'No, Steven might be back, I'll phone him again.'

Julie had no feelings for her stepmother either one way or the other. Steven called her the wicked witch of the North when he wanted to be funny, but to Julie she was somebody who kept her father company without being any danger to herself. She was reasonably attractive, reasonably popular in the circle in which they moved, but then her mother had hardly figured largely in her schooldays or her father's business life.

The evening before his second marriage he'd been anxious to reassure Julie that she'd always be the first one, she had nothing to fear from Valerie.

She returned to the lounge and decided to try the television. It was some trite film she'd seen before and there didn't seem to be anything else she wanted to watch.

She thought about Elvira, probably bored to tears in that big house attempting to satisfy her grandmother's questions about her life.

Elvira's mother had been Steven's youngest sister and he'd often kept her entertained with stories of Gloria's love affairs and her life in general. It was always Gloria who had been the belle of the ball, the madcap girl who had ridden her horse recklessly across the fences at the point-to-point meetings.

There had always been a tinge of envy whenever Gloria had been discussed, and now she was far enough away in a different world with a man they had never met.

'They're as jealous of her as they are of me,' Julie had once said to Steven, and after laughing he'd said, 'They're not jealous of you, Julie, they're just amusing themselves.'

'I'm a bookmaker's daughter and they'd have liked it better if you'd married that upper-crust girl who chased after you. Why didn't you marry her?'

'Because I've never done what was expected of me.'

'When I met you I thought you were going to be a lawyer, I wanted you to be a lawyer, not involved with gambling, which doesn't always work out. My father is angry that you're doing this.'

'He won't be when I hit the jackpot.'

'But will you, Steven? It's a long time coming.'

As she sat curled up in her easy chair she thought about the long and often bitter arguments they had had across the years. Their son was often difficult, too much like Steven. The fact that he had decided to go off climbing instead of attending his grandmother's birthday party had caused anger and bitterness in the family, what next?

She was dozing fitfully when her father telephoned, and hearing her muffled voice he said anxiously, 'You all right, Julie? This is Dad, Val said you phoned.'

'Oh, it's nothing much, Dad, but I need to see you. I have thought I'd call at your office on Monday morning if that's all right with you.'

'Yes, why not, I'll look forward to it. Nothing wrong I hope.'

'No. Just something I want your advice about.'

'You know you can always have that, love. I believe you've been to a birthday party.'

'Yes, Steven's mother.'

'Good was it?'

'Yes. Loads of people there. Didn't you know it was her birthday?'

'Well, Charlotte and me are not exactly bosom chums, Julie. Is Steven there?'

'No, he had to go out to see somebody, he'll be back presently.'

'Did Val tell you we're thinking of getting away for a little while? When did you and Steven last have a holiday?'

'Oh, you know Steven, too much going on here that he doesn't want to miss.'

'Why don't you come along with us, it'd do you good – new place, change of people, we're thinking of France.'

'Oh, I don't know, Dad, wouldn't Val mind?'

'She wouldn't have to mind.'

'Well, I'll think about it. See you Monday morning, Dad, around ten.'

That was just like him, taking his wife for granted. Of course Val would mind but it was something she just might think about. Steven was in no hurry to return to the house and she was tired. It had been a long day and instead of mooning about downstairs she decided to go to bed.

She stood for a while looking out of her bedroom window at a pale crescent moon silvering the rooftops of the cottages in the lane, a lane singularly quiet for a Saturday night. Steven and his cronies would be in their favourite haunt on the High Street. There would be laughter and ribaldry, talk of racing and cricket, golf, and Steven would no doubt elaborate on his mother's party, most of which he needed to invent.

She wanted to tell her father about Charlotte's house. When she married Steven Chaytor, spoilt, ambitious Julie had been as concerned with the things that came with him as she had been with the boy himself. She fancied herself as the lady of the manor; she was destined for it.

The fact that Steven had disappointed her sorely would be brushed aside, everything else in her life that she had found abhorrent had suffered a similar fate.

She wanted the house, her father would want it for her – oh, perhaps not just yet – but soon, after all Charlotte was eighty and she could be persuaded to move on, diplomatically, into something smaller.

Neither Glenda nor Georgia would want it. Kate was ambitious, but not for property, and Glenda's daughters had married well but were hardly manor house material. There was Alex of course.

Alex was an unknown quantity; she was always aware of the cynicism in his eyes, the teasing banter in his voice, and he too was ambitious, ambitious and successful.

She couldn't picture Marian taking Charlotte's place. Marian was distant and hardly welcoming. Marian was wrapped up in her children, the church and her home. Not really the sort of wife Alex could have been expected to have but because nobody really knew Marian perhaps she was the one to be feared.

She dreaded Sundays. Steven was not a churchgoer, he'd always maintained that he'd had too much of it as a child, and now he could please himself, so it was either the golf club or something to do with horses.

She could go to church of course, but most of the conversation afterwards would have to do with Charlotte's party, and she'd had a surfeit of that.

She supposed she could go up to the manor, see Elvira again, make an excuse that they'd not seen each other for years and they needed to chat more.

It was no good visiting her father, he and Val usually drove off somewhere for lunch and in any case she needed to see her father alone, not when Val was there.

At half past ten she decided to go to bed. She didn't want any more conversation with Steven, he'd be too argumentative or too morose, however his cronies and the pub had affected him.

She couldn't sleep so she thought about the house. She wanted it, and she visualized what she would do with it. Of course Charlotte's furniture was in keeping with the building and with the tradition that surrounded it, but it needed to change. Burr Walnut and a preponderance of oil paintings were boring – who bought display cabinets these days, and bronze and marble statues were silly, they had no place in houses now.

She'd change the carpets for one thing. Persian designs and Indian carpets too were no good – she wanted fitted carpets and silk curtains instead of those heavy velvets her mother-in-law was so fond of. And what about the kitchen? The kitchen at the manor was medieval with its vast Aga range and huge Welsh dressers. She'd have a white kitchen with all new units, something light and airy.

She switched on the light when she heard the sound of a car outside, surprised to see that it was after twelve o'clock. She knew that a few of the men went into the landlord's private rooms after closing time so she guessed that he would either lurch his way upstairs or sit in front of the television with the whisky bottle in front of him.

Her thoughts strayed to the birthday party, and particularly to the guests on the top table reserved for family.

Charlotte was eighty but she still possessed that genteel aristocratic beauty that found its place in the portrait at the head of the stairs in the manor. Neither of the two daughters present had captured their mother's looks or charm. Glenda was sweet, unremarkable, and Georgia was haughty and distant.

Glenda's daughters and their husbands were ordinary – nothing wrong in that – but the house would be wasted on them; and Kate was too like her mother, too ambitious, and if the rumours were right, too wrapped up in somebody else's husband.

Maybe Alex was to be feared. Alex would look after Alex and he had children to consider even if his wife was hardly a problem.

Of course Elvira wouldn't come into it. Elvira had been the wild child, simply because her mother had hardly ever been around, besides she was simply another granddaughter, while Steven was her son.

Charlotte had looked so complacent, so sure that everything

in her world was sacrosanct – surrounded by family who loved her, friends who respected her, a pefect summer's day and nothing but perfection everywhere. But then their own son hadn't been there.

It was no use, she couldn't sleep, she had to go downstairs to see what her husband was doing, so she slipped into her dressing gown and went to stand at the head of the stairs. She could see that the light was on in the living room and hear the television. As she had thought, Steven sat slouched in his chair, his glass had been knocked over and its contents were still dripping on to the carpet.

In some anger she shook him, so that he cursed angrily before he opened his eyes to glare at her furiously. 'What ails you woman? You've spilled my whisky,' he cried.

'I didn't spill it, you did, do you know what time it is?'

'I'll come to bed when I'm ready.'

'Fine Saturday this has turned out to be. Here you are drunk at three in the morning, we never said goodbye to your mother and other people do things on Saturday night – what do we do? Nothing.'

'I thought you'd done enough for one day.'

'We never seem to do anything or go anywhere these days. My father's invited me to go with them to France for a few days, they have a better time than we do.'

'He's probably got more money.'

'And what about your money? When you left law wasn't it to make more money than you'd ever dreamed of – where is it?'

'You're too impatient.'

'Yes, I am, I have every right to be. I'll tell my father I'll go with them to France.'

'Please yourself. Is your father paying for you?'

'He will, but shouldn't you be doing that?'

'He's issued the invitation. Oh, go to bed, Julie, we'll talk about France tomorrow when I feel more like it.'

He sank back in his chair and she stared at him exasperated. Of course she'd go to France. Val would be annoyed, her father would ask too many questions and she'd lie about most of them.

Her eyes fell on the black hat ceremoniously perched on the chair near the window. That had been the hat destined to convince everybody that she was manor house material. She'd known there wouldn't be many hats there, so she'd stand out as elegant and worthy of the name Chaytor.

The other hats had been insignificant, but hers had been pricey and in keeping with the rest of her apparel. The fact that it had caused some amusement among her husband's family and some of their guests hadn't troubled her in the slightest. She liked being flamboyant. All her life she'd been encouraged to be the brightest, the loudest and the most prominent; she wasn't going to stop now simply because Steven had money worries on his mind.

Money worries to Julie were trivial. Not changing the car this year, perhaps one holiday or none at all, not so many dinner parties and Steven scanning her dress bills instead of saying 'Have what you want, dear' – there'd be time to make up for it next year.

It was all very tiresome, she didn't interfere with his business why should he interfere with things she wanted to do to the house.

Her mind strayed to Gloria. She had been two years younger than Steven and the two of them had more or less always done what they'd wanted. Of course being the man he had had to think about making a living whereas Gloria had found some man or other to look after her, but she'd fallen on her feet and Julie had no difficulty in believing that Steven would too. Neither of them were like Charlotte, and although she'd never known his father she'd heard enough people telling her that he'd been a perfect gentleman.

What made a perfect gentleman? – not having money worries, not gambling what money you had, and not cheating on your wife or neglecting your family.

She couldn't think that Steven had ever been interested in other women. He'd seen to it that their son had received a good education even when careerwise he was something of a playboy.

Her father was too generous with him; when she saw him on Monday she'd have a word with him about that, and she would go to France, give them all something to talk about.

Seven

Alex followed Elvira into the drawing room, saying with a smile, 'I'm curious, I thought you'd be coming back here, where did you get to?'

'I drove around. The sky was beautiful and I felt I needed to see more of the village, after all a short afternoon hasn't really been enough.'

'Well, I'm here to keep you company.'

'Don't you think you should be keeping your mother company, she was very upset.'

'Elvira, my mother's upsets will be over in five minutes when Kate assures her there's nothing to be upset about.'

'Can you really think that Dora's going to let it rest there?'

'I think her husband can persuade her to.'

She stood looking out across the gardens now silvered by moonlight and she was remembering this room as a schoolgirl, sometimes lonely when her grandparents had gone to some function or other, at other times watching her grandmother working at her tapestry, or sad and unhappy after her grandfather had died.

Most vividly she remembered her parents bringing her to the manor on their way to the hunt ball. Her father had looked handsome in his hunting pink evening jacket, and her mother incredibly beautiful in her ball gown. They had looked so well together and yet in reality they had spent very little time together. Had her father ever really cared, had either of them ever really cared about their daughter?

Her thoughts were interrupted by Alex saying, 'How about a drink? I remember Granny always kept a good supply of scrumpy.'

'Should we be raiding her wine cupboard?'

'Well of course, she'll be most upset in the morning if she thought I'd been gallant enough to keep you company and hadn't thought to offer you a drink. What will it be, G and T, sherry, wine, there's sure to be one we fancy? Your mother always fancied German wine, I'm not surprised she married an Austrian.'

'How do you know what my mother fancied?'

'My dear, she was young enough and popular enough to enter-tain me and my chums, who all adored her. They fancied her like mad, the fact that she was my aunt didn't put them off, and I felt unduly flattered.'

'Did you think I'd grow up like her?'

'Not really. You were a bit of a tomboy. The boys liked you but you weren't a sexy sort of girl. In any case you only had eyes for Roland Bannister and he was ear-marked for the Mansell girl.'

'Funny how we tend to put people in parcels with names on them, and then the parcels remain closed for so long.'

'And when they're opened the contents have altered.'

'Something like that.'

She smiled as he placed a glass of wine on the table near her chair. 'I've opened the wine, Elvira. When you next see your mother ask her if she remembers the group of boys she used to dance for and sing to.'

'Did she really do all that?'

'Of course.'

'I wonder what I was doing then?'

'Asleep in your bed, and now here you are all grown-up and surprisingly mature.'

'Tell me about you and Marian.'

'I'll tell you what it was like when I was growing up: money married money, land married land. The Steadly family were rich, they had one daughter, Marian, and she was eminently suitable material for one of the Chaytor boys.

'Actually I was the only Chaytor boy, like Steven had been the generation before. Steven didn't actually take to any of the blue-blooded girls the family had picked out for him, instead he went for a bookie's daughter, pretty, a father well heeled, but not quite out of the top drawer.'

'And Marian?'

'Ideal wife material, but sometimes it isn't enough. You know, Elvira, we have absolutely nothing in common.'

'You have the children?'

'She leans on those children, smothers them with affection, but I'm the bread-ticket and only that.'

'I'm sure that's not right. You see them, play games with them, talk to them.'

'Not very often these days because Marian has something they need to do or be seen doing. Something at church, to do with church, even the vicar thinks they should see more of me and the rest of the family. Even today, Elvira, they seemed singularly alone and apart from the other children.'

'I think it's strange that you're here with me when Marian is at home with the children. A little bit like Dora actually except that you're not with the other woman.'

He laughed. 'I never thought of it like that though actually Marian and Dora are a little bit alike. In one way they would have differed.'

'What way is that?'

'Marian would never have forced her way into the other woman's home to accuse her of having an affair with me. No, she'd have played the martyr, poured out her heart to the vicar and assured his congregation that she was a brave, principled woman tied to an unfeeling womaniser, but she'd survive.'

'I can't believe you really mean that.'

'It's a pity you're not here for longer, then you'd see this disintegrated family as it really is.'

'Is Granny aware of the problems?'

'I'm sure she isn't, I expect she regards us all as organized, decent people who would never let the family down by being anything less than perfect.'

She didn't want to ask Alex about Roland and Joyce, but her meeting with him on the hillside had disturbed her strangely, but how to go about it without rousing his cynical amusement.

'Isn't there anything else of interest that you feel I should know about?' she finally asked.

'Such as?'

'Well, when I left your mother's house I saw Roland Bannister driving away alone from Aunty Bessie's. Wasn't there supposed to be another party?'

'You say he was alone?'

'Yes, I'm sure he was. Perhaps not, perhaps Joyce was with him.'

'Or maybe Roland had had enough partying for one day. I've

never been to one of Aunty Bessie's parties but I can guess what went on there.'

'You make it sound like an orgy.'

'Anything but, my dear. No, the Mansell clan would be there in full attendance. And the discussion: Joyce's attire, her charm, her beauty, how wonderful to witness her demeanour.'

'All of which Roland would agree with.'

'But don't you think it could all have been a little boring to say the least. They've been married five years, five years of Joyce's acumen could begin to be a bit tedious don't you think. At least it would be for me.'

'He was probably going home to walk the dog.'

'They don't have a dog. Dogs shed hair, leave muddy footprints, jump up on impeccable clothing.'

'They don't like dogs?'

'But didn't Roland have a dog – you liked his dog.'

She'd loved him, a black Labrador she'd wished was hers even when her mother said dogs were too much trouble.

'You're making everything and everybody seem sinister, Alex, and I'm sure they're not. Tomorrow when I talk to Granny it'll all seem different.'

He laughed. 'But you'll remember our conversation, Elvira, you'll remember when she talks to you about Kate and her ambition, that Dora was practically hysterical about her, and her rapturous twaddle about Steven will only make you remember things about Steven she doesn't know anything about. At least I doubt if she'll know why Roland left Aunt Bessie's alone.'

'Aren't you going to call to see your mother on the way home?'

'Certainly not. Kate will still be missing and she'll have me out there warning her. Oh no, my dear, but it will be interesting to see how Kate gets out of this one.'

'You're not very sure that she will.'

'With mother perhaps, but not if the firm gets a hint of it. No firm of lawyers likes scandal – money's involved, and reputation, and for a firm that handles everybody else's reputations losing their own will not be tolerated.'

'I have the feeling, Alex, that you're really enjoying all this and I'm wondering why when it's your own family at risk.'

'Don't you remember? Elvira, I was always able to laugh at

other people's problems, and in those days I was a bright happy-go-lucky lad with few problems; now I'm a bored, cynical man with too many problems.'

'Probably imaginary.'

'I don't think so. I have a good career, enough money, a beautiful house and friends, some of them good ones, so why am I restless? Why am I not sitting at home on a Saturday evening blissfully content instead of pouring my heart out to you?'

'Alex, I don't really know you.'

'So why don't we talk about you, then. Tell me about the man or men in your life, how you spend your time, where do you live and who do you live with?'

'I live in a small cottage in a small village very similar to this one but it's in Cornwall near the coast.'

'Cornwall! Cornwall for heaven's sake, what are you doing there?'

'I did very well with art at school, it was probably the only real thing I did well at. I went with my mother to an art exhibition in Truro and I met this man there who had a small college in Cornwall for would-be artists. He offered me a job after he'd seen some of my work.'

Alex laughed. 'Probably after he'd taken a shine to your mother.'

'I told you – he liked my work.'

'And you're still there?'

'Yes. Some of the students are very good, others are struggling, but yes I'm still there and I get to paint and show my work. It's a great painting place.'

'And what about the time when you're not painting? Don't tell me there isn't some man to go home to, Elvira, you're twenty-six, beautiful and intelligent, there has to be someone.'

'Maybe, maybe not.'

'I've told you my problems.'

'Well, perhaps I don't have any. Won't your wife be wondering where you are?'

'Do you want to get rid of me?'

'I think it's time you went home. I'm here for a week, we'll see each other again I hope.'

'I was rather hoping to have another drink, but perhaps not. You'll explain to Granny in the morning, I hope, that we helped ourselves to her wine cupboard.'

'You don't think she'll mind?'

'I think she'll be relieved that I stood in for her as host. You can't say the night's been boring, Elvira. Why did your mother call you Elvira; it's a name I've never heard of?'

'She was a fan of Noel Coward, and I rather think he used it in one of his plays.'

'Perhaps you'll see me off then, I think the servants will be in bed by this time.'

As they stood together in the courtyard she looked up into his smiling face and he reached out and drew her into his arms. It was a warm, brotherly embrace and, as he released her, he said, 'Goodnight, Elvira, it seems a long time since I held a young beautiful girl in my arms, pity you're family.'

She laughed, and watched while he ran quickly down the steps towards his waiting car.

It was the sound of his car that awakened Charlotte. Moonlight filtered gently through the curtains and she reached out for her walking stick as she struggled out of bed.

Who could possibly be leaving at this hour? She saw by her clock that it was almost one o'clock and she was glad of the lamp on her bedside table as she made her way to the window.

The car was heading for the gates, pausing for a moment before heading for the village, and she wondered which one of the family could have been thoughtful enough to think of Elvira. She felt very guilty, they'd had no time to talk and she would be leaving in the morning.

She struggled into her dressing gown and decided to investigate. Her visitor had only just left so Elvira must still be downstairs and she badly wanted to talk to her. From the top of the stairs she could look down into the hall where one light still glowed and she could see that the hall door was open to allow moonlight to flood through. She stood on the stairs waiting, and then she saw Elvira coming back into the hall and quietly closing the door behind her.

She moved slowly down the stairs and Elvira looked up and seeing her there ran quickly across the hall and up the stairs.

'Granny, wait,' she cried. 'I'll help you. Please don't come any further.'

She took her grandmother's arm and slowly they descended

the stairs and entered the living room. Charlotte's eyes fell immediately on the table near to the chair where Alex had been sitting, and where the wine bottle and his empty glass still rested. At least it was a relief to see that whoever their guest had been had not been afraid to enjoy some refreshment.

Elvira saw her grandmother settled in her easy chair before saying, 'Didn't you sleep well, Granny?' Before she answered she said quickly, 'Granny, we raided your wine cupboard, I hope you don't mind.'

'We, dear?'

'Alex came. He made me promise to apologize but it was kind of him to keep me company, I enjoyed it.'

'I'm glad he looked after you, my dear, although I'd never actually thought of Alex as a good Samaritan. Perhaps I misjudged him.'

'He was entertaining, very amusing actually. We talked about the family, the old days, all sorts of things.'

'I didn't think you actually figured in the old days with Alex, dear.'

'No, perhaps not, but we really did find a great many things to talk about.'

'His wife, his sister?'

Elvira looked at her anxiously, wondering how much she knew about the family and, seeing her doubtful expression, Charlotte said, 'They think I live my life in a close, sheltered world without evil, where people behave beautifully towards each other and never fall from grace. Elvira, I'm eighty years of age, I have tried to be a good woman, I loved your grandfather and we had a good marriage, but I've seen the sort of things that happened to other people and thanked God that like things hadn't happened to me.

'I worried about your mother, I've worried about Steven and others in the family and yet none of them talk to me. It's rather as if I've got to be spared from all that goes on in life and yet I'm not such a fool that I can't see it for myself.'

'Then why don't you tell them, Granny?'

'I've tried, they don't listen, I've got to be shielded from such things. I've been a terrible hostess, Elvira, and I did so want to talk to you about all sorts of things: you, your mother, the lives you lead – and you're leaving in the morning.'

'No, Granny, I'm staying for the rest of the week. I've managed to arrange it.'

'Oh, I'm so glad, so tomorrow we'll talk. I have to go to church though, the vicar told me there'd be a special mention for my birthday and he's such a nice man I don't want to let him down.'

'We'll go, Granny, and I can see more of the others.'

'Do you know when I heard the car I really thought it might be the Bannisters' car.'

'Joyce and Roland, but why?'

'Oh, think nothing of it, dear, it was just a thought.'

'But why should they come, didn't they have Aunty Bessie's birthday party to go to?'

'Of course. I know her birthday's the same day as mine. When you were all small and came to my party Joyce had to leave early to go to her Aunt's party, then she used to come back here with a multitude of presents that her relatives had given her, simply to show us.'

'Presents for Joyce, but wasn't it her aunt's party?'

'Oh, my dear, that little girl was idolized and she was such a pretty little thing. She never went near the horses and she hated dogs. She was so pristine, never got her dress soiled, her hair always so neat and tidy and the ribbons tied so perfectly.'

'Didn't you wish I was like her?'

'No, dear, you would have had an awful lot of living up to do and I doubt if your mother would have wanted it. That job would have been left to me.'

'Let me take you back to bed, Granny. We can do all our talking tomorrow and the rest of the week.'

No longer tired, all Charlotte wanted to do was talk to this new granddaughter and before Elvira could pull her to her feet she said, 'I'd love a cup of tea, dear, before I go to bed, wouldn't you like one?'

'Are you sure, it's awfully late?'

'I know, but a cup of tea would be so nice, and just to talk for a few more minutes. You know where the kitchen is or shall I get it for us?'

'No, I'll do it. Are you quite warm?'

'Oh yes, it's been such a beautiful day.'

How well she knew the kitchen with its old Aga range and

the Welsh dresser with its preponderance of willow pattern. She should have known that her grandmother's housekeeper would be methodical, cups and saucers and cutlery in the right place, and tea in the right canister. Fortunately there was a new electric kettle that she knew hadn't been there in the old days.

She laid out biscuits on a small tray suddenly realizing that she'd had very little to eat. She'd been late for lunch, merely helping herself to one or two sandwiches later in the afternoon but she didn't really feel tired. She'd spent the night in a London hotel before travelling to the party and she'd enjoyed a good breakfast, and as she waited for the kettle to boil her thoughts strayed to the evening she'd just spent.

She thought about Dora and her distraught anger, her aunt's insistence that her daughter could do no wrong, and Alex's cynical feelings about his dysfunctional family, as he'd called them, but most of all she thought about Roland standing alone on the hillside, his expression thoughtful, and strangely sad. He'd seemed like a man surrounded by a great loneliness until suddenly his remoteness had gone and he felt the need to assure her that all was well.

Eight

Sitting across the breakfast table from her grandmother Elvira thought she looked considerably happier and brighter than she'd looked the day before. She was wearing three rows of pearls against her black dress, entirely elegant, and Elvira said, 'You look very nice, Granny, black flatters you, just as it suits my mother.'

'Yes, my mother always said that blondes looked well in black, brunettes should wear red. I'm no longer blonde, I was only just over forty when my hair turned to silver.'

'Am I driving you to church, Granny?'

'Oh no, dear, I've still got the old Bentley your grandfather was so fond of. She's my best friend although I no longer drive her.'

'You mean you've got a chauffeur?'

'Nothing so grand, dear. No, I have Vincent. He does all sorts of things around the house: gardening, a bit of decorating – and there's always something going wrong somewhere.'

'Do the rest of the family go to church?'

'Georgia and Glenda, I'm not so sure about the younger element.'

On their way to the car Elvira speculated as to which young element might be there. Kate and Alex she had doubts about, the rest she tried to visualize, but as they drew up at the church gates it was Aunt Georgia who hurried forward to greet them.

She said quickly, 'I wondered if you'd be coming this morning, Mother, particularly after yesterday.'

At that moment a woman came forward, embracing Charlotte, and Georgia whispered urgently, 'You haven't said anything to Mother about last evening, Elvira?'

'Of course not.'

Much relieved, Georgia said, 'Well we don't want to worry her with something like that. I can't think what came over Dora, it was all so ridiculously untrue.'

'Will Kate be here this morning?'

'I doubt she'll have the time, dear. She's so terribly busy with this case she's working on, I don't see much of her. She's up there in the study surrounded by paperwork.'

'Even though it's Sunday.'

'Oh, Elvira, Sunday's just another day to Kate. I didn't even bother to ask her if she would be coming to church.'

Charlotte had walked on ahead still chatting to the woman who seemed to be doing most of the talking, and Georgia said 'That's Bessie Mansell Mother's talking to, they're probably discussing their parties.'

'Aunty Bessie?'

'Yes. She does go on a bit, you'll have to rescue Mother, Elvira.'

Elvira was introduced to Aunty Bessie who said quickly, 'Oh, I do remember you, dear, but I wouldn't have known you now.'

'No, it's ten years since I've been here.'

'Weren't you a friend of Joyce's? She was such a beautiful girl, wasn't she, we all adored her.'

More people were walking up the path now and Georgia said quickly, 'Oh no, Dora's here, I hope she doesn't make a scene here, she was so unpredictable last night.'

She hurried in front of them and Charlotte said quickly, 'What's the matter with Georgia? Who is she running away from?'

By this time Dora had caught up with them, favouring Charlotte with a brief smile, before stalking into the church.

Charlotte sighed. Dora was the matter with Georgia. How could anyone live in a village the size of this one and not know something about conflicts and scandals going on in it? And how much more worrying when one of the scandals concerns a member of the family.

Glenda came hurrying up the church path and Charlotte said quickly, 'Are you all alone, dear?'

'Oh, I'm sure one or two of the others will be coming. I'm surprised you're here, Mother, shouldn't you be resting today?'

'Don't fuss, Glenda. Have you forgotten the vicar is giving me a special mention this morning?'

'Oh yes, of course. Well, do go and sit down, we'll talk later. Elvira, what time are you leaving?'

'I'm not, I'm here for a few more days.'

'Oh, that's nice, dear. We're all dying to hear about your mother and her new life in Austria, about you too, dear.'

'I'm sure you'll find Mother far more interesting.'

'Well, wasn't she always.'

As they sat waiting for the service to start Charlotte whispered, 'I see that Georgia's on her own, I didn't expect Alex but I thought Kate might be here.'

'She's busy with work, Granny.'

'Among other things I've no doubt,' Charlotte said dryly.

The service was predictable, like all those other services she remembered, and the vicar's eulogy on her grandmother's life fulsome and charming.

There were so many people milling around after the service was over. People spoke to her that she didn't remember but who said they remembered her, and Aunty Bessie asked, 'Do you go to church where you live, Elvira?'

'Yes, sometimes.'

'Oh, I never miss. Joyce goes to the church near their house. They live in that lovely house over in Ashlea. You should visit her while you're here. Everything is so perfect, you'll be very impressed I'm sure, but then that's Joyce for you. She'd be delighted to see you, Elvira.'

'A week isn't really very long to do everything, Mrs Mansell.'

'I'm Miss Mansell, dear, I'm Joyce's father's sister.'

'Oh, I'm sorry.'

'I was engaged to be married once, a young officer in the Cheshire Regiment. Unfortunately he was killed in the war, just twenty-four years old.'

'I'm so sorry.'

'You're not married, dear?'

'No. I must go, Miss Mansell, Granny is waiting for me.'

Vincent was already holding the car door open for them when Julie greeted them rather breathlessly, flamboyant and sporting extravagant jewellery, a great deal of it.

She kissed Charlotte who said, 'I didn't see you in church, Julie.'

'No, I was late getting there so I sat at the back. We had to call for petrol – you know Steven, he's always late or has forgotten to fill the car up the day before.'

'Is Steven here then?'

'No, he had to get back, I've got a lift home with the Stewarts. You're looking much better than you did yesterday. We do worry about you, Mother, that house is so terribly big for you, it must need a lot of looking after.'

'I have very good servants, Julie.'

'I know, but they're not getting any younger and the young ones move on don't they. Like I said we do worry about you, dear.'

'How very thoughtful of you, Julie, but there's really no need. I think your friends are waiting for you.'

Julie kissed her effusively and turning to Elvira said, 'Do look after her, dear. I'm sure you agree with me about the house, a sweet little bungalow somewhere nearer the shops would be ideal.'

Sitting in the car Charlotte sat smiling. 'I've been hearing more and more of this recently, mostly from Julie.'

'I wonder why.'

'Oh, Julie always has a reason, it could be that she would like my house, perhaps she feels they have every right to it.'

'Uncle Steven is your son, Granny.'

'Well, obviously I can't go on forever but I can't see Steven taking over. Neither of the girls will want it, and certainly not your mother. How can it possibly compare with life in old Vienna.'

'Granny, it's too far off. You've years to go yet. I suggest we forget about Julie and her fantasies.'

Charlotte laughed. 'So, what shall we do with the rest of our day? I always loved Sundays, now I think it's a good idea if we drive off somewhere for lunch, I don't feel in the mood for visitors and I have a feeling there'll be some.'

'Then we'll go in my car, Granny. It's nothing like this one but it's a dear little car, you'll love it.'

'Then we'll tell the servants we're going out, and Vincent can have the rest of Sunday to himself.'

Glenda reflected that she had never seen her sister in such a hurry to leave the church. Normally she'd spend so much time chatting to all and sundry, but this morning she'd darted off as though she was being pursued. She'd been going to suggest that they called to see her mother sometime in the afternoon and perhaps have a chat with Elvira.

Georgia didn't want to talk to anybody, she wanted to get home to confront her daughter.

She'd been in bed when Kate had come home but she hadn't been asleep, she'd been too busy thinking about Kate and James Harrison. Where had she been until three o'clock in the morning? Obviously not in some hotel bedroom, and from the look on Dora's face her anger of the evening before was still there.

Kate watched her mother hurrying up the garden path and sat down in expectancy of the accusations to come. Meeting her mother's stern eyes she said quickly, 'Say what you have to say, Mother. I know I was late home, or rather early if you like to put it that way, but I am old enough to have a life outside my profession.'

'Kate, where were you? Dora Harrison was here, absolutely furious. I didn't know what to do with her. Elvira was here too, she witnessed it all.'

'What was Dora doing here?'

'I'd invited her, but when she came it was terrible. She accused you of having an affair with her husband, said you were together, that it's been going on for months. Do you know what it will do to your careers, everybody's going to know about it.'

'Then they'll all say I'm another Gloria, this family's had its fair share of scandal.'

'You're not in the least like Gloria.'

'How do you know, Mother? I always had a secret longing to be like her.'

'But James Harrison of all people. Aren't there enough men in the world without your going off with him?'

'I haven't gone off with him, Mother.'

'No, but you're in danger of doing something as stupid.'

'Such as what?'

'Well you work for the same firm, the best firm in the city and you're both jeopardizing everything you've worked for. How serious is it?'

'It seems to me we spend our lives sorting people's problems out, fraudulent and adulterous, scandalous and infamous, call it something we fell into; besides, James isn't happy in his marriage, you've seen Dora, can you imagine what she's like to live with?'

'The woman's unhappy. Her husband's having an affair and you're the cause of it. She'll take it further, ask for a divorce and then what?'

'Don't the guilty partners usually live down their misdemeanours by getting married and settling down to blameless respectability?'

'And will you?'

'No, Mother. I wouldn't marry James Harrison if he was the last man living. He's just somebody who was there, not badlooking, fairly decent as a lover, but not a husband, not my husband.'

'So you thought you could get away with it because you're colleagues, you work together, nobody to ask questions, until his wife started asking them.'

'It'll be Dora's word against ours, and everybody knows what Dora's like. We'll end it, he'll know how to pacify her, it'll all work out.'

'I wish I had your convictions. Alex knows about it, he came while Dora was here.'

'Gracious. How many other people were here to see Dora?'

'He is your brother.'

'And hardly likely to be too concerned about my fall from grace. He has enough problems of his own anyway.'

'Problems, what problems?'

'Oh nothing, Mother, nothing for you to worry about.'

'You mean he's got another woman?'

'If I was a man married to Marian I'd have several.'

Georgia sat down weakly on the nearest chair. Never in a million years could she ever have thought to be having this sort of conversation with Kate. Kate who had always been so correct, clever and ambitious, discreet and proper. The little girl who never stepped out of line, dressed classically and discreetly passed her exams with flying colours and who chose her friends from like-minded people.

Her mind went back over the years to her sister Gloria's indiscretions, but then Gloria had not been anything like Kate. Gloria had been beautiful, flirtatious, and men had flocked around her like flies around the honeypot.

Scandal and Gloria had touched them all, even Elvira's father, and that had hurt most of all when she reflected on how much she had been in love with him.

Oh, surely it wasn't going to start all over again, and not here with Kate. She didn't want to have to tell her mother, and yet Charlotte would know best what to do. Her mother was wise about such things, years of being a magistrate had surely instilled some sort of reasoning into her life.

'We've got to talk together about all this, Kate, I don't feel I'm any use. It's a pity there isn't somebody like your grandfather left, Steven's hopeless and I'm not very sure about Alex.'

Kate looked at her long and hard before saying, 'I'm going into the study, Mother, I need to get on with some work.'

As she sat looking through the window, work didn't seem very important. It was another beautiful day, and because it was Sunday families were walking to the park or climbing up the hill; there was the sound of children's laughter and even thinking about work seemed incongruous.

She had never meant it to come to this. It had been fun, a little game to be played in the midst of other people's more painful disasters.

Kate had never been the sort of girl who needed men prominently in her life. Even as a schoolgirl she'd been serious-minded, ambitious, and boys had thought her too distant although she had been attractive.

While her friends were into Saturday dances and parties, Kate had preferred to study, the future was more important than the present.

Winning a scholarship to Oxford had set her apart, and reading law had proclaimed her to be something of a blue stocking, even more so when she joined the most prestigious law firm in the city.

Right from the first few months she and James Harrison had been thrown together. He was good-looking, clever, and serious; that he was also married had never fazed her in those first few months. He was simply a colleague, another man, she felt herself to be immune from such dangers, and then, more and more, amusement turned to passion, and even then she failed to see the dangers.

She met Dora Harrison on several occasions and thought she was not bad-looking, reasonably intelligent and to a man of James's intellect rather boring.

They'd been careless. Neither of them had thought for a moment that Dora would read something more devious into the time they were spending together.

Dora had a good life, she had money and position, James was always generous and she wasn't the sort of woman who craved excitement. James grumbled about the odd dinner party she hosted – he said they were unnecessary and boring – largely in the company of family they seldom saw or women like herself whose husbands were well off and holding down good jobs.

To Dora Kate was simply another lawyer, somebody her husband saw every day at the office and no more important than any of the men. When had she begun to change her mind and had anybody else thought fit to have put lingering doubts in her head?

What sort of reception had she given her husband the evening before, or had she had the courage to wait up for his return home in the early hours of the morning?

She heard the sound of voices in another part of the house, and then the door opened and Alex stood smiling at her, the brother who had always had the power to infuriate her, even when he was the only member of the family she really liked.

'So, you're home this time,' he said dryly.

'I've been here all morning.'

'I suppose Mother's told you about our visitor last evening.'

'Have you come here to gloat, Alex?'

'By no means, I've come here to commiserate.'

She frowned and gave her attention to the notes on her desk.

'Kate, what are you thinking about,' he said, 'or didn't you think she had it in her to fight back?'

'Fight back?'

'Of course. She's a wife, a woman with children, and if you think she's going to hand her nice cosy little world over on a platter you can think again.'

'We're friends, colleagues. It wasn't serious.'

'Serious enough to keep you out all night, serious enough to start people's tongues wagging.'

'Gossip never loses anything.'

'But can you afford gossip? Think about it: Dora goes to the firm, no smoke without fire they think, and then you and James are questioned, you deny it, Dora has proof, what then?'

'You tell me if you're so clever.'

'It's not a case of being clever, Kate, it's a case of looking after number one. Personally I'd get out of this mess as quickly as possible, consign James to the dustbin and placate dear old Dora the best way you can.'

'Suppose she doesn't want to be placated.'

'Oh, I think she will. Think about the smart house and the neighbours, the children's upper-crust school and the Jaguar on the drive. Of course there's always the possibility you'd lose and she'd get her hands on the lot, but would she be willing to risk the scandal, face two legal eagles who know their way around the block.'

'You're too cynical for me, Alex.'

'Mother saw Dora at church this morning, apparently she still looked extremely angry. I called to see Elvira last night, it was a chance to enlighten her on the state of our dysfunctional family.'

'Well, her mother gave us a head start.'

'Yes, but wasn't she worth it. As a twenty-year-old I dined out on Aunt Gloria. I think every village within miles must have been envious of our reputation for unseemly behaviour.'

'And you compare Aunt Gloria with me?'

'Oh no, dear, you're in danger of injuring a great many people. Gloria merely enchanted us.'

'I can do without your sarcasm, Alex.'

'I know, and I'm sorry to be so caustic, but you are my little sister and we are family. Think what it would do to dear old Granny, to say nothing of other calamities hiding round the corner.'

'What calamities?'

'Nothing specific, but one hears it on the grapevine.'

Nine

Julie contemplated her wardrobe as to what she should wear for her visit to her father's office. He liked her to be smart, and although she didn't like to be seen entering a bookmaker's office on Monday morning his staff were invariably respectful and welcoming.

Steven was already at the breakfast table, his head buried in the racing pages of the daily newspaper, and as she helped herself to toast and marmalade she couldn't help reflecting that it hadn't always been like that.

There'd been a time when she'd waved Steven off to his office in a firm of solicitors feeling proud that he had chosen such a respectable career; that was until the day he had come home to say he had left the firm because he had other things in mind. He knew how to make more money, he had friends who knew well how to speculate wisely and who would help him.

All Julie knew was that their standard of living had gone down. Gone were the expensive holidays and the talk of boats in the South of France, the expensive car, her car in particular and the furs and jewels he had once lavished on her.

Now he simply said that foreign holidays bored him, they were bourgeois and predictable. He didn't need a flashy car that guzzled petrol and she had enough jewels and furs. Women didn't wear furs like they once did, and the ones she already had were sitting in the wardrobe like some discredited meat market.

More and more she wanted to talk to her father about Steven but she was too loyal. One thing was sure: she had to talk to him about the house, that was something she was determined to get.

'You know I'm going to see Daddy this morning, Steven, will you drive me into town?'

'I'm sorry, I can't this morning, I have somebody coming to see me.'

'Why don't you see about getting my old car repaired or getting me a new one. Your mother's still got that Bentley, Kate has a car and so has Elvira,'

'Kate has a job and so I presume has Elvira.'

'I have a job, looking after you, going to all those meetings you were so anxious for me to take on. I suppose I'll have to get a taxi.'

'There's a very efficient train service and there are buses. Glenda uses them frequently, why can't you?'

'I really am going to do something about my car, Steven, either getting that old thing in the garage repaired or having a new one. I'm not asking for anything expensive, just a little runabout to get me from A to Z.'

'And I have other things on my mind, besides, I still owe money on that sports car you insisted we got for Barry.'

'I'll talk to my father, you know how fond of Barry he is, he might lend us something towards it.'

'And I'd rather you didn't involve your father, Julie, he knows enough of my business already.'

'Oh, I can see I'm getting nowhere with you this morning,' she cried. 'I'm going. I hope your visitor finds you in a better mood than I have.'

He stood at the window watching her stride along the drive. As always she looked stylish in a navy-blue linen suit and white hat. Once he'd admired that stylish city smartness. She'd been so different from the girls he'd known in those days, country girls who rode horses and went to point-to-point meetings, girls the family approved of, and then had come Julie with her sophistication. It hadn't really been sophistication at all, simply a brash assurance that city girls felt they should have.

As Julie walked through the city streets she found herself remembering the young girl she had been, a product of a good school in the city, not always a moneyed home life, but one that had evolved over the years.

Pretty, spoilt by both her parents and a girl who'd thought herself too good for the boys who had flocked around her in those days. She'd aimed for better things, and she'd thought to have found one in Steven Chaytor. They'd met at a race meeting. He'd been there with a bevy of friends, drinking their champagne and talking horses and hunt meetings. She'd been there with a boy who fancied himself as a social climber, but across the room their eyes had met and she'd smiled. Now, on this beautiful June morning twenty-one years later they were both wondering where it had all gone wrong.

Her father's premises were in a small square off one of the city's main streets and as she strode through the main entrance hall members of the staff greeted her with smiles and good wishes. She was the boss's daughter, smart and extremely well married.

Her father sat behind his huge desk, a cigar in his mouth and clutching his telephone. She walked round his desk and kissed him on the cheek then she sat opposite to wait for him to finish his call.

At last it was over and, putting back the receiver, her father said, 'Well how are you, love, looking very smart I must say.'

'Nothing much changes around here, Daddy. They're very busy out there.'

'Ay, well, that's what we want.'

'How's Val?'

'Very well, and looking forward to the trip to France. Have you decided to come with us?'

'I really don't know, Dad. Are you sure she wouldn't mind?'

'Like I said she won't have to mind. You're my little girl, I've invited you. But we'll want to know soon, love.'

'I'd love to come, Dad, but I'm not sure about Steven.'

'I haven't invited Steven.'

'No, but he seems to have so much on at the moment, I don't know how he'd feel about my being away.'

'Do him good, love, might make him appreciate you more.'

'How long would it be for?'

'A week, perhaps not that, but we like the place, it would do you good. I've thought you've been looking a bit peaky lately.'

'I've got something on my mind I need to talk to you about.'

'Barry or Steven?'

'Neither actually. No, it's the house. I love that house, Daddy, and what's going to happen to it when Charlotte dies?'

For several minutes he stared at her incredulously before saying, 'Have you discussed it with Steven?'

'A little. He isn't interested, but, Daddy, he's Charlotte's son, he's the one who should have it, there's nobody else.'

'But isn't the old lady still there? It's my guess she'll never leave until she's carried out.'

'It's too big for her, she needs something smaller, nearer the village, nearer people, an old lady rattling alone in that stately pile waiting for death.'

'Charlotte looked very much alive the last time I saw her. She's well looked after, she's got servants and friends and family. She'd hate something smaller, she's never been used to it and what's more I don't think you'll get Steven interested.'

He was looking at the set of her mouth, adamant, wilful, the little girl who had cried for the moon and got it, the child who had been raised that way and he felt a vague repentance that he'd been too indulgent and allowed her too many times to get away with it.

'What do you want me to say, love, do you want me to agree with you? But if I do you've got the old lady to contend with and it's not going to be easy.'

'I saw her in church yesterday, I told her she looked tired, that the house was becoming too much for her.'

'And what did she have to say?'

'Nothing. Elvira was with her, and there were so many people around. I'm sure she'll think about it though, perhaps when Elvira's gone home.'

'Elvira, who's Elvira?'

'Steven's sister's daughter. You remember Gloria, Dad?'

He chuckled. 'Doesn't every man in the vicinity remember Gloria, most of them had never even spoken to her, only wished they had. In any case there are other members of the family that need to be considered, she's probably made her will.'

'Oh, Dad, what members of the family. She's three daughters who wouldn't be interested, one lives in Vienna, two of them are widows, and their children couldn't afford it.'

'Could Steven afford it?'

She stared at him, momentarily confused. 'What do you mean by that, why couldn't he afford it?'

'Julie, I've been hearing things about Steven's finances at the moment, he's into a dodgy game, one minute he can be sailing on cloud nine, the next he can be sinking in quagmire.'

'I don't know what you mean.'

'Oh, I think you do, Julie Where is your car, where's that Aston Martin he was so proud of, and what did he put in its place – that decrepit old Ford he picked up at some sale or other?'

'How do you know all that?'

'I make it my business to know what is happening in my daughter's life. At the moment I'm not happy with what I see.'

'He's going through a bad patch at the moment. The good times were great, they'll come back.'

'But will they come back to enable you to contemplate living in your mother-in-law's stately pile?'

Her face was sulky, this conversation with her father was not going the way she had thought it would go. In some anger she said, 'If we're so hard up as all that then I don't think I should even think of going to France with you, we'll need all the money we can get.'

'It wasn't going to cost you anything, remember that I invited you at my expense.'

'I do have my pride, Dad.'

'Pride's all right if you can afford it, love. I hope everything turns out well for Steven, Julie, but he's not been used to the hard times. He was brought up to the good life, adversity isn't easy when you've not grown up with it, and if you can think back a bit, love, you'll know I can talk about all that.'

She did know. She remembered the shortage of money, the fact that her mother had taken in sewing and her father had worked nights and weekends to bring in a little extra. But her father had known how to handle poverty, slowly climbed above it, and become the rich man who'd worked for it; Steven had been defeated by it.

Her father got up out of his chair and, pulling her to her feet, put his arms around her. 'We'll talk about it in France, love – you need a holiday. I'll be in touch during the next few days with all the news.'

Julie had meant to make a day of it. Lunch and shopping, after-noon tea perhaps at The Grand and then, when the evening traffic had left the city, a leisurely train journey back to the village.

She was no longer interested in shopping. She had enough clothes and that outfit she'd bought for Charlotte's party had been ridiculously expensive.

She walked disconsolately down the main street, disinterested in the shop windows. The conversation she had had with her father had not been the one she'd envisaged. She'd expected him to encourage her about the house, tell her what a good idea it was, and the talk about Steven had been something she hadn't wanted to hear.

She knew Steven was having problems, everybody had problems but they didn't last. Steven had told her that their life was going to be wonderful. There was no money to be made in his line of business whereas there was a mountain of it simply waiting for them in his new venture.

She hadn't asked any questions. She'd always relied on him, he was an intelligent well-educated man who obviously knew what he was about and for a time life had been wonderful, now she had only to look at his face to see it often sunk in despair.

He would never tell her that things were going wrong, he was too proud and she was too afraid. What did her father know about Steven? She daren't mention him to Steven who would hate that he should know anything at all.

She turned into the square, and decided to have coffee in the small coffee shop opposite the law courts. It wasn't her usual place, but she wanted somewhere quiet where she was unlikely to meet anybody who knew her.

It had been a mistake, however, and as she sat at a table near the window she looked with dismay at the couple who were deep in conversation at a table near the wall. Kate and James Harrison. They hadn't seen her, but if she moved now they might.

Whatever had possessed her to decide on this cafe so near the law courts. She might have known she'd see these two but at the moment they were totally engrossed with each other.

What were they doing here, shouldn't they be in court? But then she'd been hearing rumours about them for weeks, probably the rumours were true after all. The coffee was too hot to drink quickly, but in any case it might be better for her to let them leave first and she wished she had something to read.

It was the old man on the next table who dropped his newspaper and his spectacles that caused Kate to turn round and then she cried, 'Aunt Julie, what are you doing here? Not your usual place.'

She got up to help the old man retrieve his belongings, then they both joined her at her table.

'We didn't see you come in,' Kate said with a smile. 'Didn't you see us?'

'Well, no. Like you said this isn't my usual place.'

'Aren't you shopping this morning?'

'No, I've been to see my father, I felt like a change.'

'Oh, we use this place all the time, we're not due in court until later. How is your father?'

'Very well. We're contemplating a few days in France.'

'Lovely. And you do have the clothes for it, Aunt Julie.'

'Yes, I rather think I have.'

'Uncle Steven going with you?'

'I hardly think so, he's far too busy to get away.'

'Granny's party was nice, did you enjoy it?'

'Oh yes, it went very well.'

'We'd better be getting across the square, James, nice to have seen you, Aunt Julie.'

She watched them walking towards the law courts with the feeling that her presence in the cafe hadn't been entirely welcome. They were hurrying, with a lot to say to each other, and she decided that she too should be making for the railway station. She had no wish to visit the shops she usually favoured but she realized she would have at least half an hour to wait for her next train.

She didn't really want another coffee but it was better than idling about on the platform. She found a table near the window and was about to sit down when a man's voice said, 'Julie Marsden, I thought I recognized you.'

She looked up to see a big man looking at her with a broad smile, and without invitation taking the seat across from her.

'You don't remember me do you?' he said with a smile. 'Well, it's been a long time. Johnny Letchworth, schooldays, rugger balls and Saturday morning at the tennis club.'

She did remember him now, even though he'd put on a lot of weight and the years had taken their toll. He'd been one of the boys at school that she'd fancied in those early years, that was until she'd been introduced to what she considered to be better things.

She smiled at him. 'I do remember you now, Johnny. What are you doing with yourself these days?'

'I'm into building and doing very well. I started small but I've got my own firm and we're kept pretty busy. And you?'

'Very well, I've been to see my father.'

'Ah well, he's had a bit of my money over the years.'

'I can well believe it, he had some of your money when you didn't know what you were doing.'

He laughed. 'So, what's it been like living with the upper crust, the tally-ho high-flyers we all felt abandoned for?'

'I didn't realize that was how you felt.'

'So what's it been like all these years. Do you have a family?'

'A son, Barry. He's on holiday at the moment.'

'Got a job?'

'He's at university.'

'I've got a lad too. He works for me, which is very good since he's likely to inherit the business.'

'That's good then.'

'Isn't your husband in law?'

'He was, he's in finance now, more lucrative.'

'Bit of a gamble, though.'

'I don't really know, I leave all that to Steven.'

'Well, it's nice to have seen you, Julie, must be getting along now.'

He smiled and shook her hand, and she watched him walking along the platform to the doors beyond. He was a parody of the boy she'd known years before, stouter, ruddier, but just as brash. It was something she recognized in Steven now, where once he'd been courteous and quietly polite, now he was often strident, as though he had to prove something to the world, when before he had never needed to.

★ ★ ★

When Julie arrived home Horrocks, their daily, was still in the kitchen and Julie said, 'You're still here, Mrs Horrocks, I thought you'd have left ages ago.'

'I've been washing up his luncheon plates. I've missed my bus so I have half an hour to spare. I thought I might as well do these.'

'I'm sorry, Mrs Horrocks, I'll pay you extra. What time did he go out then?'

'Soon after two.'

She never knew where he went these days. He didn't have an office apart from the study upstairs and he hated having to answer her questions. How was it that her father knew about him? Her father knew about gamblers, but she shied away from placing Steven in that category.

If Barry had left his car keys she could have driven his car into the village, gone to see Charlotte perhaps or some other member of the family, but Barry had taken the car keys so that his mother couldn't get her hands on them.

After Mrs Horrocks left she wandered into the garden. The gardener had been that morning so there was little for her to do. She contemplated walking in the park or even on to the hill, but then she heard the sound of the telephone, so thinking it might be Steven she hurried back inside.

It was a man's voice, sharp and decisive, asking, 'Can I speak to Steven Chaytor?'

'I'm sorry, Steven isn't in, can I take a message?'

'Who are you?'

'I'm his wife.'

The voice became less strident. 'Oh, I see. What time will he be in, Mrs Chaytor?'

'I'm not really sure. Will you give me your number and I'll ask him to telephone you?'

'No. I'll ring him back this evening. Tell him Norman Leigh rang.'

She'd never heard of Norman Leigh. More and more men were telephoning now that she'd never heard of, but when she asked Steven about them he merely said they were business associates and she wasn't likely to know them.

She was glad it was a hot day and a cold meal seemed eminently suitable. Even so it was seven o'clock when he deigned to appear and by this time Julie was becoming both anxious and angry.

Before she could say anything he said, 'I'm sorry I'm late, I should have phoned. I'm not really hungry, have you eaten?'

'No, I was waiting for you.'

'What are we having, not something cooked I hope?'

'No. Some man called Norman Leigh telephoned, he said he'd ring later.'

'Is that all he said?'

'Who is he?'

'Just a business colleague. I have to go out anyway, so if he calls again just say I've been called out.'

Why didn't she believe him? Why had this day gone wrong when she had set such store on it?

Ten

James Harrison and Kate left the law court together and James found himself parked next to Roland Bannister's car with Roland sitting inside it leafing through a sheaf of documents.

He tapped on the window saying, 'Still working, Roland?'

'Not really, just leaving,' Roland answered, then seeing Kate said, 'Everything go all right?'

'No, it's going to drag on a bit, what about yours?'

'Over with.' He smiled and drove slowly out of his space.

As he drove home he contemplated what he knew about the Kate and James affair. Most of the people they met every day knew about it, they hadn't been exactly discreet and it was time they sorted themselves out. Neither of them could afford to put their careers on the line, and Kate had never seemed to him the sort of woman who might do it.

James had confided in Roland one evening after he'd stayed on in town, drunk rather too much, and seemed reluctant to go home to face his wife. Roland had surmised that he was more in love with Kate than she with him. According to James, if it all came to light there were other law firms and he was good at his job, he'd move on. Kate wouldn't need to worry about money as he had a private income – she didn't need a job. But Roland could have told him then, if he'd been prepared to listen, that Kate would never accept it.

James evidently loved her, whereas Kate thought of him as an amusement, a risky enjoyment to alleviate the boredom of their working time together.

Roland had offered no advice and decided to keep well out of it. Kate was a true member of the Chaytor family, and he'd known them too long and too well.

Kate and James were the last people on Roland's mind as he drove home from the city that Monday evening. Joyce was entertaining her mother and two of her aunts in order for them to see the presents stacked up in the hall.

After the viewing they would be invited to take any they wanted home with them, others would be donated to charity or as prizes at some of the committees she favoured. Joyce didn't need presents, the wardrobes were full of them; they were simply an advertisement that she was loved, cossetted and idolized, and for six long years Roland had been consistently reminded of the fact.

Everybody who knew them regarded them as the golden couple who had everything: money, a good marriage, good looks and many friends. But underneath it all he had a beautiful wife who was in love with herself and brought nothing into his life except a feeling of acute boredom.

He had time to recollect as he drove slowly in the build-up of evening traffic. He'd been told it was a marriage made in heaven and he'd largely believed them for the simple reason that she was there waiting and Elvira had never come back.

They'd be there at the house waiting for him to arrive home, just as they were for any occasion they could think of throughout the year, and he would do his part, smile into her eyes, echo their blandishments and wish he was a million miles away.

There were several cars outside the house when he arrived home, and he guessed they would be sitting on the terrace enjoying the early evening sunshine. Before he joined them he went into his study and poured himself a glass of whisky. One had to be fortified for an evening such as this one.

He sat down to drink it, and was staring disconsolately through the window when the door opened and Mrs Taylor's head appeared. She'd been with the Mansell family for years. She still referred to his wife as Miss Joyce although she always called him Mr Bannister. She'd transferred from her mother's house on Joyce's wedding day and, to Mrs Taylor, Miss Joyce was still the little girl who was both beautiful and perfect.

Smiling broadly she said, 'The ladies have had tea on the terrace, Mr Bannister, but I can serve yours in here if you'd like that.'

'Thank you, Mrs Taylor, just a light meal, I had a good lunch.'

'Oh, it's been lovely, sir, all those beautiful presents and most of them gone to charity. Miss Joyce insisted I had that lovely shawl, cashmere it were, I've never had anything like it.'

He smiled and she went on, 'She allus gave her presents to people who didn't have much, oh, some of 'em she kept, but that was Miss Joyce for ye.'

He knew that they would linger on in the garden and one after the other they would enthuse on his wife's generosity.

He ate his solitary meal and poured himself another glass of wine. It was then that he heard Joyce's voice in the hall and next moment she was smiling at him across the room. 'Oh, I'm so glad Mrs Taylor has been looking after you, Roland. They're still here, I doubt if they'll be in any hurry to get away.'

'It doesn't matter, dear.'

'You'll come and speak to them though, you know Mummy likes to show you off before her friends.'

'I'm hardly exhibition material, dear,' he said dryly.

'Oh, but you are, dear. The best-looking man. Haven't we always been the perfect couple.'

How many times had he heard it, from Joyce, her family, and a great many others.

'I've been discussing it with Mother, dear, and I really think I should invite Elvira over for afternoon tea while she's here. It's so long since we've seen her, and who knows how long it will be before we see her again.'

'Don't you think she'll be kept pretty busy with the family? A week isn't very long.'

'But I was thinking about Thursday or Friday, she'll have had plenty of time to see the family. We know so little about her life since she moved away.'

'And maybe that's how she wants it to remain.'

'Oh Roland, she'll love talking about her man friends, her lifestyle, her romances.'

'Romances?'

'Well, yes. Surely there have been a great many of them, after all you must surely remember Elvira's affairs.'

'Aren't you confusing her with her mother?'

For a moment she appeared nonplussed, then with a smile she said, 'Oh, perhaps I am, but she was a jolly carefree girl. Didn't she rather like you, Roland?'

'If she did it didn't stop her staying away. I expect that disconcerted innumerable busybodies.'

'Well, I do intend to invite her over one day, Roland. I'm going to join the others now so do join us soon, dear.'

Of course, to be trotted out like some trophy and with Mrs Mansell saying as usual and smiling sweetly, 'You all know Roland except perhaps you Mrs so-and-so, Roland is a barrister, always destined for each other.'

Everyone would smile, Joyce would take hold of his hand, and all their guests would think themselves extremely fortunate to have been invited to spend the afternoon in such idyllic surroundings: a perfect setting for the perfect couple.

Why was he so cynical? He'd lived with it for six years, accepted it as normal, so why now, and then he was remembering a pair of dark-blue eyes looking at him with something the past ten years had been unable to sweep away.

He dutifully appeared on the terrace to mingle with Joyce's guests but he was quick to explain that he needed to excuse himself on the grounds that he had some paperwork to attend to and then perhaps later take a stroll through the village.

He seldom strolled through the village, indeed his favourite place was the winding road that led to the hill, but of late he had been very aware that Kate's car had been parked in the lay-by soon to be joined by James Harrison. It had annoyed him, he'd felt stupidly that they were intruding into a spot that he'd considered singularly his own.

He joined his wife to say goodbye to their guests, and Joyce said somewhat wearily, 'I'm going to bed, dear, I really do feel tired. Mother's so energetic – I don't know why she has this effect on me.'

'Well, I'll just take my stroll, I feel like some exercise.'

Gently he kissed her cheek, watched her slowly climb the stairs before letting himself out.

The sky was tinged with pink remnants of the sunset as he climbed towards the hill, looking cautiously towards the car park, which was empty, and he sighed with relief that he could continue his walk towards the top of the hill. He could enjoy the quiet, smell the gentle perfume of wild flowers and think about things he should have forgotten years before. As he looked up at the giant oak tree he wondered if the initials he and Elvira had carved on its trunk still lingered beneath the moss that had accumulated over the years.

Why did he torture himself by coming to this spot when memories were painful, memories of guilt as well as passion? They had been so young. Elvira only fifteen and he nineteen. So many people had said that Elvira was like her mother, wayward and too easy and over the years he had asked himself how many other men had enjoyed making love to her. She'd offered no resistance and even when it was over and they had remained in each other's arms, there had been tenderness and in her eyes he had only read joy and warmth.

He'd believed she was coming back. She was leaving to join her mother for a few weeks during the school holidays, but then all he learned was that she was not coming back, she hadn't even taken the trouble to write to him.

Joyce had always been there, her family and his were delighted to push it for all it was worth, and he was hurt and bitter enough to permit it.

Of course he cared for Joyce. He agreed with everybody else that she was a nice girl. They were both young and love would grow. Their marriage had been the melding of two monied families as organized and steadfast as everybody had expected and yet here he was alone on a calm summer evening asking himself where it had all gone wrong.

The house had been Joyce's choice, one she had set her heart on from the time she had walked past its portals on her way to school. Then there had been Tessa his dog. He had had Tessa from being a puppy and to placate Joyce he had had to give her to his cousin, either that or have her put to sleep.

After that came the adoration lavished on his wife who had expected it because it had always been hers; the presents, the innumerable parties and holidays, always in the company of the rest of her family and now after six years, the boredom.

Joyce was a good woman, she enjoyed working for her charities and now more and more she was taking on much of the work that Mrs Chaytor had done for the community.

There were times when he saw the speculation in the old lady's eyes when she looked at him. Was it sympathy? he wondered.

He started to walk back along the narrow lane and it was

then he saw the small car climbing the hill. He knew it wasn't Kate. Kate wasn't into small cars, she preferred something more prestigious and Harrison drove a large black Range Rover which was considered a bit of a nuisance at the court's car park.

He waited near the stile, watching until the car came to rest in the lay-by. He couldn't be sure but, anxiously, he believed it might be Elvira. Whoever was driving the car was in no hurry to get out of it, perhaps a new generation of lovers anxious to find somewhere quiet, but somehow he didn't believe it.

He knew now that he had walked up the hill hoping that she might come. How he was afraid. The lights on the car were switched off and he found himself hating his racing heart as he watched the figure of a woman getting out of the driving seat.

He didn't at first recognize her. She was wearing a short white coat over a summer dress, but as she walked towards the lane he knew it was Elvira, auburn hair blowing gently in the breeze, the smooth grace of her walk – and then she looked up and saw him.

At that moment the years slipped away and he was nineteen again waiting for a girl to come laughing up the hillside. He had known then how the day would end, now he could only feel uncertainty and regret.

He did not go to meet her but watched as she climbed steadily towards him, and then she said softly, 'This must be quite a favourite spot for you, Roland, quite a peaceful end to a Monday in town.'

Her words had been banal, hardly what he'd expected, and in similar vein he said, 'I do quite often come up here, like you say it makes a peaceful end to the day.'

'I didn't see your car.'

'No, I didn't bring it. We've just said goodbye to our visitors. Joyce was tired but I thought I'd get a breath of fresh air.'

'That's what I felt. Granny went to bed. We've had quite a busy day and she was tired.'

'What did you do with your day then?'

'Oh, we drove around – she rather likes my little car – and we had lunch out. Then this evening Aunt Glenda came around, suggesting that perhaps Granny had done too much and should go to bed early.'

'They do tend to live our lives for us, Elvira. How long do you intend to remain up here?'

'Oh, for a little while. You were leaving I think.'

'I'll stay and keep you company, Elvira, but if you'd rather be alone you only have to say so.'

How stilted it all was, and still there was danger. She walked past him towards the giant oak, only to stand looking up at it, the gentle moonlight silvering its branches, and Roland said softly, 'The initials we carved on the trunk are covered with moss. I can't really remember how far up they were.'

She reached up and gently touched the trunk. 'About here, I think,' she said. 'Ten years isn't really very long in the life of a tree this size.'

'No, I suppose not.'

'There are probably quite a few initials carved up there.'

'Possibly. Not mine, yours perhaps?'

'You mean you would expect other people to have carved mine?'

'I don't know, Elvira, you were a popular girl.'

She didn't answer, but stood looking upwards at the tree and he waited near the stile unsure as to where the conversation was leading.

She turned and walked towards him, saying briefly, 'I'll take you back to your house, Roland, unless you'd prefer to walk.'

'It isn't far, Elvira, I came out for a stroll.'

They walked down the hill in silence. It had all gone terribly wrong, stupidly wrong, and they had almost reached her car when he said, 'Joyce was hoping to invite you for tea one afternoon, Elvira, would it be convenient?'

'Well, I don't really know what plans Granny has. If she would like to telephone me I'm sure we can fix something up.'

'Yes, perhaps that would be best.'

'Goodnight, Roland – sure about the lift?'

'Yes, thank you, Elvira, goodnight.'

She sat in the car watching him walk away from her. He was not hurrying, and she was hating him for his cool remoteness. Well of course it couldn't have been anything else, what had happened between them was a long time ago. He'd thought she was a flighty girl who'd probably had similar flings with half a dozen boys, and he loved Joyce, dear sweet uncomplicated Joyce who loved him to the exclusion of everything and anybody else.

As she drove the car down the lane he stepped back against

the hedge, his smile one he would have bestowed on any other driver on that narrow lonely lane, and because there were tears in her eyes she did not see the wooden post until the noise of her car striking it brought her to a halt.

He was opening the car door saying, 'Are you all right, Elvira? I'll take a look at your car – I don't think it will be much.'

She was trembling as she wiped her eyes hurriedly, while he looked at the front of her car before coming back to her.

'A couple of scratches. If you take it down to Standing in the morning he'll soon touch it up for you. These posts are a bit of a nuisance on this narrow lane.'

She nodded, and seeing her expression he said quickly, 'Are you sure you're all right, Elvira? I'll come with you, we'll just sit here for a couple of minutes until you're feeling better.'

He got in the front seat and they sat in silence until she reached out to turn the ignition on, then he noticed that she was trembling and he said, 'Wait a little while, Elvira, you really are upset, I think that little bleep really did upset you.'

It wasn't the bleep, she thought angrily. It was meeting him on the hill, like meeting a stranger and the painful normality of their conversation.

'We'll call in the Bull's Head on the way back,' he said. 'You could do with a brandy.'

'And have them all see a very respectable married man in the company of a less than pristine woman,' she replied sharply. 'They always thought that of me without knowing me. I was like my mother, and my mother was never one of them. You evidently thought that too, Roland.'

'I never listen to gossip, Elvira, and I never heard anybody say that about you. I didn't live in this village, I only came during school holidays. I knew you, I liked you, and then—'

'Then?'

'I thought I loved you. When the summer was over I went back to university and thought you would be coming back here. You didn't and I firmly believed that what we had had together had meant nothing to you. I drifted into feelings for Joyce. Everybody wanted it, she wanted it, and I thought what the hell, as a matter of fact I hoped you'd come back to find it was all too late.'

She sat quietly beside him, her eyes looking down on a familiar street. But she was not seeing it, instead all her thoughts were on another time, another place, and she knew now that they would go on accepting their lives with only vague regrets that it could all have been so different.

After the long silence Roland asked, 'How do you intend to spend the rest of your time here, Elvira?'

'Being with Granny, some of the others, tea with Joyce I expect, and it all sounds very mundane, doesn't it?'

'I suppose so. I'll walk home, Elvira, it isn't far. Perhaps we'll meet again before you go home. Where is home by the way?'

'For the moment a small village in Cornwall . . .'

'Are you happy there?'

'I have friends there, I'm happy enough but I'm not sure how long I'll be living there.'

'Why is that?'

'My mother would like me to go to Austria. She loves it, she thinks I'd love it too.'

'Your mother has a husband but would you have anybody there apart from your mother?'

'I know people there, over the last ten years I've met a great many people.'

He smiled, then softly he said, 'Goodbye, Elvira, perhaps we will meet again before you leave, but not here on the hillside, too many memories.'

She sat in the car watching until he was out of sight, and she had not thought that after all these years the pain could still be there.

The old Elvira had been a child, loving him and hating him, convinced that he had made love to her when he really loved someone else. Now the woman Elvira could only reflect on the vagary of youth that had deceived them both.

Eleven

Charlotte was enjoying her time with Elvira: the excursions into the countryside, the discovery of inns and tearooms, their conversation when Elvira talked about the times she remembered, her mother's life in Vienna and, when Charlotte evaded talking about her family, Charlotte's anxieties and the hope that Elvira would not stay away from them too long.

'What shall we do today?' Elvira asked over the breakfast table on Tuesday morning.

'I really don't mind, dear. Isn't there something you want to do without dragging your old granny along?'

'Of course not. And I'm not dragging you along, you're such good company, I enjoy being with you.'

'Then we'll go off on our own, no Glenda or Georgia.'

'And no Steven.'

She did not miss the swift spasm of anxiety that crossed her grandmother's face. All was not well with Steven, and quickly Charlotte was saying, 'Well, of course he's always so busy, and Julie is often out.'

'Well, why don't we just drive off somewhere: a mystery trip.'

'Oh, yes dear, that would be lovely. I'll just decide what to wear for the occasion.'

That was the moment the telephone rang and Charlotte said, 'You answer it, dear, put them off whoever it is.'

It was Joyce, whose voice she recognised immediately, gentle, faintly persuading.

'Elvira, it's Joyce Bannister, I'm so glad I've caught you in, I was hoping I would. I would like you to come and have tea with me one afternoon, bring your grandmother if she would like to come. I thought Thursday or Friday, tomorrow I have court in the morning and need to shop in the afternoon.'

'Shall we say Thursday, Joyce. What time?'

'Oh, around three, dear. Roland eats out on Thursday so won't be coming home until late in the evening. We could spend more time together and have a nice chat.'

'Yes, thank you for inviting me, Joyce.'

'And you'll ask your grandmother?'

'I will, and I'll let you know.'

Elvira had already known what her grandmother would say. 'Oh, dear, you go without me, I am rather tired. It will be an afternoon when I can put my feet up and you and Joyce can have a good chat about young things.'

'Young things?'

'Well, yes. Fashion and what you like doing most. Joyce is a very nice girl, but sometimes when I'm talking to her the conversation dries up and I'm not very sure how to carry on.'

'But you don't see much of her?'

'No. It's always better when Roland's there. He chats about all sorts of things; she just seems to chat about herself.'

'I'll make some excuse for your absence, Granny.'

'Did you go out last night, dear, I thought I heard the car?'

'Just for a little while. I love the sunset and the weather is so beautiful.'

'Did you meet anyone?'

'No.'

'Not even Alex?'

'Not even Alex. Although he has seen fit to drop in on us I only tell him what I want him to know.'

They both laughed and Charlotte reflected that Alex had at last met one member of the family who had his measure.

Julie surveyed her husband's morose expression and wished he would go out. It was never like this in the old days when he would eat breakfast and leave for the office. Now he sat slumped in his chair with the morning paper in front of him, or listening for the telephone with every expectation that it would ring.

'Are you going to sit there all morning?' she asked him sharply.

'I'm waiting for a call.'

'And then what?'

'I don't know. I may have to go into town.'

'It never used to be like this. You went to the office and I knew when you'd be home, now you're either here mooning about or you're out and I never know where.'

'I told you what it would be like. You knew what to expect.'

'Not this I didn't. My father's worried about you, he doesn't like what you're doing.'

'He doesn't know what I'm doing, and why do you discuss me with your father? What I do is none of his business.'

'It is when it concerns his daughter.'

'Just because your father's on cloud nine doesn't mean he has to poke his nose into my affairs. Tell him to keep out of it, Julie . . .'

Just then the telephone rang and he hurried out of the room to answer it. Next moment he was back saying, 'I'm going out, Julie, you have the house to yourself. If your father rings up tell him I'm out – working.'

'Working?'

'That's what I said.'

'Will you be home for lunch?'

'Highly unlikely.'

With a brief smile he walked towards the door, then as if suddenly remembering he asked, 'When are you thinking of going to France?'

'Dad's making all the arrangements, I'm not really sure.'

'Oh well, see you later.'

That was how it always was these days, and she stayed at the table until the sound of his car faded and Julie was left with the feeling that the rest of her day was unimportant.

Throughout their married life she had never questioned Steven about anything to do with his chosen career, so why was she filled with overwhelming doubt and anxiety about their life now? Why this sudden need to go into his study and once more search for answers? All the drawers in the old oak desk were now locked, something she had not expected because Steven had always been careless about keys and locks.

She searched in drawers in the bedroom, even in the garage, and then she suddenly remembered his habit of keeping keys in the pockets of old coats and it was in one of these that she located a bunch of stained and grubby keys which had not been used for some time but which were obviously duplicates of others in constant use.

The click of the lock assured her that she had found a key to fit and then she stared with dismay at the untidy mess littering the drawer. Most of it she didn't understand. Julie had never been happy with figures but as she delved deeper and deeper she could understand the letters asking for late payment, threats from sources she had never heard of, and then bank statements showing that they were hardly solvent.

She sat in stunned silence. How had it come to this? Hadn't she been the golden girl, marrying Steven Chaytor from the manor house, handsome popular and rich? She'd had it all, the jewels and furs, the parties and balls, the holidays in exotic places that lesser folk had never even heard of.

All that crowd who had never quite understood how a book-maker's daughter had aspired to wind up on those dizzy heights, yet now it seemed to Julie that her world was crashing round her feet.

Of course Steven must have made money, as there was the sum of a hundred and fifty thousand pounds paid into the bank, so surely he must have done something right, but after that entry it had all been paid out. Oh surely there was another account. Steven would have answers but she couldn't ask without him knowing she had been prying into his desk.

How much did her father know about their affairs? She needed to ask him – and where was his mother in all this? Surely if Charlotte knew they were losing money she would have come to their assistance. After all the rest of the family were affluent.

She'd go to see Charlotte, her excuse could be that she would like to see Elvira before she left. She telephoned first to make sure they were in, but to her annoyance the housekeeper informed her that Mrs Chaytor and Miss Elvira had already left the house.

She couldn't spend the rest of the day doing nothing. She decided to telephone her father. He was the only person who might know anything and even then his voice was hesitant as she asked firmly, 'Dad, do you know anything about Steven's business?'

After some hesitation he said somewhat gently, 'Only hearsay, love. Steven's business is not my business.'

'But you said something yesterday about him. I need to know what's going on.'

'Nothing for you to worry about, love, I shouldn't have said anything.'

'But there is something. He's so difficult at the moment . . . we don't talk any more , , , he's grumpy and he gets so angry all the time.'

'If he's angry with you, love, I'll come over and sort him out. I'm not having him upsetting my little girl.'

'Oh, Dad, I don't want you interfering, that would only make matters worse.'

'Well, we'll think about this visit to France. I'll be in touch as soon as I've sorted something out.'

The last thing she wanted was her father's interference. Of course it would sort itself out. Steven had always bounced back from whatever catastrophe he'd got himself into, but to Julie the day ahead seemed endless.

She saw that their gardener was closing the shed door and appeared to be leaving, so she hurried out into the garden to ask, 'Are you leaving already, Henry? You usually stay until two o'clock on Tuesday.'

'Well, Mr Bannister said half a day on Tuesday will be fine, and from now on I'm only comin' once a week.'

'But you come three times a week, Henry, why has he stopped it?'

'I don't know, Mrs Chaytor, ye'll 'ave to ask him.'

With a brief smile she watched him turn abruptly away. A few hours on Tuesday morning was not enough for a garden the size of theirs and warning bells were not singing in her head, they were literally clanging.

As she turned to walk away a large black car drew up at the gate and she stood waiting until a man climbed out of the driving seat and walked towards the gate, pausing when he saw her standing on the path.

'Are you Mrs Chaytor?' he asked abruptly.

'I am.'

'Is your husband in? I need to speak to him.'

'No, I'm sorry, he's out this morning. Who are you?'

'The name's Norman Leigh. I telephoned you a few days ago and asked if you'd tell your husband to get in touch with me. He hasn't and I need to see him very urgently.'

'I'm sorry, Mr Leigh, I don't know exactly when he'll be back.'

'I'll be in the Bull's Head this evening after eight o'clock – ask him to see me there and tell him it's very urgent, either that or there's worse to follow.'

He looked at her long and hard before turning away and getting back into his car.

He'd been rude and abrasive. She didn't know him, but it was evident something was very wrong between him and Steven. She watched his car turning into the village and it was then that she saw Dora Harrison walking towards her along the road and she was unprepared for the long hard look from Dora's unfriendly eyes.

She didn't really like Dora but anybody, whether she liked them or not, would be company on this awful morning.

'Dora, do come in for coffee. I haven't seen much of you recently, how are the children getting along?'

Dora paused. She didn't want to chat to Julie Chaytor but it would be one more opportunity to tell one of the family what she thought about Kate Deptford-Smythe.

If she'd expected Dora to cheer her up she realized she had been very much mistaken. Almost immediately Dora said, 'I suppose you heard of the problems I'm having at the moment, Georgia must have informed the entire village of my visit. She was out of course, but I told the rest of them why I'd gone.'

'Who was out?'

'Why, Kate. Out with my husband. If you didn't know about the carryings on you're the only one who doesn't.'

'I don't see a lot of the family, except at functions like last Saturday.'

'Surely you've heard something about it. The entire village is talking.'

'Kate and your husband? No, but don't they work together?'

'That's why they've got away with it for so long, but not any more. Now something's going to be done about it.'

'But are you sure, Dora? I never thought Kate was interested in men, she seemed such a career girl.'

'That's what I thought. Oh, she's ambitious all right, but they've both of them covered their tracks pretty well.'

Why had she been stupid enough to invite Dora in? She had

enough problems of her own to worry about without this gloomy woman rambling on about her own problems.

In a vain effort to change the subject she asked, 'How are the children, Dora?'

Dora wasn't having any of it. 'You'd think he'd be thinking about the children, wouldn't you, but all he thinks about is that woman. You ask Steven, I'm sure he'll know something about it.'

'He's never said anything.'

'Well, you know the family, always so pristine and upper crust. Apart from the old lady there's been enough scandal to fill the newspapers.'

'What scandal?' Julie asked somewhat fearfully.

'Well, wasn't there Gloria. Three husbands.'

'Actually, I always rather liked Gloria.'

'Oh, she was charming, beautiful, but you have to admit she certainly played the field. I suppose it passes from one generation to the next.'

'But Kate isn't at all like Gloria.'

'She doesn't have to look like her. Actually Elvira was there when I went round the other evening so she heard it all.'

That should keep her away for another ten years, thought Julie. Then remembering that she was the hostess she said, 'I didn't get to talk to you at Mother's party, did I?'

'Didn't you think it was rather ostentatious to hold such a large affair for an old lady of eighty?'

'Steven thought so, but Glenda wanted it and she did most of the arrangements.'

'It seems to me that Glenda and her family are the best of the bunch, no scandal attached to them.'

'I'm sorry about James, Dora, but I can't think that he'll jeopardize his career or his marriage for an affair, nor will Kate.'

What does Julie know about anything? Dora was thinking. Aunt Julie'd always been the city girl with that bookie for a father, hardly raised to Chaytor standards and there was talk now about her husband having money problems.

She hadn't been a very sympathetic ear, but then why would she, the Chaytors stuck together, even when they were interlopers into the family.

It became evident that Julie was averse to discussing Kate so

Dora said, 'I wonder if Elvira's seen anything of Joyce and Roland Bannister. Didn't she once have a thing going for Roland?'

'Over ten years ago perhaps.'

'Well, yes, but a tale never loses anything.'

Both women were bored by their time together. Julie had wanted someone to take her mind off her anxieties and Dora had wanted somebody to listen to her woes; they had both failed each other and were relieved to say their farewells.

It was four in the afternoon when Steven arrived back home, going immediately into his study, and then Julie remembered she'd left the keys in the lock.

She prayed that he wouldn't go into the desk drawer; she'd been so anxious to see the gardener she'd forgotten about the keys, but it was a forlorn hope.

Steven flung the door open, his face red and stormy. Throwing the keys at her feet he cried, 'What are these, why have you been prying into my drawer?'

'Because I'm worried, I think you're hiding things from me.'

'None of it is your business.'

'I'm your wife. I spoke to the gardener and you've told him he's not needed as much – something's going on and I need to know what it is.'

'You'll hear soon enough.'

'Steven, we're short of money. I thought you said everything was going to be fine.'

'So you've been looking at my bank statements. If you've sussed them out then I don't need to tell you anything.'

'What are we going to do?' she asked weakly.

'God knows. Borrow I suppose.'

'Wouldn't your mother help us?'

He laughed. 'Hardly, I'm already in her debt to the tune of a hundred and fifty thousand.'

'That's why you didn't speak to your mother on Saturday, because you can't pay it back.'

'That's right, I can't pay it back.'

He returned to his study slamming the door shut behind him and it was then Julie remembered her visitor of that morning so she followed him in asking, 'Who is Norman Leigh?'

He stared at her before saying, 'What do you know about him?'

'He's the man who telephoned you and I told him you'd ring him back. He came this morning, said he'd be in the Bull's Head this evening and he wants you to be there.'

'Does he indeed.'

'Who is he?'

'Just somebody else I owe money to, not a very nice man.'

'But you'll meet him.'

'Did he threaten you?'

'Threaten me?'

'Yes, he's that kind of person.'

'Steven, I'm frightened, what have you got yourself into? My father's worried about you.'

'And I'm saying your father should stay out of it. I'll see him this evening, there's no need for you to be frightened, Julie. I'm tired. Just leave me alone for a while.'

'But you'll eat something?'

'I'm not hungry. I'll have something at the Bull. Why don't you take a look round the garden. I've dispensed with Henry for much of the week, there's surely something you can do.'

She listened to his footsteps crossing the hall and guessed he was going to the bedroom, then she went out into the garden but she had litle enthusiasm for weeding flower beds and Henry had been very thorough in the short space of time he had been there.

Who was this Norman Leigh with his cold penetrating stare and harsh demanding voice?

Tomorrow she'd go to see her father whether Steven liked it or not. Her father was the man she'd always depended on through all the trauma of growing up.

She couldn't go to France, surely her father would see that, but when he had said he'd sort Steven out he was quite capable of doing it. Her father hadn't got where he was by being gentle.

Twelve

Joyce Bannister and Marian, Alex's wife, had been invited to attend the auditions for the musical society's production of *The Mikado*, so their husbands decided they would have dinner at the Bull's Head. Roland had said he would pick his wife up at Alex's house later in the evening.

The two men had known each other since schooldays. Alex was accustomed to Roland's reserve and Roland was familiar with Alex's cynical sense of humour.

The Bull's Head was well known for its excellent food and Alex said, eyeing the food set before him, 'Makes a nice change from Marian's culinary skills, she doesn't have much imagination.'

Roland smiled. 'Joyce is quite a good cook, the only problem I have is that her mother insists on coming round, cooking the meal to give Joyce a treat, and then staying for the evening.'

'Glad I don't have that problem, my mother's too busy keeping an eye on Kate.'

When Roland didn't reply he said, 'I saw you talking to Harrison in court the other day, it seemed fairly serious.'

'He's very serious, she isn't.'

'That's what I feel about it. If he doesn't watch out his career can fly through the window and I doubt if Kate will be sitting there waiting for him.'

'No.'

'If he'd listened to me I could have told him that it was simply a passing thing as far as my sister was concerned, but I doubt if he'd have listened to me.'

'He wouldn't listen to me. I simply hope it's not gone too far.'

Alex was deciding it was time to change the conversation so he said, 'What kind of illuminating conversation will our wives be entertaining themselves with?'

'Joyce is very interested in the society.'

'Really. Have you seen anything of Elvira since her arrival on the scene?'

'I saw her on Saturday afternoon and I've seen her once or twice in the village.'

'She had a thing about you you know.'

'It was a long time ago.'

'No chance of a recurrence then?'

'I'm an old married man.'

'Old married men have been known to fall by the wayside. When I was a boy I worshipped her mother along with a string of others. It didn't matter that she was my mother's younger sister and she used to tease me rotten. All the same I always liked Elvira, she was lively and funny. I used to wish she looked like her mother; she didn't then, but she does now. She must have somebody in her life, perhaps we'll never know.'

Roland didn't speak. He wanted the talk to move on, he didn't want to discuss Elvira because Alex was too astute. Instead he said, 'I thought I saw Steven going into the bar next door. I can never understand why he gave up law.'

'For something more lucrative, he said, something less boring.'

'And is it do you think?'

'Not from what I hear.'

'I'll have a word with him in the bar later.'

'Good idea.'

'Joyce has invited Elvira to afternoon tea on Thursday, talking about old times I expect.'

'And do you intend to be there?'

'To indulge in girl talk?'

'To see the two of them together, the wife and the girl who had hopes in that direction.'

'She was a schoolgirl for heaven's sake. Were you thinking of being a husband at sixteen?'

'I wasn't thinking of being a husband at twenty-six and now that I'm thirty-six I'm feeling even less than one.'

'Bad as that is it?'

'Well, it was mapped out for us, Roland. I was never in love with Marian . . . nice girl, good family background, plenty of money, marriage for all the right reasons – except the main one.'

'Too late to be bitter, Alex. What about those people who marry for love and it doesn't last.'

'So which is it with you? You married for love and it hasn't lasted or, like me, people who were older and wiser dreamed it up for you.'

'And perhaps we've already talked too long about something we walked into with our eyes wide open and it is much too late to change.'

Alex smiled and, refilling Roland's wine glass said, 'You're probably right. We'll take a look in the bar to see what Uncle Steven's doing, probably telling his cronies where they've all gone wrong and attempting to influence them one way or another.'

It was fairly quiet in the bar but they saw that Steven was sitting near the window with another man, and that they appeared to be arguing.

'Do you know the other fella?' Alex asked.

'He looks familiar, but I can't think who he is.'

'Not a very amicable man from the looks of things.'

'No, it would appear not.'

'Oh well, we won't interrupt them, see how it goes.'

The man was prodding the table with his finger to emphasize his words, and Steven's face was stormy,

'If it gets any worse I'll go over there,' Alex said. 'I don't like the look of things.'

Other people in the bar were looking at them now, and their voices were raised. At last the stranger got to his feet and in a loud, angry voice said, 'Friday, Chaytor, no later. I'll be in here at eight o'clock, if you're not here I'll come looking for you wherever you are.'

Not looking at anyone, he stormed through the bar and out of the door while Steven called the bartender over to order more drink.

'Well, well,' Alex murmured, 'what do you make of that?'

'Something very unpleasant. I doubt if he'll want to discuss any of it.'

'He won't. When I was a kid and behaving very badly I was always accused of being like Uncle Steven when he was a boy. I am like him in some ways, cynical, chancy, but I'm more astute, less likely to tilt at windmills.'

They chatted together and with others who had joined them at the bar, and Steven sat alone drinking so that eventually Alex said, 'I'm going over there, Roland. If he's in the car he's not going to be fit to drive home. He's behaving like an idiot but I do feel some sort of responsibility.'

'He'll not like your interference.'

'I know, if he's difficult we'll leave him to it.'

It was evident that Steven was much the worse for wear and Alex said softly, 'We're ready to leave now, can we give you a lift home?'

'Lift home? I'm not ready for a lift home, anyway I've got the car.'

'You're hardly in a fit state to drive.'

'Don't tell me whether I can drive or not, I was driving before you were old enough to buy a car.'

'Well, if you continue drinking say you'll walk home.'

'I'll please myself what I do . . . too much interference. Julie's father's bloody well sticking his oar in, and now you, just you look to yourself and leave me alone.'

Alex walked away, and all he could do was have a quiet word with the barman even though he doubted it would do much good.

When Alex arrived home with Roland, Joyce and Marian were discussing the auditions and Marian said sharply, 'You're late, Alex, had you forgotten that Mrs Connelly was looking after the children?'

'No, I hadn't forgotten. She knew I was eating out and that I would have taken her home.'

'Well, she got the bus, fortunately I'd arrived home.'

In the quiet of a small sitting room Alex said, 'When you have children, if you have children, they will often be the weapon she uses against you when she can't find any other.'

Roland didn't think that Joyce had ever wanted children. To her family they would have been perfect, and Joyce wanted no competition. He hated having to think of her in that vein, but it was difficult to think of her in any other.

He didn't want to talk about Joyce, children, or even Alex's problems, so instead he said, 'I think I do know the chap Steven was talking to. He's called Norman Leigh, been in the hands of the police several times, and he's appeared in court on money laundering charges.'

'What's Steven doing with him? I have heard rumours about his money problems but I wouldn't have thought he was into anything dodgy.'

'Sometimes it's difficult to stay out of dodgy enterprises in the life he's opted for. I would think his father-in-law might have warned him.'

'But would he have taken any notice of his warnings? You heard what he said.'

'Perhaps we should join the girls, I rather think Joyce will be wanting to drive home.'

The two women were still discussing the auditions and Joyce said, 'I did so want to be an actress after I left school; girls were going to drama schools but mother was totally against the idea.'

'Why was that?' Alex asked curiously.

'She maintained that there was something about acting that was not quite nice. I probably wouldn't have been much good at it anyway.'

'You could have been brilliant,' he said with a smile.

'I was never as good as Elvira, she was so full of life and she could dance. I was the quiet, genteel one.'

'Elvira had a perfect mentor in her mother. I doubt if Gloria would have had reservations about her becoming an actress. I once went to a fancy dress ball when Gloria went as Madam Du Barry, a quite beautiful French courtesan.'

They all laughed, and Joyce said, 'And Elvira came to the end-of-school party in three-inch heels and earrings that reached her shoulder. She was frowned upon all evening.'

'I remember that,' Marian said. 'She really didn't care. And do you remember the black chiffon evening dress which made her look thirty?'

'And very beautiful,' Alex said.

'Oh, all the boys were smitten. I really do wonder what she's up to now. Did you say she was having tea with you on Thursday, Joyce?'

'Yes, but how can I make her talk about herself?'

'You'd have had no trouble in the old days.'

Roland had taken little part in the talk about Elvira but he was remembering Elvira, warm and alive and consumed with passion. Six years of marriage to Joyce had had no power to erase that one memory from his mind. Looking at his face Alex was aware of a strange sort of sadness and regret, mingled with impatience and Roland said, 'I think perhaps we should be getting off home now, Joyce, haven't you got court in the morning?'

'Heavens, yes. Some rather dreadful burglary at two of the shops in the High Street. Do join us for tea on Thursday if you feel like it, Marian, you'll be very welcome.'

'I won't promise now, Joyce, but I'll telephone you. I have a dentist's appointment at three o'clock.'

As they got into the car Joyce said, 'I hadn't realized it was so late, one gets talking and the time flies by.'

The road was quiet as they drove towards the village and yet as they crossed the bridge and started to climb they were aware of another car coming towards them, driving very fast and swerving erratically so that Roland had to veer on to the grass verge and Joyce screamed in fear.

He recognized the car as Steven Chaytor's, and he stayed on the verge listening to the screeching of brakes and then the loud explosion as the car hit the bridge. And then silence.

'I must go back,' Roland said quickly.

'No, please, Roland, take me home first, then come back.'

'That was Steven Chaytor's car, Joyce.'

'You can come back – you can ring the police from home.'

'Oh, very well.' He got back on to the road and Joyce said, 'You needn't drive so fast, Roland, somebody will have seen the accident by this time.'

She hurried into the house and Roland telephoned the police then turned to see Joyce looking at him with wide trembling eyes. 'Do you have to go back, Roland? I'm frightened.'

'There's no need for you to be frightened, Joyce. Steven Chaytor could be dead, I have to go back.'

'He was driving like an idiot.'

'I know, but you can't expect me to ignore the accident. Go to bed, I'll be back when I know what's happening.'

She went into the kitchen and made herself a cup of tea; she was still trembling. Steven had been driving too fast, it could have been them who had had the accident. She wouldn't be able to sleep and there was court in the morning. She hadn't been a magistrate very long and she had to do well. Tomorrow was an important case and she'd been welcomed most enthusiastically on the bench, it would be so awful if she couldn't concentrate on really important matters. She wished her mother was there; her mother would encourage her, have tremendous faith in her to do well.

Three police cars had already arrived at the scene of the accident and as Roland got out of his car Alex drove up beside him.

'I heard the crash from inside the house,' Alex said. 'He must have been driving like the wind.'

'And swerving all over the road. He was probably drunk.'

'I wish I'd insisted on driving him home, but he wouldn't have it.'

'It's not your fault, Alex. Here's the ambulance.'

One of the policemen recognized Alex saying, 'I'm sorry, Mr Chaytor, it's your uncle I'm afraid.'

'Yes, is he very badly hurt?'

'Too late I'm afraid. Driving like the clappers, he didn't have a chance.'

'I suppose the police will inform Julie.'

'They will, but I should go there too, this is awful.'

'Then I'll come with you,' Roland said.

Alex informed the police of their intentions and with something akin to relief the young policeman said, 'His wife will need somebody at this time, sir, this is when relatives help most.'

Julie had gone to bed early but she wasn't asleep. Her thoughts were on Steven meeting that dour, unpleasant man in the Bull. She couldn't think that their meeting would be amicable, she needed to talk to her father again, but what could he do? Steven resented his interference, but what sort of help could he expect from his family, even from his mother, too busy with her birthday party and entertaining Elvira. Elvira's mother hadn't even taken the trouble to attend the party, married to some foreign aristocrat no less, and probably loaded.

The lights from the cars on the drive lit up her room, and she got out of bed and went to the window. Three cars stood in front of the house and one of them a police car. Suddenly the terrible fear she had been feeling all day consumed her now.

She ran downstairs still struggling into her dressing gown and she threw the door open wide as the policeman was reaching out for the bell.

She stared at them fearfully and then she saw Alex and Roland Bannister. Then Alex came and put his arms round her saying, 'Come in here, Aunt Julie, we have something to tell you.'

'It's Steven, isn't it?'

'Yes. I'm afraid so.'

'Is he hurt, is he dead?'

'He had an accident near the bridge. I'm so sorry, Julie, there was nothing anybody could do.'

She sat down weakly in the nearest chair and Alex said gently, 'You need to telephone your father, Julie, can I do it for you?'

'I don't know, it's late.'

'That doesn't matter, he'll want to be here with you.'

'What happened?'

'He was driving too fast. You tell her, Roland, you met him on the road.'

'He was driving very erratically, Julie, he crashed into the bridge. Alex and I met him earlier on in the Bull's Head with another man and he did appear to be drinking rather heavily. Can I get you a brandy, Julie? This must have come as a terrible shock to you.'

'I just want to see my father – oh I don't know what I want, who's going to tell the others?'

'I'll tell Mother and Aunt Glenda, but I'm anxious about Granny.'

'She'll be in bed by this time. Elvira will be there, perhaps she can tell her first thing in the morning.'

They had forgotten that the police were still there, and they stood hesitantly in the hall before Alex said, 'Thank you, officers, there's nothing more you can do here at the moment.' Then, after they had left he said, 'I'll telephone your father now, Julie. Perhaps you'll tell Elvira what's happened, Roland.'

One look at Roland's face told Elvira that he had terrible news to impart but her first thoughts were for her grandmother. She was remembering Steven as she had known him years before. Handsome and popular, always surrounded by a flock of girls in spite of his young wife and son.

Her grandmother had adored him, now Roland was asking her to tell her grandmother that he was dead. It would break her heart.

Roland went over to the drinks cabinet and poured out a brandy, saying, 'Here, drink this, Elvira, you've had a terrible shock.'

'Have you seen Julie?'

'Yes, I went there with Alex. He's with her now, trying to telephone her father with the news.'

'And the others?'

'He'll tell them, either tonight or early in the morning.'

'I should let my mother know, he was her brother.'

He wanted to put his arms around her and comfort her but he was afraid of his emotions, emotions that could plunge them into memories that had never gone away, memories that would give them an excuse to mingle grief with passion, desire with sympathy, and in the morning nothing would have changed, he would go home to Joyce and look upon it as unimportant as the last time.

Wasn't that how Elvira had imagined he'd thought about it? Simply a little dalliance with a girl who treated love with the same frivolity she treated everything else in her life.

He shouldn't be here, he should be home with his wife, but she didn't want him to go, so she asked questions about the accident, about Julie, about anything that came into her head and Roland only cared that he was there, with his arms around her and then from somewhere upstairs they heard the sound of a door opening and Charlotte's voice calling, 'Are you there, Elvira? What time is it?'

Elvira leapt to her feet, her face white with anxiety, and Roland said, 'Be careful, Elvira, don't tell her immediately, bring her down here. We'll tell her together.'

Her grandmother was halfway down the stairs and gently Elvira took hold of her hand saying, 'Be careful, Granny, let me help.' She looked down into the hall and saw Roland standing there, saw that it was all happening again, that Elvira was Gloria with all her indiscretions and recklessness. What was Roland doing here? What was going on? But Elvira was guiding her slowly down the stairs and Roland came forward to take her arm.

With a voice trembling with emotion she said, 'What are you

doing here, Roland, why are you here with my granddaughter at this hour?'

Elvira pushed her down into her chair, looking sadly at her accusing face, then quietly she said, 'Granny, it's not what you're thinking . . . we have some very bad news for you. Roland came here to tell us.'

'News? What sort of news?'

She was aware of Elvira's hand warm and firm in her own, and Roland's face grave and earnest until, gently, Elvira said, 'Granny, it's Uncle Steven, he's had an accident . . .'

'An accident?'

'Yes, Granny. I'm sorry, but nothing could be done, he's dead.'

It was all there in her face: shock, bewilderment, and then, strangely, acceptance. Why had she known that something to do with Steven was waiting for her? For weeks now she'd felt that Steven was going further and further away, and now he'd gone forever . . . no more fear, no more worry, just nothing.

Thirteen

It was early afternoon when Elvira was able to get in touch with her mother because all morning had been given up to family discussion, and she had never admired her grandmother more. Even though Charlotte was devastated at Steven's death, and in spite of the weeping and arguments going on around her, she had remained quietly aloof from it.

Steven had been her son, adored as a child and perhaps less so as a man but Charlotte today was remembering the boy he had been, and then Georgia asked crossly, 'Where's Julie in all this? She should be here with the rest of the family.'

Looking at her quietly Charlotte had said, 'Julie is with her father, hurting more than any of you, but it's her father she needs most at this terrible time.'

Glenda's daughters had sat quietly beside their mother taking no part in the arguments and recrimination. Kate had sent her apologies that she was wanted in court, but Alex was able to tell them all he knew concerning the accident.

None of them was aware that it was Steven who had been causing Charlotte so much grief. For months Charlotte had felt that there was something wrong in his life and she'd felt incredibly helpless when he'd made such an issue of avoiding her.

At last they'd all left after Alex had said the funeral arrangements could be left in his hands and any other matters that needed seeing to.

When he left, Charlotte said dryly, 'I'm really rather proud of Alex, he's a tower of strength at the moment, but how about you, Elvira, you intended to go home at the weekend?'

'I'll stay on until after the funeral, Granny. I can't leave you now.'

'But your job, dear, are you sure it will be all right?'

'Yes, Granny, please don't worry.'

But it was early afternoon when the vicar and his wife arrived and she felt able to leave her grandmother in their company. Then she had to telephone her mother.

Her mother's first words brought a smile to her face, as she said gaily, 'Darling, don't tell me you're still with Mother, I thought you were only spending the weekend there.'

'No, Mother, I stayed on. I have some very bad news for you I'm afraid.'

'You mean you've fallen in love with quite the wrong man.'

'No, Mother, it's about Uncle Steven, he was killed in a car crash last night.'

There was silence for several seconds before her mother said, 'Steven is dead. He was two years older than me and he's dead. I can't believe it.'

'Don't you think you should come here for his funeral, Mother?

'Oh, Elvira, no. I hate funerals, and I can't bring him back.'

'Mother, he's your brother.'

'Darling, I don't live in England, I don't live in the next village and I'm sure none of them will expect me to be there.'

'I expect you to be here, Mother.'

'Darling, don't be pompous. Is everybody else all right, is Mother well? Oh, I don't know what I'm saying. I'm shocked. Talk to me later after I've had time to think about all this.'

'Very well then, this evening after Granny's gone to bed.'

'Tell me, is the village the same, and how about that boy you were so besotted with?'

'We don't need to talk about him, Mother.'

'But you've seen him?'

'And his wife and a score of other people. I'll ring you this evening, Mother . . . you'll be there?'

'Yes.'

She was gone. And in the next few minutes the vicar was asking, 'Do you think your mother will be here for the funeral, Elvira?'

Before she could answer him her grandmother said, 'She lives someway away, Vicar.'

'Oh indeed, but they were quite good friends when they were children.'

'A long time ago, and Gloria was never one for living in the past.'

All the rest of the day people came and went and one or two of them lingered on so that it was late when she was at last able to telephone her mother.

Her first words were, 'Elvira, I know you're going to ask me to come over for Steven's funeral, but you know I'm busy with other things and my being there won't bring Steven back.'

'You've made your mind up, Mother?'

'Oh, darling, please don't sound so disenchanted, you know me better than anybody; I'm selfish and maddening but I'm truly sorry for all my failings. I loved Steven, and I'm sorry for what's happened, while you're praying for Steven pray for me too, dear, I certainly need it.'

The line went dead and Elvira didn't know whether to be sorrowful or angry. Gloria would never change. All through her life she'd been the capricious, mercurial one, reaching out for the moon then wanting more, and yet Elvira had adored her.

Other people's mothers had always been there for them; not so glamorous, not so exciting, but when she had been there she'd been wonderful. Some people had felt sorry for her, others envied her, it didn't make any difference: nobody would be surprised if she came or if she stayed away.

They all departed except for Great Uncle Nigel and his wife, and Charlotte said feelingly, 'Don't feel you have to stay here with us, Elvira. Drive off somewhere or take Bengie for a walk, poor little thing he's wondering what all the trauma is about.'

Elvira decided to drive off somewhere. Bengie was happy in the car and she could find somewhere on their journey to walk. As she drove past Steven's house, however, she saw that there was a large car parked outside and, making up her mind quickly, she decided to call.

A large man met her in the hall, a man with a stern, unsmiling face who was quick to inform her that his daughter was not receiving guests as she had had a bereavement.

'I'm sorry,' Elvira said quickly. 'I know about Uncle Steven, I'm Elvira.'

For several seconds he simply stared at her, then he said, 'Well, you'd best come in. I'm Julie's father.'

She hadn't known what to expect from Julie: histrionics, drama or grief, so she was unprepared for Julie sitting stony-faced and bordering on anger.

'So they sent you,' Julie said sourly.

'Nobody sent me, Julie. I came because I saw the car outside. They said you'd be with your father.'

'What was it like up there this morning?'

'Quite dreadful. I'm so sorry, Julie, for you and for Grandma.'

'I suppose Alex is in charge now, he's in for everything.'

'He's been very kind, Julie.'

It seemed to Elvira that instead of grief there was resentment but she would have been surprised to know that Julie's bitterness had little to do with Steven's death. The house, the Chaytor house she'd always coveted, now somebody who had no right to it would get it.

She was conscious of the man standing uncertainly at the door and Julie said irritably, 'Dad, I know you have to get back, you can go now. Elvira's here and I don't really need anyone.'

'I'll decide whether you need anybody or not. I don't suppose your mother knows anything about this catastrophe?' he said, fixing Elvira with a stern look.

'I telephoned her in Vienna. She's very, very sorry.'

'And it's my guess that that's all she'll be.'

Why did everybody know her mother so well, what had she ever meant to this cold hard-faced man that made him so sure about the way she would behave?

From her chair near the window she watched him striding to his car and Julie said, 'He's not really uncaring, he's a good Dad, he's just so angry that I'm suffering over Steven.'

'It's terrible that he had to die, Julie.'

'Oh, not just his death, the way he's been these last few months. He owes money all over the place – I'm not sure how I stand or even if I'll have a house to live in.'

'Does Granny know any of this?'

'She lent him money, she must do.'

'You can't be on your own here, Julie, will you come to Granny's with me? I'm sure that is what she'd want.'

'Dad'll be back this evening, I don't want to see anybody else right now.'

'Can I get you anything, Julie? I can stay as long as you like.'

'I'd just rather be left alone for now, Elvira. Thanks for coming, I won't always be like this.'

There was nothing for Elvira to do but leave, but she did so reluctantly. She had had little experience with death; she'd been a child when her father died and he'd been such a remote man in his young daughter's life.

There seemed to be so many days left but she had promised to stay until after the funeral and she had to keep that promise.

As she drove towards the village she saw Dora Harrison walking quickly towards her. She looked strangely untidy and nervous and Elvira felt a sudden rush of compassion for her. She'd been so angry the last time she'd seen her, so helpless that she had little armour against a younger woman who was intent on stealing what was hers.

Elvira was not to know that at that very moment Kate was leaving her office followed by an irate James who desperately wanted to talk to her.

She'd asked permission to leave early and here was James standing by her car pleading with her that they had to talk.

'James, I can't talk now,' she cried. 'I promised mother I'd be home early. You know what it'll be like there, they'll all be devastated.'

'I know, I'm sorry, Kate, but we have to talk about us. We can't go on like this and I can't go on with Dora any more, it's impossible.'

Kate was frightened. It was never meant to be like this. They'd been friends, colleagues, then lovers, but as far as she'd been concerned the love affair had been part thrilling, part amusement. She'd known James when he was single and she hadn't wanted to marry him then, so why now? As a lover he filled a gap in her life until somebody else came along; as a husband he was someone she didn't want.

James had arrived as far as he wanted to go in his career. He was a well-respected solicitor in a very prominent firm, and even when she was becoming equally acclaimed, it wasn't enough. She'd gone into the affair like a silly teenager and now she could see the terrible scandal it would cause. James was a fool if he thought either of them would survive it and she had no intention of being so reckless.

She pulled the car door out of his grasp, only too aware of his pleading eyes and the fear in them. 'Please, James, do let me go, we can't talk now, I have to leave.'

'And we have to talk, Kate. I'll get the car and follow you home, we'll talk on the hill, only for a few moments, but we do have to do something about things.'

'I can't talk today, James. Don't you realize how things are at home. Uncle Steven's death is more important than our affair.'

'Is that all it was, Kate?'

'It's all it can be, you have a wife and children.'

'It didn't bother you before.'

'Please, James, go back to the office, let me go.'

'I've done all I need to do at the office, Kate, I'm following you home, we need to talk today. I spoke to Dora last night and she knows the position. There's no going back.'

She got back into the car, and before he closed the door he said, 'I'll meet you on the hill, Kate, I'll go mad if I don't talk to you . . . so it's either there or at your mother's house later this evening.'

As she drove home through the evening traffic she couldn't believe that something she had embarked upon with light-hearted flippancy meant so much to him. She didn't know whether to console him, make new promises, or end it for ever.

It was quiet on the hill. People spent time there during the weekend but today they had the lay-by to themselves.

James parked next to her then he strode over to her car and opened the passenger door. As he climbed in beside her he said, 'It's quiet up here, Kate, we can talk all we want to.'

He was unconcerned that she needed to get home; he was unaware about anything outside his own emotions and Kate was unsure how to handle him. She had never been frightened before, had always been the confident strong one, but now she was unsure if confidence would be enough.

'I told you I've spoken to Dora,' he began. 'She did know about us and I thought it had gone on long enough. We have to reach some sort of decision, Kate, before I see her tonight.'

'What sort of decision?'

At that moment she couldn't think of anything to say. She had to know more from James about his wife and children, and she stared at his hands nervously clenched on his knees, his face strained and anxious. Then he said, 'Kate, I love you, I want us to be together, surely you must know that.'

'Oh, James, I'm very fond of you, but I really didn't want it to get this far.'

'You mean it didn't mean anything to you.'

'Not for you to leave your wife and children.'

'Then why did you let it get this far, why did you encourage me in the first place?'

'Because I was foolish. I wanted you to love me; it was something different in my life. For years I've thought about nothing but my profession; I've worked hard at it – I never had boyfriends, my job was more important. And now I've got what I wanted, but I want more, James. To put an end to it now would be stupid, it would be stupid for both of us.'

For the first time in her selfish, egotistical life she began to realize what she had done. It was evident in his bewilderment, the shock of hearing that the woman he loved had no feeling for him beyond the passions of the moment.

He had never truly loved his wife, but he had respected her as a truly decent woman and the mother of his children. Now here was this woman he had made up his mind to leave her for, telling him that he had meant nothing to her.

Nervously she reached out to clutch his hand but he withdrew it sharply, the bewilderment in his face replaced by a sudden and angry hatred.

'James, I'm sorry,' she cried. 'I like you, I'll always like you but I thought you thought like I did, just something away from normality. We listen to it everyday, the trauma of broken marriages, the arguments and insinuations, the insults and accusations, but ours was different, ours would never come to that. James, I'm frightened, I like my life, I've worked hard for it, some little love affair isn't going to take it away from me.'

For several seconds he looked at her long and hard, then without a word he left her. He got into his car and drove away without a backward glance and she sat watching until he joined the line of traffic through the village high street.

★ ★ ★

Dora's car stood on the driveway but there was no sign of the children and the house seemed strangely quiet and orderly. Normally when he arrived home from his office the table would be set out for dinner and there would be sounds from the kitchen; today, however, the table had not been laid and there was no smell of cooking. His anger gave place to a strange emptiness until he heard the sound of drawers and cupboards being opened and closed upstairs.

She was in the bedroom packing things out of the drawers into a large suitcase and there were smaller ones on the floor, opened and waiting to be packed.

She looked up briefly before continuing with her task and James said, 'What is all this, Dora, where are you going?'

'I'm going to stay with my sister in Gloucester, she's expecting me.'

'Where are the children?'

'Marian took them, she said they could stay with her until I went for them.'

'And who will look after them while you're in Gloucester?'

'They're coming with me.'

'What about their schooling?'

'My sister's a headmistress, she said she'd make arrangements for them to enrol at her school. There'll be no problems.'

'Don't you think we should talk about this, Dora? You can't just go off like this and take the children with you.'

'I thought we'd done all the talking we needed to do last night.'

'I've done a lot of thinking since last night.'

She sat down on the bed and stared at him grimly. 'You mean somebody's done the thinking for you, James. I know Kate. I've known her longer than I've known you, that's if anybody's ever known her. Even her own brother thinks she's an oddball.'

'Oddball?'

'Yes. While we were out partying, playing tennis, among other things, she was stuck up in her room studying. We all knew she'd do well . . . then it was time for her to have some fun, with my husband to start with.

'Last Saturday when I went to her mother's house I was upset and very angry. I'd watched you all afternoon at her grandmother's party, flattering her, being with her, and flattered that she was with you, now somehow it doesn't matter any more. You can have your Kate, James, although I very much doubt if she'll be willing to put you before her career.'

Something in his expression brought a sudden smile to her face. 'So I'm right, James, you have not had second thoughts on all this, not you, her.'

'I'm a lawyer, Dora, I don't want to have my private life talked about in court like all those others I have to listen to. I've been a fool, I realize that now. Learning it hasn't been easy.'

'What do you want from me, James? That I forgive you, that I overlook the last couple of years, and all our friends and neighbours will think I'll stand for anything – poor old Dora, willing to forget and forgive just so long as he stays with her.'

'We'll go away, Dora, we'll take the children to Provence – you love it there – and when we come back it'll all be forgotten, there'll be some other people to talk about.'

She stared at him in pitying silence, then, slamming the lid of the suitcase down, she said, 'Somehow I don't care about you, James, but I do care about the boys. This marriage is something I have to think about and I can't think about it here with you breathing down my neck, and that woman living round the next corner. I'm going to stay with my sister and whether I come back or not is something else.'

'When will you go?' he asked her.

'I've ordered a taxi to take me to the station. I'm going for the boys.'

'You don't need a taxi, Dora, I'll take you and the children to the station.'

'No, it'll upset them. Anyway the taxi's here now but you can help me with the luggage if you like.'

She'd gone and the house felt empty. Last night they'd talked and today he'd believed would be a new life. Would Kate be congratulating herself that she was well out of a relationship she didn't want or would she still be worrying that his wife would take her revenge. When she'd had time to think about it she could do that, when she'd become accustomed to living without him.

At that moment he didn't really care. He would be hurt by her decision, but Kate would be hurt more intensely because it would injure the only thing that was important to her: her career. Let Dora do her worst, revenge would be very sweet.

Fourteen

Afternoon tea with Joyce had been a civilized and tasteful affair. Joyce had taken great pride in showing her over the house where everything was immaculate, without blemish and strangely soulless. Now they sat in the drawing room to enjoy polite conversation.

'I'm sorry your grandmother hasn't come with you,' Joyce said. 'Poor Mrs Chaytor, she must be feeling very distressed about her son's death.'

'Yes, she is. My aunts are with her, so she isn't alone.'

'We were driving home from Marian's that night and Steven almost hit us. Roland had to go on to the verge to avoid him. It was fortunate that Roland was able to give some help to Alex.'

'Yes, it was.'

'Well, perhaps we should talk about something a little more cheerful then. How do you like the house, Elvira? I always loved it when I was a child, I used to visualize living here when I passed it on the way to school.'

'Yes, it's a lovely house, you must be very happy here.'

'Oh we are, but mother and father keep on talking about going to live in France. We do have relatives there and my parents have always thought it very beautiful where they live.'

'And will they, do you think?'

'Perhaps. They'll want us to go with them.'

'But will Roland be able to work there, does he want to go?'

'Perhaps not really, but if I want it I'm sure he'll get used to the idea. Doesn't your mother live abroad, Germany . . .?'

'Austria . . . Vienna.'

'She must have got used to it.'

'Oh, she has, but then it was very different for Mother, she married an Austrian who lived in Vienna. They have a lovely old house in the city and another in the country. She's very happy there.'

'I do vaguely remember her. She was very pretty, very fashionable.'

'Yes, I suppose she was.'

'Did I tell you about Aunty Bessie's party? I had so many presents, I had another party to give some of them away for charity. Aren't people kind?'

'But wasn't it Aunty Bessie's party?'

'Yes, of course. Oh, she got presents too, but it's always been like this, when I was a little girl and went to parties I came away with more presents than anybody else.'

Nothing had changed, and she was looking at Joyce the schoolgirl again with her string of doting admirers, the girl who had everything, even Roland Bannister.

'I wonder what Julie will do now?' Joyce asked. 'How simply terrible to be without him, but her father spoiled her terribly, didn't he?'

'I really don't know.'

'But you're Steven's niece.'

'And I left the village ten years ago and missed a great deal of the life here.'

'Why did you go away, Elvira? We all thought you'd be coming back.'

'My mother decided I should stay with her, it was what I wanted too.'

'Oh, my mother would never have left me, she's always been there, but it was nice of your mother to want you at last.'

'Yes, it was.'

'I must go before Roland gets home, Joyce, I don't want to hold your evening meal up.'

'Oh, you won't, dear. Roland is eating in the city, he'll probably be with Alex and I'll probably be in bed when he gets home.'

'It will be so late?'

'I go to bed around ten, usually to read. Roland and I lead very well-ordered lives.'

'Yes, I'm sure you do.'

What sort of conversation could one really have with Joyce when she was so terribly obsessed with herself. There was a kindness about her, a sweetness that had always been there as a child but behind that beautiful, gentle face was there a depth of mind, a profundity of thought? Joyce had been like this ever since she had known her. While she'd been light-hearted, often silly, Joyce had been quiet and thoughtful, but whereas Joyce hadn't changed, Elvira knew she had, and in doing so had become the woman she now was.

'Oh, we must have a glass of sherry,' Joyce said quickly. 'Mummy always says we must offer our guests sherry before they leave.'

'But I'm driving, so not for me, Joyce.'

'But you're not leaving just yet, dear. Sherry you must have.'

While Joyce poured the sherry Elvira consulted her watch. It was half past five. How long would she be expected to stay and what could they talk about that they hadn't already discussed?

Joyce didn't have much to say about her husband, it was all about her parents, her relatives, and herself. Elvira wondered how much they loved each other. She was remembering Roland's remoteness, the question that had plagued her the most, Why did you never come back?

Joyce prattled on and she realized she didn't really need to contribute much to the conversation. The Chaytor family were quickly exhausted but the Mansell family Joyce considered to be infinitely more interesting, in the nicest possible way of course.

She talked about people Elvira had never met, but people who had prospered, been somebody, contributed much to the world at large and Elvira thought about Roland. How much of this could he stand, did any of it really matter?

It was half past six and Elvira said, 'I really think I should leave soon, Joyce, I think my aunts will probably have left Granny's by now.'

'When is the funeral?'

'I'm not sure, possibly Monday, Alex said.'

'Of course we shall be there. How terrible to think that only last Saturday the same people were enjoying themselves at your grandmother's party.'

'I know. Perhaps it's as well we can't see into the future.'

'Yes, that's what Mother always says.'

They embraced at the door and Joyce said, 'It's been lovely having you, Elvira, please don't stay away another ten years.'

Suddenly she was driving away with a sense of freedom, but she didn't want to drive home just yet. The aunts had said they would stay until Granny decided to retire and she thought that perhaps she should visit Julie, only to find that her father's large car was parked on her driveway.

At this time most of them would be busy with their evening meal so she decided to visit her favourite place. Roland would not be there if he was dining in town with Alex so she would have the place to herself to absorb the evening sunshine and the scent of clover.

The afternoon she had spent with Joyce had somehow depressed her. Joyce had been gracious, as always the sandwiches and the pastries had been perfect, but it had all seemed so manufactured, rather like a scene from a play when the lines had been studiously researched.

She had the distinct impression that Joyce and Roland were two people their world wanted them to be, while in reality Joyce was happy with her life and Roland strangely unsure.

She was suddenly aware that a long black car was climbing the hill and she recognized it as Roland's car. There was no way she could leave the lay-by without him seeing her and she wondered why she had been so foolish as to come here.

He drove slowly, staring at her before he raised his hand in greeting; then he was leaving his car and walking towards her. He smiled before opening the passenger door, saying evenly, 'I really couldn't think you'd be here, Elvira, I simply hoped you would be.'

'Well, I didn't expect to see you. Joyce said you would be dining in town with Alex.'

'That's what I told her, but it wasn't true I'm afraid. I haven't seen Alex, he's no doubt busy with family matters. I didn't want to see you at the house, I simply hoped you'd be here.'

She had nothing to say, and he said evenly, 'Have you enjoyed your afternoon with Joyce?'

'Oh yes, of course. She was very nice.'

'Joyce is always very nice, my dear.'

'Then why do I get the feeling that it bothers you?'

'Perhaps because it's sometimes a little wearying. Didn't you find it so?'

To change the subject she said hastily, 'I thought perhaps Kate might be here, isn't this one of her rendezvous places?'

'It is, but I rather think that affair has run out of time.'

'You mean it's over?'

'Dora's gone and taken the children with her – for the moment that is, I saw James and Kate in court, studiously avoiding each other.'

'Isn't he going to bring his wife back?'

'Perhaps, I don't know.'

For some time they sat in silence then Elvira said, 'When I drove here on Saturday I thought I was returning to a place where everybody would be happily celebrating my grandmother's birthday, instead so much has gone wrong. Kate and James, then Steven. Alex and Marian aren't exactly all that they should be, and then there's you, Roland.'

'What have you discovered about me?'

'That's just it, I don't know.'

'Are you telling me my wife doesn't seem very happy?'

'I don't think there is anything that would disturb the serenity of Joyce's life. I gathered that in one brief afternoon, but she was talking about moving to France, that surprised me.'

He laughed. 'We shall not be moving to France, Elvira. Her parents do have relatives there but Joyce wouldn't go, nor I.'

'But she seemed very interested.'

'Joyce's life is here with her committees, her days on the bench, the friends and people who idolize at her feet. It's a dream world when she talks about France.'

'Why don't we walk up the hill and enjoy what's left of this beautiful June evening.'

A warm perfumed breeze swept across the hillside and they stood at last under the giant oak tree and Roland said, 'I wonder just how much it has grown since we adorned it with our initials.'

'Well, they're well and truly covered with moss now and well out of reach.'

'Oh, I don't know, I've got a rake in the car, I could easily get rid of the moss. Perhaps those initials should see daylight again.'

'I don't think so, they meant nothing then, they mean nothing now.'

'Is that really what you thought, Elvira?'

'That is exactly what I thought . . .'

'I thought so too. Now you've merely confirmed my thoughts.'

Angrily she said, 'I should go, Roland, it's late.'

'That's what you said that afternoon. Why were you so angry, Elvira?'

'It's not important, it's long gone.'

'If it's so unimportant now, then it doesn't matter if you tell me. I'll tell you why I was angry: I thought I was just another notch on your chain and I'd been stupid enough to fall for it. Now it's your turn.'

'I was angry that you'd made love to me when you loved Joyce. Now we're even.'

'No we're not — why should either of us have been angry if it didn't matter? I loved you, Elvira, and you went away. I was going to tell you when you came back but I never got the chance.'

She stared at him in sudden amazement, then she said, 'Roland, I didn't know, I never even thought you could love me because it was always Joyce. I loved you, I always loved you, and then the years altered so many things and now we're two different people and what happened that afternoon happened to two other people, both young, both terribly wrong about everything. You have your life and I have mine.'

'Even when my life is not what I hoped it would be?'

'Even then.'

'And what about your life, Elvira? I don't know anything about your life, if there is some man in it, anything at all.'

'And it's better that it stays like that, Roland.'

Suddenly he reached out, crushing her in his arms, bruising her lips with his kiss, and for one wild, brief moment she clung to him, then came sanity and, wrenching herself free, she cried, 'Roland, it's too late, it's all too late.'

She ran back to her car relieved that he made no move to follow her. They would meet no more on the hillside, there could be no hopes for a dream that was dead.

As Elvira drove back along the lane that led to the manor she found herself remembering that last day before she had gone away. She had been swinging on the gate of the cottage nearest the house and an elderly woman had admonished her saying, 'Why are you swinging on my gate? None of the others do. You're the one they're going to have trouble with.'

Her words had endorsed the hurt and anger of that afternoon. She'd been the wild one, the one nobody took seriously, just like her mother, and she'd gone back to her room and cried herself to sleep.

Now as she crossed the hall she could hear voices and it was obvious her aunts were still with their mother.

She didn't want to talk to them until she'd collected her senses. Aunt Georgia in particular she didn't really like, and Aunt Glenda would fuss around her and ask questions about her so-called 'new life'.

She'd loved being with her grandmother; Charlotte had been kind and funny, her brain as active as it always was in spite of her age, even when behind her smiles and laughter she had sensed a feeling of unease and sadness.

Had it been something to do with Steven, or perhaps Kate, perhaps even to do with her health, which she didn't want to talk about; she only knew that these extra days were something she hadn't wanted.

She would like really to get in touch with her mother but she was not ready for Gloria's whimsical sense of humour and the amused assumption that even tragedy could be irrelevant. She had not seemed unduly upset at the death of her brother, but would anything really disturb her mother's attitude to life?

She went into the kitchen where the housekeeper was busy with the evening meal and smiling she asked, 'Are they staying for dinner, Mrs Horton?'

'I suppose so, Miss Elvira, I'm getting it ready anyway. Will you be joining us?'

'I'm not really very hungry, but I suppose I shall have to. I had tea with Mrs Bannister.'

'Oh yes, so you did. Mrs Bannister all right then?'

'Yes, she's very well.'

'Nice lady, bit airy-fairy like.'

Elvira smiled. 'I suppose she is, I've never heard her described like that before.'

'Oh, I've always thought so, even as a little girl. Always the princess, never the scullerymaid.'

Just then her grandmother came into the kitchen and, seeing

Elvira, she said, 'I didn't realize you'd got back, dear. Did you enjoy yourself?'

'Yes, Granny, it was very nice, very civilized.'

Charlotte laughed. 'Uncle Nigel and his wife are here so your aunts are going home. Not too much food, Gladys, I don't think any of us are very hungry.'

Elvira went back with Charlotte to the drawing room where her brother and his wife greeted her warmly and her two aunts smiled briefly before heading for the door. Glenda turned to say, 'I'll come in the morning, Mother, around ten o'clock.'

'No, Glenda,' her mother said firmly. 'You really don't need to be dancing attention on me like this, I'm perfectly well and we've got to get through Steven's death the best way we can. Poor Julie and the boy should be our concern at the moment.'

Glenda merely nodded and closed the door after her.

'I think Julie's father was at her house today, Granny, it looked like his car on the drive,' Elvira said.

'He'll be very good with her I'm sure, he's always been very proud of her.'

'I haven't seen him for years,' Nigel said quietly. 'We'll meet at the funeral no doubt.'

'Oh yes, I'll be glad when it's all over, the time seems to go on so long. I remember when we were visiting friends in India it was all over so quickly because of the hot climate; one day they were dead, the next day they were buried.'

At that moment Elvira could think only that there were still three more days to go and as if she could read her thoughts Charlotte said, 'After all this, dear, you won't be sorry to be going home. When do you intend to leave?'

'Monday afternoon or Tuesday morning, I thought.'

'I suppose it depends how soon the funeral is over, doesn't it?'

'Yes.'

'I'd leave it until Tuesday morning,' Nigel said feelingly. 'Funerals tend to go on a bit, you'll feel more refreshed after a night in bed.'

Charlotte smiled. 'Trust my brother to see the logic,' she said, 'but I do agree with him. What a week it's been.'

Mrs Horton produced the sort of meal Charlotte had asked for and even when she was unable to do it justice the other three enjoyed it.

Elvira realized that she was, after all, feeling hungry as it was some time since she had enjoyed Joyce's dainty afternoon tea and as she helped herself to more vegetables Nigel said, 'I've always thought women's tea parties were a waste of time, my dear, too much sweet stuff and not enough savouries.'

'It was really very nice, Uncle Nigel.'

'Oh, I'm sure it was, everything to do with Joyce is sure to be very nice. Did you see Roland at all?'

'Joyce said he was dining in town – with Alex I believe.'

'So you didn't see him?'

'I left to come home. I thought Granny might be on her own.'

He smiled, so why did she feel he didn't believe her? She thought about the traffic on the road before she climbed the hill and realized that one of those cars might have been his. He could have seen both their cars on the hillside, but in the next moment he said, 'We don't see much of Marian these days. She's friendly with Joyce – they sit on one or two local committees together. Does she come here, Charlotte?'

'Occasionally. She does have the children to look after and like you say a host of committees, and like Joyce she's a magistrate.'

'Hmm. I wonder how they have time.'

'Well, I know for a fact that Joyce Bannister loves it,' Isabel said. 'She's been reared to appreciate the limelight.'

It seemed they all had to contribute something to the evening ahead. Nigel was amusing, Isabel gossipy, and yet when they finally decided to leave Elvira heaved a sigh of relief.

After her grandmother had retired she read for a while, but the book was uninteresting, a novel Charlotte said somebody had lent her and which she hadn't been able to get interested in.

The kiss on the hillside had disturbed her strangely, she hadn't wanted it to happen, it reminded her too much of things best forgotten and yet there had been a poignancy to it, not passion, not romance, but on his part a strangely bitter regret.

Fifteen

Julie surveyed her son's face across the breakfast table and her first thoughts were that he was confused, So many different emotions had crossed his face over the last half-hour, first sorrow at the loss of his father, and then had come the doubts and perplexity. How would his father's death affect his life? His wonderful week in the Alps had not conditioned him for his grandfather's strictures on the state of their finances, or his mother's grief tinged with anger.

Never for a single moment had he expected there might be money problems. He'd always believed there had been too much of it, with his mother's extravagances, his father's involvement with blood sports and pursuits that cost money with people who had enough of it.

It was a question that was difficult to ask, but it couldn't be avoided.

'We are solvent I hope, Mother?' he asked quietly.

'For the moment.'

'What does that mean?'

'Barry, I talked about this with your father and he was always difficult. Why don't you go to see your grandmother this morning? I'm worried about her, she's eighty years old and frail. Why doesn't she exchange houses with us? We could live at the manor and she could come here.'

He stared at her in disbelief.

'We! Go to live at the manor?'

'Of course. It's what I want, what I've always wanted, and you are her grandson, Barry.'

'You think now's the time to talk about it?'

'The best time to talk about it.'

'Mother, I can think of nothing I'd hate more than living at the manor. It's too big for us, we haven't got the staff to care for it and according to Grandfather we haven't got the money.'

'Your grandfather would help out, and your grandmother would want us there, the house has been in the Chaytor family for years. How can it possibly go to anybody else?'

'Has my grandmother said she wants to move out?'

'No, not at the moment, but she will see the logic of it.'

'But why us?'

'Because your father was her only son, because he was a Chaytor, because I want it.'

He stared at her in pitying silence. 'What about Alex, he's her grandson too?'

'He's not a Chaytor, you are.'

No wonder his father had a traffic accident, he thought. If his mother's been arguing with him about such nonsense he'd have been devastated, besides there were more important things to think about than his grandmother's house. Next thing his mother'd be asking him to quit university because of their money shortage, and then the holidays abroad, and in some annoyance, he said, 'Mother, what about my education, about that trip to Chile next year? I've already put my name down for that with the other chaps.'

'Isn't this more important?'

'No, Mother, it isn't. I've got to think about earning a living and that means a decent degree.'

'It doesn't mean going to Chile on some hare-brained scheme that'll cost money.'

'Grandfather has said he'll finance it.'

'Your grandfather will see that the house is more important than your trip to Chile. You can do that some other time when we've sorted the house out.'

'Mother, as far as I'm concerned there's nothing to sort out. It's Granny's house, she doesn't want to move, I don't want to move, and we can't afford to even think about it. You're upset and not thinking straight, you've had a terrible shock, it's father's funeral on Monday so let's talk about something sensible until then.'

'You're like your father, Barry, totally unfeeling. I thought that when you went climbing rather than go to your grandmother's birthday party, and I was right.'

'I talked to Granny about it before I went. She didn't see the need for all that pomp anyway.'

'There were a great many people there who thought you were wrong to miss it, I'm sure.'

'But not my grandmother, and she's all I'm concerned about.'

'Oh, it's no use talking to you the mood you're in. I'm serious about the house, Barry, and I'm not going to forget about it. You should go up to see her today, your cousin Elvira's with her.'

'Elvira! How did she manage to get here?'

'By invitation like everybody else.'

'Oh well. I really don't remember her, I was only a kid when she left, I don't even remember her mother.'

'That doesn't surprise me, she was hardly ever here.'

'Oh well, I might just go up to see Granny and meet my long-lost cousin. I promise you, Mother, there'll be no mention of the house or any other hare-brained scheme.'

'Like your trip to Chile?'

He smiled and she glared after him as he left the room.

Her father had said he would see her later in the morning and she was hoping he wouldn't bring her stepmother with him. She had a lot to discuss with her father and she couldn't say nearly all she wanted to say when Val was there. Up to a point they got along but underneath Val resented the things her father did for her, the gifts and money he gave her, and there was no need for it. Val was well taken care of, she didn't go short of anything.

She watched Barry driving off to see his grandmother, and she began to grow impatient waiting for her father. Of course Friday was a busy day for him, but he had plenty of staff and surely with the funeral on Monday she had to be his priority.

It was half past eleven when she saw his large black car driving through the gate, and her heart sank when she saw Val sitting in the car with him.

She was three years younger than Val and Val was stylish and attractive. As they walked to the house Val pointed out something that interested her in one of the flower beds, and seeing her standing in the doorway her father waved to her.

'Sorry, I'm a bit late, love,' he said and kissed her cheek. 'Val was at the hairdressers and I went round to pick her up.'

Why did she need to come anyway? thought Julie, and Val said, 'How are you, Julie? Barry get home all right?'

'Yes, thank you. He's gone to see Grandmother.'

'We passed the manor on our way here, I must say the gardeners really keep it looking very pristine. The old lady must be extremely proud of it.'

'Even when it's much too large for her.'

'Does it matter? She has plenty of help, and a doting family. She'll not leave it, why should she?'

She didn't miss the look her father bestowed on her to shut her up but, oblivious to it, Val said lightly, 'I'd forget that if I were you, Julie, concentrate on something more modern for you.'

'More modern?'

'Well, this has been up a few years hasn't it?'

'Are you staying for lunch or shall we eat out somewhere?' Julie asked.

'Oh, do let's eat out,' Val said, 'that new place over at Coylton. I've heard it's very good, and with the funeral on Monday, sitting here we're sure to be pretty dismal.'

'I'm not sure about Barry.'

'Well, leave him a note, or better still telephone his grand-mother and tell her where he can find us – are you expecting anybody else?'

'No, not that I know of, the funeral director said he would call in the morning.'

'Did you tell him to send the bills to me, Julie?' her father said.

'Don't his family feel they should contribute?' Val asked sharply. But looking at her pointedly her husband said, 'Leave this to me, Val, it's got nothing to do with you. Now we'd better be on our way, that new place seems to be doing very well and I like getting a comfortable table before the rush sets in.'

'I'll just ring the manor to tell Barry what is happening,' Julie said. It was the housekeeper who answered the telephone and she was informed that Mr Barry would be eating lunch with his grandmother and she would pass the message on.

Charlotte was fond of Barry, he was very like the boy Steven had been and she listened with interest while he talked about his climbing holiday and his longed-for trip to Chile.

Wistfully Charlotte said, 'I travelled quite a bit when I was younger, dear, but I never got to South America.'

'That's what's so exciting about it, Granny, somewhere new, the Andes, the Amazon, different places.'

'Oh, no doubt we'll be hearing all about it when you return.'

'Granny, are you happy living in this large house, you're not contemplating moving are you?'

'Good heavens no, dear, where would I go?'

'I thought perhaps something smaller.'

'I've never even thought about it.'

He looked across the table at the cousin he hadn't seen for ten years and from the girl he remembered it was hard to recognize her in this beautiful young woman.

'You're not a bit like I thought you would be, Elvira,' he said smiling.

'Nor are you, Barry.'

'Well, I was only twelve when you went away, you were about fifteen.'

She smiled.

'God, how I hated you in those days,' he said with a grin.

'Really, Barry,' his grandmother said, while Elvira merely looked at him enquiringly.

'Why did you hate her?' Charlotte asked.

'She could ride better than I could, she always had the best horses and all the lads preferred riding with her rather than me.'

'I rode my mother's horse when she wasn't around to ride him herself,' Elvira said. 'I thought you were a conceited brat so that evens us out, I think.'

'My mother says you teach school.'

'Actually, I don't. I paint pictures and teach occasional classes for a friend of mine.'

'Does it pay well?'

'I get by.'

'What do you paint?'

'Landscapes, anything that takes my fancy.'

'Do you sell them?'

'Some of them. And what about you, Barry, what do you propose to do when you return from Chile?'

'I'm reading law. Dad wasn't enthusiastic about it, he didn't stick with it anyway. But I had a great time in the Alps, I didn't expect to be coming home to this. I was sorry to miss your party, Granny, it was quite an affair, I believe.'

'Too much of an affair, Barry, not something I really wanted.'

'Oh, I don't know, make the most of things while you can, that's my motto.'

'I hope your mother is bearing up well. Your grandfather is very kind, I need to speak to him after the funeral on Monday.'

'Will your mother be there?' he asked Elvira.

'I'm not sure, she does live a long way from here you know.'

'Oh yes, Vienna, isn't it? I remember her once at a Christmas party, black silk and diamonds, there were the other aunts all terribly pristine and there was this gorgeous creature like something out of *The Merry Widow.*'

'You remember an awful lot for a boy of ten or so,' Elvira said.

'Well, that was me. The youngest, sitting on the stairs with a mince pie and watching what the grown-ups were doing.'

Elvira laughed. Wasn't it something she'd done so many times, wrapped in admiration for her mother's accomplishments on the dance floor and the retinue of young men she collected.

Thinking it was time to change the subject Charlotte said, 'Are you intending to go straight home, Barry? They'll probably be back there by now.'

'No, Granny, Grandpa and Val will be there, steeped in gloom and, oh well, I suppose it's natural, but mother can go on a bit and there are times when she talks a lot of rubbish. What are you two doing?'

Barry shrugged his shoulders as he looked at Elvira, and Charlotte said, 'Well, I have letters to write, why don't you and Elvira drive around somewhere, the countryside is very beautiful at this time of the year.'

'Fancy that, Elvira?' he asked.

'Of course, if you don't mind having somebody you once hated on board.'

As she climbed into his sports car he said, 'What do you think of her? I was hoping to get a new one later in the year but I doubt if finances will run to it.'

'What's wrong with this one?'

'Nothing actually, but last year at this time everything was great, I could have mentioned a new car and Dad would have said yes, now they tell me he's been losing money for months, probably years.'

It was Saturday market in the village. The main street was busy and it was only when they were driving past Alex's house that he said, 'See anything of them?'

'I've seen Alex several times, not very much of Marian.'

'She's never much to say for herself . . . isn't he quite a favourite with Granny?'

'I don't think she has any favourites.'

'Not even you?'

'Until last Saturday I hadn't seen her for ten years.'

'I really didn't go to Granny's party because I didn't feel like it. Climbing was great, but I could have got out of it. I know it sounds awful, but I don't really know the cousins' husbands. Alex isn't a bad sort but I don't like his wife, and the Bannisters are so superior.'

'Why the Bannisters?'

'Well, he's OK but Joyce is like Miss Goody Two-Shoes.'

'That's a funny thing to say. Most people like her very much.'

'Of course, just as they like ice cream and candyfloss.'

'How come you know so much about her? They're quite a bit older than you are.'

'One of the chaps I've been away with is Roland's cousin. He says Roland was brainwashed into marrying her . . . his parents . . . her parents – why didn't he run?'

'They've stayed together, they're obviously happy.'

'I suppose that's right. After all they've no children, he could leave if he was unhappy.'

'Perhaps if he had somebody to leave her for?'

'That's a point. Do you know him, Elvira? Perhaps you could be a likely contestant.'

'And perhaps you fantasize too much.'

'Well, you're pretty, the right age, the right sort of family background even for the Bannister family, and you should think about it.'

'I'm leaving on Monday, and not before time with your sort of reasoning.'

They laughed, and after a few minutes Barry said, 'I'm enjoying being with you, Elvira. Oh, I know I should be steeped in misery over Dad's death and I probably will be when it's had time to sink in, but today at least let's enjoy the sunshine. Fancy a cup of tea at that little cafe there?'

So they enjoyed tea and scones in the company of a group of ramblers and later, as he deposited her back at the manor, Elvira reflected that it had been the day she'd enjoyed most since her return to the village.

'See you Monday,' he said and he kissed her cheek. She stood on the terrace until his car had driven down the long drive towards the gates.

As she crossed the hall she met the housekeeper, who smiled and said, 'Your grandmother has visitors, Miss Elvira, Master Alex's wife and her little girl.'

She remembered the little girl, filled with instructions as to where she should go and who she should meet at the party, and she recalled Marian's swift smile and cool acknowledgement.

Her grandmother looked up with a smile saying, 'Isn't this nice, dear, Marian and Josephine thought they should call to see me. Did you enjoy your afternoon with Barry?'

'Yes, Granny, we called for tea and scones somewhere and he was very entertaining.'

'Entertaining!' Marian said. 'Really, one would expect him to be heartbroken, never entertaining.'

'He's very upset, he doesn't have to parade it,' Charlotte said quickly.

Looking at Elvira Josephine said, 'I met you at great grand-mother's party. I told you where to find her didn't I?'

'Yes, you did. I do remember you.'

'You're Elvira?'

'That's right.'

'Are you going to the funeral? I'm not going, Daddy says funerals are no place for children.'

'I'm sure he's right.'

Marian, who was busy officiating at the table and passing a cup and saucer over to Elvira said, 'Hand the scones out, Josephine. I don't suppose you're hungry if you've already had tea, Elvira?'

'No, not really, a cup of tea will be nice.'

'Yes. Did you enjoy tea with Joyce the other day?'

'Yes, it was very nice of Joyce to invite me.'

'Isn't her house lovely? She has such good taste, everything in its place and so artistic.'

'She made me very welcome.'

'Oh, she would. She doesn't have children to worry about, and she does so much for the church activities for charity and any other organization wanting help. We're both magistrates you know but if one of the others isn't able to attend for one reason or another it's always Joyce who manages to cover for them. At times I feel so guilty.'

'But why should you?' Charlotte said quickly. 'The children could be unwell, don't they come first?'

'Well, of course, but I do so admire Joyce, we all do.'

Meeting Elvira's eyes, her grandmother said, 'You'll soon be leaving us, dear, it hasn't been exactly an uneventful week.'

'No, Granny, but a death in the family is something we could have done without.'

'I know . . .'

'What exactly are you going back to?' Marian asked. 'I asked Alex but he doesn't seem to know very much.'

'I have a small studio where I live and I paint. I also teach a little when I'm not commissioned to doing anything else.'

'So you're a teacher?'

'Not exactly. I merely help out with students who show some sort of potential.'

'You paint, don't you, Josephine,' her mother said. 'She helped paint some of the scenery for the Christmas concert last year.'

'I'd like to have seen it, Josephine.'

'It was all right I suppose, I'd rather have gone to skating lessons.'

'And they can be very dangerous,' Marian snapped.

'Oh, Mother, I hate it when you fuss so.'

Afternoon tea progressed with Josephine doing most of the talking until, surprisingly, she said, 'Auntie Joyce is showing me how to do tapestry but I'm not much good at it.'

'But of course you are,' Marian said. 'Just think about those you admire when we go to see Auntie Joyce. One day you'll be able to do one quite similar for me.'

'You call her Auntie Joyce?' Elvira said.

'But of course. Joyce and I have always been friends.'

'Alex and Roland seem to see quite a bit of each other,' Charlotte said quietly. 'Perhaps their profession brings them together.'

'Yes, they meet at the law courts, and when Joyce is busy with other things it suits them to dine out together. Alex finds any excuse he can think of to chat with the men in the evening instead of spending time with me and the children at home.'

There was an uncomfortable silence until Elvira said quietly, 'And Roland, it would seem he too enjoys chatting to the men.'

'Well, of course, but Roland adores Joyce, always has.'

Sixteen

Elvira was eating breakfast alone when the housekeeper said, 'The mistress isn't feeling very well this morning, Miss Elvira, it's all been too much for her. I really don't think she should go to church.'

'I've been thinking church this morning might be too much for her, particularly with the funeral tomorrow. I'll go up to see her.'

'Well, I've said my piece, miss, but you know how stubborn she can be and she thinks it's probably her duty to go to the service.'

'I'll see her and try to persuade her otherwise. There'll be enough of us at church, I'm sure.'

She found her grandmother sitting at her dressing table, wearing her dressing gown and looking decidedly pale and fragile.

'Granny, you're not going to church,' Elvira said. 'Think about tomorrow and rest today.'

'But I should be there, Elvira, they'll expect it of me, and most of the village will be there.'

'And they'll be at the funeral tomorrow, Granny. I'll offer your apologies and surely they'll understand, after all they know the sort of week you've had.'

'But Steven was my son, Elvira.'

'I know. The whole village loves and respects you, Granny, you've done a lot for this village and I'm sure they appreciate it. Today you have to rest so that you can face the enormity of tomorrow. They'll understand.'

The village would understand but whether some members of the family would understand was another matter, and Elvira, after one week in their company, was not so sure.

As her grandmother's representative she sat in the front pew with Julie, Barry and Julie's father and stepmother. There were those sitting behind who resented it, particularly Marian and Georgia, and Barry whispered to her, 'You're getting a frosty reception, Elvira, but don't let it worry you.'

'Granny wasn't well, I persuaded her not to come.'

'I'm surprised how well the old girl keeps going.'

'She won't if you call her the old girl.'

'I'll try to remember that.'

Julie was wearing purple. The other members of the family couldn't remember seeing it before, but probably tomorrow she'd be in deepest black, equally expensive.

The church was crowded, the sermon brief, but the heartfelt sympathies of the vicar on everybody's behalf were received gratefully by the family in a well-rehearsed speech narrated by Alex.

'I've been instructed that it's my turn tomorrow,' Barry confided. 'Good preparation for my career as a barrister.'

'Alex performed very well,' Elvira said.

'Absolutely. He's the one with the experience.'

After the service they milled about the churchyard speaking to the villagers who came to offer their condolences. Elvira was amazed that she remembered so many of the older ones, while they professed surprise that she seemed so adult and pretty.

Joyce embraced her briefly and Roland held her hand for longer than was necessary. He asked about her grandmother, spoke briefly about his memories of Steven, but neither of them were in his thoughts and she knew it. It was Alex who said, 'Make the most of it, Roland, there's only tomorrow left before she goes off into the blue.'

Roland smiled briefly and turned away.

Again it was Alex who said, 'What are you going to do with the rest of your day?'

'I'm going to pack my small suitcase in preparation for my journey home. That shouldn't take long.'

'And then what?'

'Look after Granny, hope she's feeling better, think about tomorrow.'

'I hate funerals. The sadness, the insincerities, the wishing it was over. Marian's at her best at times like these, she's the real drama queen, enjoying every minute of it.'

'I wish you didn't talk about her like this.'

'Elvira, I wish I didn't have to. I wish I could be like Bannister, keep the traumas well hidden, be good at pretending, but I can't.'

'Maybe there aren't any traumas.'

'I can assure you there are. I wonder what they are in your life?'

'Marian is waiting for you near the car, Alex, shouldn't you be going?'

He laughed, so much that those around him looked at him in surprise, then, kissing her cheek swiftly, he whispered, 'You're right, we should be sunk in gloom. See you tomorrow, Elvira, give my love to Granny.'

As she walked to her car an elderly lady she vaguely recognized caught up with her and with a smile said, 'My but it's a long time since I caught you swinging on my gate, Miss Elvira.'

Elvira paused. 'I know I should know you, but it's been so long.'

'Mrs O'Connor. I live in the cottage near the gates to the manor.'

'Of course, I do remember you now. We used to steal your apples and I do remember swinging on your gate. I hope it's not too late to say I'm sorry.'

'No need, you were only a young lass and you had plenty of help from the other children. My but it's been a week hasn't it? Your grandmother's party and now her son's death.'

'Yes, it's unbelievable really.'

'Will ye be staying here now then?'

'Only until tomorrow, perhaps Tuesday at the latest.'

'And when shall we be seeing you again?'

'I don't really know, Mrs O'Connor.'

'Is your mother likely to be at the funeral?'

'My mother? I'm not sure, she doesn't live in England now.'

'Is that so? I remember her, my but she was a beautiful woman. I remember your father too. Is she living in America?'

'No. She lives in Austria.'

'Austria, is it. My niece lives in Spain, is it anywhere near that?'

'No, Mrs O'Connor, quite some way from Spain. Are you going back to the cottage, Mrs O'Connor? If so I can give you a lift.'

'Well, thanks very much, Miss Elvira, that is nice of you.'

She'd have something to tell her friends in the morning, particularly that old busybody Molly Woods. Taken home by Miss Elvira, hearing about Miss Gloria living abroad in Austria, wherever Austria was, and Miss Elvira looking so smart and beautiful. Molly Woods could talk all she wanted about her sister Rose but she'd never been given lifts in their motor cars.

When they reached the cottage Ann O'Connor said, 'Can I offer you tea, Miss Elvira?' But Elvira said with a smile that she was anxious to see if her grandmother was feeling better.

Her grandmother was sitting in her favourite chair so that she could look through the window and she seemed rather better than she had earlier in the morning.

She was anxious to hear about the church service: who had been there; who Elvira had spoken to; had people commented on her absence – and considerably relieved when Elvira told her that most people had thought she had behaved sensibly in remaining at home.

'The housekeeper insisted that I had something to eat round about eleven, just poached egg and toast, but I'm not really very hungry for lunch. Oh dear, don't say we're having visitors, there's a car coming up the drive.'

Elvira joined her at the window to look at the large car driving slowly towards them and her first thought was that it was Roland's car. She'd seen them at church so why should they feel they must visit, either separately or together.

The car came to a standstill on the square in front of the dining room and her grandmother said hurriedly, 'Do meet them at the door, dear. If the maid opens the door she'll usher them in with a great welcome and I really don't feel like seeing anybody just now. Who is it do you think?'

'I thought it was the Bannisters' car.'

'Really. Are they both here?'

By this time a woman was walking across the terrace before she was hidden by the bushes and Elvira said, 'I think it's Joyce, Granny. I'll meet her at the door and take her into the conservatory. Don't worry, I'll explain that you're still not feeling very well.'

She was puzzled as to why Joyce should be visiting so she stood waiting at the door until their visitor came into view and she realized that this was not Joyce, she was taller, more elegant, and then with a cry she ran out of the house and the woman paused and held out her arms while Elvira cried, 'Mother, it's you, it's really you.'

Gloria looked at her daughter with a wry smile. 'I didn't make up my mind until yesterday morning. Ludvig has business in London so I decided to travel with him and drive on here.'

'I was so sure you wouldn't come.'

'I know, and I thought I should surprise you. Is Mother in?'

'Yes. She wasn't very well this morning so she didn't go to church. She'll be so glad to see you, Mother, she didn't for a moment think you'd come.'

'Anybody else here?'

'Not at the moment, but later on I've no doubt they'll be here.'

'Particularly if they know I've arrived, simply to pass judgement, dear. Come along, let's get it over with.'

The tears, the amazement, the questions, all came tumbling out until Gloria said, 'I'll get my suitcase out of the car, Mother, then perhaps we can have lunch and talk.'

'I'll get the suitcase, Mother,' Elvira said. 'You talk to Granny.'

This was how it had always been, Elvira reflected. The mother she adored who was hardly ever there, not because she didn't care but because she was forever searching for more – and when she found it it was never enough.

Tomorrow was her brother's funeral but it would be Gloria who would hold the critical attention of all eyes, curious and envious, and Gloria would sail through it all with consummate ease.

In spite of the tragedy that had brought them together there was a certain gaiety that Gloria had always had the power to instil in whoever she was with.

She could turn satire into laughter, amusement into cynicism, and in the end could be found a light-heartedness where fundamentally none was intended. It was Charlotte who said, 'You never change, Gloria. When you were a little girl when the others were so dismal, and often fractious, you could always laugh, look at the world through rose-coloured spectacles.'

'But the world wasn't always rosy, Mother.'

'No, dear, but it helped to think it was. Tell me about your husband, I should have met him.'

'I know, one day you will, but not just yet, not while there's misery, too many problems.'

'Is it third time lucky, Gloria?'

'Hasn't Elvira told you about him?'

'Very little, but then there's been so much to talk about, it's been the strangest week of my life.'

'Poor Steven. We were friends once, I got along with Steven better than the two girls. Were you very close, Mother?'

'Once we were, but somehow or other he drifted away. We seldom met, he didn't even speak to me at my birthday party, it was as if he had nothing to say to me.'

'And Julie?'

'I don't know. Barry was here yesterday, he's a lot like Steven was years ago but people change. I'd like to think that Barry won't change too much. You liked him, didn't you, Elvira?'

'Yes, Granny, I really did.'

'Well, I'll change out of these travelling clothes and put on something a little more flattering to make my sisters envious.'

'Oh, Gloria, that's how you always behaved.'

Gloria simply laughed. 'Where are you going to put me, Mother? Not that room overlooking the stables, I hated that one.'

'The one next to mine I think, so that I can hear what time you come to bed. You were always later than anybody else.'

A little later Elvira sat on her mother's bed watching Gloria take dress after dress out of her suitcase until in the end she said, 'How long are you thinking of staying, Mother?'

'Oh, these are not for here, Elvira. I'm simply taking them out so they don't get too creased. I can assure you the things I brought for here are very circumspect.'

'Which are they?'

'Well, this one I thought for the funeral, tonight I'll wear this and we'll go on from there.'

'This one looks adequate for Ascot.'

'Don't be tiresome, darling. I have to keep my end up and it will be expected of me. I don't want either family or neighbours to think I've come down in the world.'

'You're happy with your life, aren't you, Mother?'

'Yes, I am. Ludvig is right for me. He's good-looking, charming and affluent, what more could I want?'

'Wasn't my father any of those things?'

'Well, he was good-looking in a remote austere sort of way,

he too was affluent but he was lacking in other ways. Don't say
you didn't think so too, Elvira?'

'Perhaps.'

'And the first one was fun to be with and lacking in every
other way. With Ludvig I seem to have found the man I've been
searching for.'

'Well, I'll go and change, Mother, I'm in the room at the end
of the corridor. Will you pick me up there?'

'Yes, darling, in about an hour.'

Gloria's first words to Elvira when they met a little later were,
'Haven't you anything more elegant than that, dear?'

'You forget, Mother, that I was only intending to stay for the
weekend. I've managed to buy something for the funeral, but I'll
have to make do with the rest. Anyway, I'm leaving tomorrow
or Tuesday at the latest.'

'I can lend you something of mine.'

'No, really. I'm quite happy with this.'

She waited while her mother prowled about her bedroom,
recognizing ornaments she remembered as well as the view from
the window which overlooked the gardens; then her eyes fell
on a brightly wrapped package which she picked up to gaze at
curiously.

'Somebody's birthday?' she asked.

'Granny's, last Saturday.'

'You mean you haven't given it to her yet?'

'No, I'll give it to her before I leave.'

'Why didn't you give it to her on her birthday?'

'I bought her something else, some chocolates, some perfume.
I knew which was her favourite.'

'But why hang on to this — what is it anyway?'

'It's a photograph.'

For a long moment they stared at each other until Gloria said,
'She's turned eighty, she's lost her son, how many shocks do you
think she can take in one week?'

'What makes you think this will be a shock?'

'You must think so too, Elvira, otherwise you would have given
it to her. Wasn't this supposed to be the real present?'

'You're only surmising that, Mother.'

'Well, you'll give her the present and leave me to tell her the rest.'

'Shouldn't we be going down?' Elvira asked.

'In a little while. There are things I need to ask like, have you seen him?'

'Him?'

'Well, you never did put a name to him, darling, only that he was special. I tantalized myself by thinking about all those boys you danced with, rode with, possibly even slept with; I should have made it my business to find out.'

'Yes, Mother, you should, but you didn't did you? Mother, it's too late for questions, and I really don't have anything to tell you. Most of those boys are now respectable married men, or men who intend their solitary state to be permanent, and anything that happened to me in the past is as dead as the dodo.'

'So you can move on?'

'I've moved on, Mother.'

'Why don't we give that parcel to Mother tonight while the rest of them are asking questions and speculating wildly.'

'I don't think so. I brought it for Granny. It's up to her who she shows it to.'

They walked down the staircase arm in arm and it was the housekeeper who was setting out the table for afternoon tea who said, 'My but it's nice to see you, Miss Gloria, you don't seem a day older.'

'And you're the nicest person I've seen today,' Gloria said with a smile. 'You're looking after mother very well.'

'Thank you, but she's not much trouble, she likes everything done her way, just like it always was, but we all get along.'

'I'm sure you do.'

'Will you be staying long, Miss Gloria?'

'Not very long, I have to join my husband in London in a day or so.'

Neither of Gloria's sisters had expected to see her at their brother's funeral and their amazement was very evident. Georgia asked the most questions, and Gloria took pleasure in elaborating on her answers.

Glenda talked about her daughters, their husbands and their

children, and then Georgia, not to be outdone, spoke of Kate who was doing brilliantly professionally, and Alex who had the funeral in hand and who had been absolutely wonderful throughout the turmoil

It was later in the evening when Alex arrived, and his eyes lit up immediately at the sight of a well-remembered aunt. It was later in the evening when he was able to spend some time with her that he said, 'I'm not calling you Aunt Gloria, you look too young for that. You could be Elvira's sister.'

'Well, thank you, Alex, Mother said you were quite a charmer.'

He laughed. 'Well, have you met the rest of us?'

'Not since they were children.'

'My cousin's too circumspect, my sister might surprise you. Do you remember Marian, my wife?'

'Hardly at all.'

'But you remember Julie?'

'Not awfully well.'

'You will after tomorrow. My wife is good at playing the drama queen, likewise Julie, the rest you'll quickly forget.'

'Why do you say your sister might surprise me?'

'Ambitious, perhaps she'd like to be like you.'

'Why is that?'

'She won't be. She hasn't got your looks but she has got your ambitions. With her it was her profession, with you it was your life.'

Looking at them across the room Elvira was not surprised to find them engrossed with each other. The Chaytor family had largely produced prestigious and illustrious men. The portraits that adorned the walls of the manor were proof of this with their array of naval and military men, judges and bishops, but now and again had come along a man like Alex, undoubtedly a successful man, but somewhat removed from more proper and salubrious ancestors.

Alex and Gloria fitted into this category, although with Steven it had gone too far, and he had paid the price.

Marian watched her husband's evident enjoyment of his conversation with Gloria with a jaundiced eye. She'd heard a lot about Gloria, her three husbands and the last one a foreigner, and even a daughter who was a bit of a dark horse.

She was good-looking, but that dress was a little flamboyant, and they were laughing too much. Didn't either of them realize that tomorrow they had a funeral to go to?

Alex smiled across at her, saying to Gloria, 'I don't think my wife finds our laughter very appropriate.'

'No, perhaps we should circulate.'

'Definitely not. It's twelve years since we met, I met Marian over breakfast and she didn't have much to say even then.'

'I doubt if you'd find me quite so entertaining over breakfast, Alex.'

'No, perhaps not. How long are you here for?'

'Midweek, I have to be in London to meet my husband.'

'Your Austrian count.'

'Yes, but that isn't why I married him.'

'No.'

'He's also very nice, perhaps you'll meet him one day.'

Looking across the room Gloria said, 'My mother is looking rather tired, she wasn't very well this morning, so perhaps we should all think of retiring early.'

Seventeen

Charlotte had decided that the caterers who had officiated at her birthday party should provide the repast for those attending her son's funeral. They arrived early, and the flowers that had occupied most of the hall were now relegated to the conservatories and they were busy setting out the hall for the guests arriving later in the day.

Her chauffeur drove them to the church and they were the first of the family to arrive. The villagers had turned out in force and already Mrs O'Connor and Molly Woods were sitting immediately behind the pews reserved for the family.

Whispering to Annie, Molly said, 'My but she's hardly changed at all, they could be sisters instead of mother and daughter.'

'When Miss Elvira gave me a lift home she didn't mention her mother coming.'

'Maybe she didn't know.'

Julie arrived leaning heavily on her son's arm, followed by her father and his wife, and Molly said, 'The old lady looks a lot more dignified than his wife.'

Charlotte sat erect in between Gloria and Elvira, and throughout the service there would be many who would remark on her demeanour but would be unable to assess her thoughts.

The rest of the family arrived and the pews behind began to fill up. The service was about to begin, however, when a man who had been sitting behind suddenly got out of his pew and strode towards the door.

He had sat there watching the family arrive, his face a scowling mask, but only three people recognized him – Julie's father, Alex and Roland – as being the man they had seen talking to Steven on the night he had been killed.

Grimly Julie's father thought that his reasons for coming were decidedly sinister.

The vicar had discussed the service with Charlotte since Julie had said she was too distressed to even think about it. Calmly and eloquently Barry read a passage he had found in a book in his father's desk and after the final hymn the family were following Steven's coffin out of the church into the graveyard. It was over, and the family departed for the manor house and the villagers gathered in groups to discuss the morning's events.

At the manor house Julie sat in tearful isolation while her son brought her food. She said she wasn't hungry, but was persuaded to eat, and Marian said glumly, 'Poor Julie, I'm sure she'd rather have gone home.'

'And I'm equally sure she's enjoying the drama,' Alex said with a wry smile. 'Remember last Saturday, she was the belle of the ball, today she's living the final death toll of Cleopatra.'

'You're so unfeeling, Alex, you could at least have a word with her.'

'I've already tried to have a word with her, Marian, she didn't want to talk.'

'Oh well, I'll go and sit with her, I'm sure she'll talk to me.'

'I'm sure she will, dear, you're at your best at moments like this.'

She never knew when Alex was being cynical, possibly she told herself because he was never anything else.

Alex made his way to Gloria's side and he said softly, 'Haven't you often wondered why funerals can be more entertaining than weddings? I wonder why that is?'

'Possibly because one is the uncertainty and the other is the finality,' she replied.

'Well, Marian's attempting to cheer her up, how much success she'll have is open to doubt.'

'You might get along better with Marian if you tried to be less cynical.'

'And some day I'll tell you how often I've tried and how many times I've failed.'

'Mother's bearing up well.'

'You're changing the subject.'

'Who's the man Elvira is talking to?'

'Roland Bannister, he's a barrister like me. He was with me the night we saw Uncle Steven with some chap in the Bull.'

'Is he married?'

'He married Joyce Mansell.'

'Of course. Miss Perfection.'

Alex laughed. 'So life in the village is coming back to you. Yes, Joyce was considered the ultimate for what some mothers wanted for their sons. I can't say she was ever my cup of tea, but then neither was Marian.'

'And the woman over there is Joyce I take it?'

'That's right.'

Gloria looked at her for several minutes before she said, 'Nice, sweet and ordinary. Not to be compared with my daughter.'

'Why didn't Elvira capture Bannister then, why let Joyce have him?'

'Maybe she didn't want him.'

'Oh, I don't know. She went away and never came back. Why didn't she come back, Gloria?'

'She came to me, I am her mother after all.'

'You were a pretty absent one most of the time.'

'And you shouldn't be speaking to your aunt like this.'

'Why don't you stay on here for a while, Gloria? The place could do with somebody like you, particularly after the week we've had.'

'And I have a husband to go back to.'

'When are we going to meet him?'

'Oh, you will one day, and now I must circulate, Alex, and so must you. Which is your sister?'

'Kate. She's over there with James Harrison. They had something going for a while, but not any more.'

For a long time Kate had stood with James at the buffet hemmed in by other people. Now some of the others had drifted away and for the want of something to say he said, 'Can I get you anything?'

'No, thank you, I don't want anything else.'

'It's so sad about Steven, he was always so entertaining.'

'Yes, he was, but not so much recently, perhaps he wasn't well.'

'No.'

How difficult it was to converse with a woman you'd idolized and thought had loved you. Now here was this stony-faced woman wearing a black outfit that only added to her coldness.

He was relieved when Joyce Bannister joined them and Kate quickly excused herself.

'How is Dora?' Joyce said. 'I heard she was visiting her sister.'

'Yes she is. I'm not sure when she's coming back.'

Joyce smiled. She'd heard the rumours of course, but she didn't listen to rumours, as a magistrate she had to be very careful. She tried to like everybody, but Kate was something of an enigma. She admired her in the courtroom but although they often met socially Kate was distant. She'd never actually been friendly with her at school, and when she'd remarked on it to Roland he'd simply said, 'She isn't easy, Joyce, I've never found her so.'

How long did people stay after a funeral? Charlotte asked herself. The caterers had cleared away and she'd watched their large vans disappearing down the drive. Now only the guests were around, chatting and showing no intentions whatsoever of leaving.

Gloria was enjoying the attention she was receiving, and it would seem that everybody wanted to talk to her. Charismatic as always, she had gathered a few young men around her, in spite of the fact that their wives were none too pleased.

Elvira was still talking to Roland Bannister and across the room several other people were monitoring their conversation.

'So you're leaving in the morning?' he asked her.

'Yes, after breakfast, it's quite a long drive.'

'Is your mother going with you?'

'No, she's driving to London to meet her husband.'

'Will it be another ten years before we see you again?'

'I don't know, Roland, it shouldn't matter to you.'

'I know, the awful thing is that it does. Can't we meet to tonight even if it's only for a short while?'

She knew she could make up some excuse to go out, but her mother would be too curious – and what was the point. She would always like him, he'd been the first man she'd ever loved and something of that floundering passion still lingered, but it would be stupid to revive feelings that had lain dormant for so long.

With a sad, brief smile she said, 'Roland, it isn't possible, we'll say our farewells now and silence all that speculation in a great many eyes.'

She reached up to kiss his cheek, and he supressed every emotion he had that urged him to put his arms around her.

Tired of making conversation Charlotte had escaped into her

own small sitting room hoping fervently that for a little while at least she wouldn't be missed.

She had only just sat down when there was a soft rap on the door and it opened to reveal Julie's father standing there looking at her anxiously.

'I'm sorry to disturb you, Mrs Chaytor, but could I have a few words with you, it's pretty hopeless out there.'

'Oh yes, do come in. I was hoping I wouldn't be missed.'

'Well nobody seems to be in any hurry to leave and I didn't think it possible to talk to you in there.'

'I'm sure you're right. Please sit there – would you like a drink? Sherry is all I have in here I'm afraid.'

'And sherry is very civilized, but I've had all the drink I want today.'

They stared at each other for a long time. He admired Charlotte Chaytor without really ever having known her. He admired her dignity and composure; she'd lost her son and yet her bearing had been peerless, with none of the morbid displays of grief he'd seen, even from his own daughter.

She was looking at him enquiringly and he said, 'I hope you don't think I'm taking too much on myself, Mrs Chaytor, but Julie is my daughter and Barry's my grandson. We have to think about them at a time like this.'

'Of course, and I do think about them, particularly at this time.'

'Did you know that Steven was having money problems?'

'I was aware of it, but not until recently.'

'He never discussed it with me, as a matter of fact he didn't like me knowing about it, but in my profession word about gambling and suchlike gets around.'

'Gambling?'

'Yes. He was well into that. He got out of law and thought he could make more money on the horses and other pursuits. He did for a time until it fell apart and it all started to go wrong. I've promised my grandson that I'll put him through university so it's going to cost me, but you're his grandmother, Mrs Chaytor. Forgive me for this, I'm a blunt man, but I have to ask if they can expect anything from you?'

'I knew there was something wrong. Steven has ignored me recently, even last Saturday when they came to my birthday party.

I've been very worried about him. You're asking me to help them . . . in what way?'

'Well, money, Mrs Chaytor. I'm not a poor man, but I do have a wife and you've got to be fairly affluent to live in a place like this.'

'I admire your bluntness, and I have to be equally so. A few months ago I gave my son a cheque for a hundred and fifty thousand pounds which he said he would repay. He never has, I didn't expect he ever would, when he made no effort to speak to me.'

'I'm sorry, Mrs Chaytor, I didn't know any of this.'

'I have other children, you know, and grandchildren, I have to consider them too.'

'Well of course.'

'Has Julie any money, has she anything from Steven at all?'

'She's got the house. It's a big house with a mortgage and if she moves into something smaller it will need paying for. Barry's got a few more years before he gets a job and you know what boys of his age are like, he doesn't want to miss out on anything.'

'Particularly the trip to Chile,' she said dryly.

'Oh, ay, there's that, arranged when the lad thought his father had plenty.'

'We'll talk again about Julie's problems. I'm glad you've spoken to me today but obviously we need to talk again. Perhaps we could meet in a few days.'

'Yes, I'll be in touch, Mrs Chaytor. I'm not about to tell Julie I've spoken to you, for the moment I think we should keep it just between the two of us.'

'Yes, I do agree, and now I must get back to my guests.'

'It's nice for you to have your daughter Gloria with you for a few days.'

'Yes, although the reason for her being here is very sad.'

There were still groups of people talking together, but there were others who were intent on departure.

Charlotte sincerely hoped the others would take the hint so she went around thanking them for being there, wishing them a safe journey home, and very soon only the immediate family remained.

Standing with his grandfather Barry said, 'I think we should get Mother home, she's drunk too much wine and she's likely to say things she shouldn't.'

'Good idea, Barry, I'll collect Val and we'll get the car round. You see to your mother.'

Julie was only concerned with the beauty of the spacious hall, the wide sweeping staircase and the graciousness of a house that should have been hers.

As her son reached her side she said angrily, 'Why are we the first to leave, the rest of the family are here?'

'Grandfather's gone for the car, Val's with him.'

'This should be our house, Barry. Your father's dead but it should be yours.'

'Come along, Mother, let's get you home.'

'I mean it, Barry.'

From across the room the others were staring at them, and he was relieved to see his grandfather coming towards them.

'I don't want to go yet,' Julie said angrily, but her father pulled her to her feet saying in a commanding voice she remembered so well, 'We're going home, my girl, you've had enough.'

Considerably meeker, Julie complied, and Charlotte and Glenda went to the door with them to say their farewells.

After they had gone Glenda said, 'She seemed so angry, Mother. I know she was sad, but why so angry?'

'Grief hits people in different ways,' Charlotte replied. 'Now I expect you all want to get home. Thank you so much, Alex, for arranging everything so well, Elvira's leaving in the morning so I expect she's got packing to do.'

'Most of it's done, Granny. It's been lovely seeing you all, I'm so sorry it had to end like this.'

'When are you leaving, Gloria?' Georgia asked.

'Wednesday.'

'Oh well, perhaps we'll meet again one day, you're such a long way away.'

'Yes. If any of you feel like visiting Austria you know where I am,' she replied, while hoping fervently that none of them would. They still had very little in common, age hadn't altered their personalities, the old resentments and jealousies, and in her own foolish young days she'd played on their insecurities and her own stupidities.

She stood with her mother and daughter to wave their good-byes and Charlotte said, 'I'm afraid you're both in for a boring evening. I'm feeling rather tired, so I'll probably go to bed early and be up to wave you goodbye in the morning, Elvira.'

'You needn't, Granny, I'll come into your room before I leave.'

'I intend to be up, dear. Do you know I saw some black clouds out there, I rather think the weather is changing.'

'Perhaps by morning they'll have blown over.'

Charlotte was tired but she was unable to sleep. Her conversation with Julie's father was giving her the greatest problem. She was aware of her duties to both Julie and her grandson, but there were other members of her family with great expectations.

Glenda's husband had not been a rich man. They'd lived a comfortable lifestyle because Glenda had always been careful with their money, and after her husband died, even more so. The girls' education had been upmost in her mind, and although they had both married men in decent positions none of them could be described as wealthy.

Georgia's husband had been considerably more affluent and Alex and Kate had both done well in their professions. Even so they would expect decent legacies from their grandmother and it was evident that the money she had given to Steven had gone for good.

Elvira moved away from the window and went to sit opposite her mother, whose head was sunk in a magazine.

'It looks like rain, Mother, I hope it clears by morning,' she said thoughtfully.

'Can't you stay on another day?'

'No, Mother, I only came for one night and it's been much more. I need to get back, there's a lot I have to think about.'

'When are you going to give Mother that present?'

'In the morning. If she's asleep I'll leave it beside her bed.'

'It won't prevent the questions, Elvira, questions she'll be asking of me.'

'You'll cope, Mother, haven't you always? There's a car out there, don't say we haven't had enough visitors for one day.'

They both went to the window and after a few minutes Elvira said, 'It's Alex. I'm not surprised that he's come round.'

Gloria laughed and went back to her place on the couch.

Minutes later Alex's smiling face was staring at them across the room.

'Granny gone to bed then?' he said casually.

'Yes, she was very tired.'

'And how do you two girls intend to spend the rest of the evening, simply chatting or have you something more exciting in mind?'

'How do you intend to spend your evening?' Gloria asked. 'Not sitting here making conversation I'm sure.'

'Why don't I take you two girls out for dinner? Round about eight. You're both dressed up for it.'

'We're dressed up for a funeral, Alex.'

'Well of course, but equally elegant.'

'I hope you're not thinking of the Bull's Head. I can imagine the comments that would be passed by everybody in there about our appearance so soon after Steven's funeral.'

'Definitely not the Bull. There's that new place over at Hollington. Good reputation, and probably fairly quiet on a Monday evening.'

'Didn't you think of inviting Marian?' Gloria asked.

'She wouldn't leave the children, even though she could have left somebody else in charge.'

'Who, for instance?'

'Her mother would have come round, but Marian wouldn't want to come, she's a home bird.'

Looking at Elvira, Gloria said, 'What do you think, darling, do you feel like eating out?'

'No, mother, I'm leaving early in the morning and I have things to do.'

Elvira watched them depart convinced that they would both enjoy their evening together. They had the same sort of humour and mentality, and Alex was entirely delighted to be escorting an elegant, beautiful woman even though she was his aunt.

It was early to even think of retiring but she could have a bath, finish putting things into her suitcase and even finish the book she'd been reading.

Sitting on the edge of her bed she picked up the parcel lying on top of the bedside table. It was wrapped in gold leaf and sported a gold satin rose and she knew that what it contained would raise anxieties and problems that she'd ignored for all too long. Now, however, she knew that the last few days had finally brought her heart-searchings to a head.

She'd been so unsure how she would react to coming back and meeting her past. She'd secretly dreaded it, but now she knew for certain that it had been something she needed, something that had made her reach a decision she'd been afraid of.

She was leaving it to her mother to answer the questions her grandmother would ask, but like everything else in her life Gloria would do it light-heartedly.

There had been so many times when she'd wished she could be like her mother. Gloria had been able to treat so many of life's catastrophes with an irreverent smile and Elvira had never been sure how much she'd really cared. Gloria would know how to smile and say the right thing.

Eighteen

It was just after seven o'clock when Elvira crept into her grandmother's bedroom the next morning. Charlotte was still asleep so she placed the narrow gilt-wrapped parcel on the table nearest the bed and crept noiselessly out of the room.

She looked round her bedroom before picking up her suitcase. She wanted to remember this room, it was part of her childhood, of days and years that were intrinsically linked to what might have been and which she knew now she was right to relegate to the past.

She closed the door quietly behind her and made her way down the staircase. She decided to put her case in her car and drive it round to the front of the house. She heard sounds coming from the kitchen. Only the night before the housekeeper had said she would see that breakfast was cooked for her before leaving.

She had told the housekeeper it was unnecessary, that she would look after herself, but she would have none of that, so Elvira walked around the gardens, enjoying their freshness after the night's rain, the long expanse of lawns and the rabbits scampering across the grass, then with a little sigh she made her way back to the house.

As she entered the breakfast room she stared with dismay at her grandmother seated at the table, the gold wrapping paper spread out on the table in front of her, the contents of the parcel in her hands. Raising her head she looked at Elvira long and searchingly, then she said, 'Talk to me, Elvira, tell me about this.'

She walked slowly across the room and Charlotte held out the photograph the parcel had contained saying, 'She's beautiful, dear, but who is she?'

'Her name's Charlotte but she prefers to be called Charlie.'

'Your sister?'

'My daughter.'

Charlotte stared at her in amazement then down at the photograph in her hands. 'She's beautiful, Elvira, but how old is she?'

'She's nine, Granny.'

'And her father?'

'I can't tell you, Granny, I shall never tell anyone.'

'You mean, you don't know?'

'I mean I shall never disclose who he is.'

'Is that why you never came back here? Does he live here or is he somebody you met when you went to your mother?'

'Granny, I was fifteen, too young to fall in love and believe it's the solitary passion of a lifetime. I did think it was, now I know that it couldn't have been. I've grown up, he's grown up, we're not the same people we were then.'

'Have you met him again since you've been here?'

'Granny, it doesn't matter. He's got a life, I've got a beautiful daughter, why rake up the past now. Charlie has survived ten years without him and she stopped asking me questions a long time ago.'

Just then the door opened and Gloria came into the room, looking at them both in some anxiety before joining them at the table. She smiled at her mother and Charlotte said gently, 'You've both kept this secret all these years, don't you think I have a right to know?'

'I could have told you about the baby, Mother, that's all I could have told you. Elvira would tell me nothing about the child's father and she's never changed her mind about that.'

'But where is Charlie now, who is looking after her?'

'She's in school, Granny.'

'Boarding school?'

'Well, yes it is, but something a little more than that. It's a musical college, Granny. She's really very talented . . . she plays the violin.'

'Gracious, we've never had a musician in the family before. You learned to play the piano, Elvira, but you were never brilliant, where does she get it from?'

'Some long-dead ancestor,' Gloria said with a laugh. 'If you think it's from Charlie's father you'll be trawling the village looking for musicians so don't even try, Mother.'

'You're both too much for me,' Charlotte said. 'Do I tell the rest of the family?'

'I'd rather you didn't, Granny. They may never meet her, there'd be too much speculation and it would be terrible for you.'

'But I want to meet her.'

'And one day you will, Granny.'

'I'm eighty years old, Elvira, how many years do you think there are left?'

'Well, at the moment she's at school in Vienna. Mother sees more of her than I do, but we will arrange for you to meet as soon as possible, I promise.'

'But why Vienna, what's wrong with this country?'

'She was born in Vienna, Granny. I see her for holidays, and she's yet to discover England.'

'But you have a job here.'

'I paint pictures and sell them, I also help an old friend out in his art college.'

'Oh, Elvira, all this is too much for me, you've been here a week, couldn't you have told me all this before?'

'There's been so much going on here, Granny, somehow I couldn't burden you with any of this. I meant to give you that photograph last Saturday when it was your party but somehow I felt it wasn't right. There were all those people I hadn't seen for years, and the family that wasn't really family at all. So I got the chocolates and the flowers.'

Charlotte looked down at the photograph in her hands saying, 'She's a lot like you were when you were that age, Gloria, that's why I asked Elvira if Charlie was her sister.'

Gloria laughed. 'Oh no, Mother, Elvira was enough, you surely don't think I'm interested in a new contingent at my time of life.'

'You're only in your forties, a lot of women have children at that age.'

'But not me, Mother. Ludvig and I are very happy, set in our ways and intending to remain so.'

Elvira consulted her watch and her grandmother said, 'I asked the housekeeper to bring breakfast in around eight o'clock. I thought we needed to talk first. Are you anxious to get away, dear?'

'Yes, I think perhaps I should, I have quite a long way to drive.'

Later, as she drove through the village, she familiarized herself with old sights and sounds, from the elderly woman standing in her garden and waving her hand as she drove out of the gate, to the stalls going up in the market square, remembering suddenly that Tuesday was market day.

She drove slowly in the early morning traffic, but it was when she came to the lane leading on to the hill that she paused. She decided that just one more time she would stand beneath the old oak tree that had witnessed the memories that had troubled her for such a long time.

She stood looking up at the tree. How quickly did they grow, how far up the bark were the initials that Roland had carved that long-lost summer's day, and in the future would he ever come up here and remember.

Her grandmother had waved to her from the door, but her mother had walked to the car with her and her last words had been, 'You have a lot to think about, Elvira, have you decided to meet me in London over the weekend?'

'Yes, Mother, why is it so important?'

'Because it is. It seems to me you've dithered long enough and I think I know why.'

They had looked at each other for some time without speaking until Gloria said, 'I know I'm right, when I say you wanted to reassure yourself that you no longer cared for the boy you'd been in love with all those years ago. I'm making sense, Elvira – you tell me that it's finally over?'

There had been so many times when Gloria had been absent from her life, but she had never been able to lie to her and she couldn't have done so at that moment.

All she'd been able to say at that moment had been, 'It is over, Mother, for it to be otherwise would hurt too many people, stir too many ashes. I'll meet you in London on Saturday morning. What plans have you made?'

'We'll meet in the restaurant for lunch and I'll tell you then.'

That had been as much as Gloria was prepared to tell her, and now as she drove down the hillside she knew that finally she had put the past to rest.

She drove past Julie's house, with Barry's car standing on the drive, and she thought about Julie's histrionics coupled with Barry's embarrassment. Julie was having financial problems but thinking back on the past week there had been so many problems another of which was Marian.

She could see her leaving her house and walking qu[...]
the road and she knew instinctively that she was goin.
Joyce. Maybe they had things to do together, one of their charities or a morning on the bench, and then she was passing Joyce's
house with its pristine lawns and tidy flower beds.

Joyce would be suitably dressed for wherever they were going,
not a hair out of place, and confidently basking in the morning's
successful outcome.

What did it feel like always to be so sure, and yet never in a
thousand years would she think it was her husband who was unsure,
bored even with something that had once promised everything.

Joyce greeted Marian with a bright smile. 'I was hoping you'd
come early, Marian. What do you think of this hat, do you think
it's suitable for the WI meeting? Some of the ladies might think
it's a little over the top.'

'Oh, but it's beautiful, Joyce, didn't you wear it last Saturday?'

'No, one very similar. Have we time for coffee or should we
leave now? Isn't Elvira leaving this morning?'

'Yes. What do you think of her mother?'

'Aunt Gloria? She's very beautiful, but it's not my kind of
beauty, I prefer something a little more restrained.'

'Restrained?'

'Well, yes, not quite so flamboyant, if that's the right word.'

'Alex is besotted with her, he always was. What does Roland
think of her?'

'He's never said. Oh, I don't think he'll be too impressed, after
all she's not in the least like me. Roland's always preferred the
quiet genteel type.'

'Has he said what he thinks of Elvira?'

'Not really, only that she's changed quite a bit from how he
remembers her.'

'I wonder what's going to happen with Julie, do you think
she'll stay on here?'

'I don't know. Has she got the money?'

'From the few things Alex has said I wouldn't think so. Her
father will help I'm sure, and there's Granny Chaytor, she will
help out I'm certain, but she does have other members of the
family to consider.'

'I'm awfully lucky really, there's just me to think about, there's quite a lot of you. Perhaps we should get off now, Marian, I like to be early.'

As they walked down the drive Marian couldn't help thinking how nice it must be to be Joyce, cossetted and pampered with a husband and parents who adored her, and a safe and secure future. Whenever she said as much to Alex he merely smiled his usual cynical smile, leaving her wondering if he knew something she didn't.

Barry put his golf clubs into the car and went back into the house where his mother confronted him by saying, 'Why do you have to play golf so soon after your father's funeral?'

'Mother, my not playing won't bring him back. Besides I'm pretty new to the game, I need some practice.'

'You need to think about me.'

'I do, Mother, all the time.'

'It costs a lot of money to join that golf club, then there's your degree to think about, and that ridiculous trip to South America, you can't expect your grandfather to pay for everything.'

'When I've got the degree and a job I'll pay him back, he knows that.'

'You're expecting everything, what about me? Your father's left debts, this house needs money spending on it, and I need a car. Your father said he'd see that I got one but he never did.'

'Well at least you've given up all that ridiculous nonsense about Granny's house. We need something smaller, Mother, not larger.'

'I'm her son's wife, you're her grandson.'

'So is Alex, and with more money to pay for it.'

'I could never talk to your father, I can't talk to you.'

'Mother, I have to go now, I'm meeting chaps at the club and I'm late already. We'll talk some more tonight. Think about that trip to France.'

Of course she wouldn't go to France, she'd too much on her mind. There wasn't even any point in going to the shops, if she saw something she wanted to buy she hadn't got the money for it.

Charlotte's thoughts too were on Julie. She'd exhausted the topic of Elvira's daughter, and Gloria, smiling at her across the table, said, 'Mother, I've told you all there is to tell, she's a lovely girl, you'll love her.'

'I'm sure I will, but you haven't told me who her father is.'

'I don't know.'

'You've no idea?'

'No.'

'I'll be suspicious about every young man I see, the sons of our friends, men who are probably married.'

'Don't you think there are more things to worry about than looking for suspects. What about Julie and Steven's money problems.'

'I know. Her father talked to me about those yesterday.'

'I thought he might. I saw him looking for you, obviously extremely worried.'

'He told me Steven was gambling, heavily in debt, and that he was paying for his grandson's education among other things.'

'And he thinks you could do something to help out?'

'Yes, but, Gloria, I've already given Steven a great deal of money and I have other responsibilities.'

'The rest of the family?'

'Well, yes. I know that Glenda isn't too well placed, and the younger element might need money. There's the children's education for one thing and with that money I lent to Steven a great many things could have been done.'

'Well, you don't need to think about me, Mother, I don't need any of your money, nor will Elvira.'

'You say Elvira won't need it, but she's got a daughter to educate, and she can't be earning all that much, teaching and painting in her spare time.'

Gloria laughed. 'Mother, my daughter is really quite affluent and if she comes down to earth at last likely to be more so. You'll hear more in due course, but for now let's concentrate on Julie's problems.'

In the end Gloria said, 'Consult with the rest of them, Mother, but please after I've gone, I don't want any of them thinking I've influenced you in any way. I was the black sheep of the family after all.'

★   ★   ★

'And I'm going to spend the rest of my life wondering if every boy I see is the father of my great granddaughter.'

'You mean you're going to scan the pews in church every Sunday and every social event from here to eternity.'

'How shall I be able to help it?'

'I wasn't around much that summer, Mother. I left Elvira very much to her own devices. I was a rotten mother, you have every right to tell me so, but I've tried to be a good grandmother and I've learned not to ask questions of Elvira. Whatever happened in that lost summer, she wants it forgotten.'

'Surely we should have known if there'd been anybody special.'

'Perhaps he wasn't special. Perhaps he was just somebody she needed then, and easy to forget.'

'I'm trying to think who she's seen most of these last few days. If I'd known about her daughter I'd have been considerably more diligent.'

'Mother, I want you to stop torturing yourself about something you'll never know the answer to. Concentrate on what you're going to do about Julie, whether you can do anything about Alex's marriage, and on this very disjointed family you had such expectations of.'

'Will I ever get to meet your husband and Charlie?' she asked plaintively.

'Yes, Mother, I promise, and hopefully sooner than you might think.'

'You were always good at making promises, Gloria. Unfortunately they didn't always materialize.'

Gloria smiled and, looking earnestly into her mother's eyes, she said, 'Talk to Julie soon, Mother. Do what you want to do, it'll work out, I'm sure.'

It was later that evening when Roland Bannister ate his evening meal in the company of Alex, and as the two men sat down together Alex said, 'I see Dora Harrison's returned to the fold.'

'I didn't know.'

'Apparently the children are back at the school. I'm not sure when she came back.'

'The separation didn't last too long.'

'No. It could have been worse I suppose. Jobs were at stake as well as a marriage.'

'But Kate wouldn't have been happy with that.'

'No. You're quite a student of human nature, Roland, it's a pity it hasn't always worked out in your own life.'

'Why do you say that?'

'You know that Elvira left this morning?'

'And?'

'Come on, Roland, this is Alex you're talking to. I've seen you looking at her, I know you've been seeing her on the hill and I've seen the uncertainty whenever you've met.'

'I have a wife, Alex.'

'But would you have had this wife if Elvira had come back here? I'm not very sure about that.

'I took her mother out to dinner on Monday evening and she asked a few questions: were you happy in your marriage; how well did you and Elvira know each other in those old days – it was evident that she was suspicious.'

'Why should she be, after all it was ten years ago and Elvira had a great many friends.'

'Gloria knew that, she was searching for a special one.'

'We shall probably never meet again.'

'She'll come back again surely, why will anything be any different?'

'Just something she said.'

'What? She'll surely want to see Granny again, even members of the family, me for instance.'

'She said this really was goodbye, not just to the old days, but to the people we were now. If we met again our lives might be very different.'

'I wonder what she meant by that.'

'Some sort of finality I think. I saw her just once more and I asked her what she meant by it. She wouldn't say. We were both very emotional, she simply went away.'

At that moment Alex forgot to be cynical. He could see the sudden torment in his friend's eyes and was aware of a feeling he had never yet felt for any woman. After a few minutes he said, 'I might pop round to see Granny tonight, say goodbye to Gloria, who knows when we'll see her again?'

He reflected on his way to his grandmother's that Roland

hadn't been particularly good company that evening. There'd been a pained reticence in his conversation, the need to talk to somebody and yet the inability to do so. They'd parted in the hotel car park and Roland had appeared relieved when Alex had been hailed by two other men leaving their cars. He had wanted so much to say more, but was relieved that the newcomers had prevented it.

He found his mother and his aunt just finishing their meal and his grandmother said, 'I'm so glad you've come, Alex, you can organize something I'm not very good at.'

'Not another party, Granny.'

'No, a get-together of the family. I want them all to be here, I've something to discuss with all of them.'

She would say nothing more in spite of his questions and it was Gloria who said, 'I shan't be at the get-together, Alex, I'm leaving in the morning.'

'Doesn't any of this concern you, Gloria?' he asked.

'None at all.'

He looked at them extremely puzzled and Charlotte said, 'You'll know all about it tomorrow evening, round about eight, I think. That will give everybody a chance to have their meal and drive up here. You'll bring Marian, Alex?'

'If it's to be the entire family, yes.'

'Well, that's settled then. I'm sorry to be putting all this on your shoulders, Alex, but you do it so well. Shall we go into the lounge and have coffee there.'

Nineteen

Alex assembled the family at the long dining table and thought it resembled an important board meeting rather than a family get-together. With his usual dry humour he said, 'All we're short of is the Christmas tree. Shall I suggest we bring the meeting to order?'

His grandmother sat at the head of the table with her two daughters on either side of her. Some of them appeared puzzled, others curious, but as they looked round it would seem the only two people missing were Julie and Barry.

It was Georgia who said, 'What is all this, Mother? It all seems terribly grand.'

With a smile Alex said, 'You have the floor, Granny, you start the ball rolling.'

Charlotte looked round at their expectant faces before saying, 'Yes, well, the sooner we begin the sooner we get it over. It's largely about Steven and his troubles. I don't know if any of you were aware that he was desperately short of money; he'd gambled recklessly and lost most of what he had leaving Julie and the boy with debts and very little of anything else. I spoke with Julie's father after the funeral and he was able to tell me something of all this.'

'They never seemed short of money,' Georgia said sharply. 'Julie spent money on expensive clothes and the like, Barry went off on foreign holidays and I believe he's planning a more adventurous one. How did they manage to do all that if they were short of money?'

'He borrowed, Georgia, apparently he owes money right, left and centre.'

'Surely Julie must have known.'

'You know what Steven was like, wanting people to think that he was prosperous, that everything was going well for him. I think that perhaps Julie has been the last person to find out.'

'What has any of it to do with her father speaking to you?' Kate asked sharply.

'Because he's been helping Julie out for some time. He's paying for Barry at university, he's paid for his holidays and a great many other things. He now thinks that perhaps Steven's family might be prepared to do something.'

'Pay his debts off do you mean?' Georgia asked.

'Not entirely, but there are ways we can help, that's why I've asked you here this evening.'

'What sort of things?' Glenda asked. 'You know I haven't much money, Mother. I've helped the children, and I'm very careful with everything, I don't see how I can possibly help Julie with money.'

'No, dear, and I don't expect you to.'

'And my children are only just finding their feet, how can they be expected to contribute?'

'I don't want anything from any of you, but I have to try to do as much as Julie's father at least.'

They looked at each other doubtfully, all except Alex, who stood near the window looking out before he resumed his seat with the rest of them. His eyes met Charlotte's and with some irony he said, 'You're trying to tell us that because Steven got himself into a mess there's going to be less for the rest of us, is that it, Granny?'

'Not quite, Alex, but there is one way I can help her and I want to know what you think about it. Financially it won't affect what will be yours after I've gone, but for the imme- diate future it might lift some of the burden she's been left with.'

'You're giving her money now?' Kate asked.

'No. They're living in a house that is far too large for them, the mortgage on it has been paid thanks to her father, but they can't afford to live in it. She still has a great many debts so the house could be sold, that should take care of some of them.'

'But they'd have to buy another, even if it's much smaller it will cost money. It's like jumping out of the frying pan into the fire,' Kate said.

Her grandmother replied, 'That's very true, Kate, so I've thought up another idea, I simply wanted to know what you'd think about it. If you agree with me now, I don't want problems of bitterness and jealousy in the future.'

'Jealousy?' Georgia said.

'Yes, it happens in families, particularly when the expectations are high and we think others have got more than their share.'

'So it is money, Mother,' Glenda said.

'No, Glenda, it's this house.'

They all stared at her in amazement until Alex said, 'Don't tell us you're selling this house to give the money to Julie. Really, Grandmother, that would be the most ridiculous thing I've ever heard of.'

'No, Alex, of course I'm not selling this house, I'll never leave here. This has been my home for sixty years, it will be my home until I die.'

'Then what?' he said curiously.

'Ask Julie and Barry to live with me here. She's still Mrs Chaytor and Barry's the only man in the family with my name.'

'But Alex is your grandson too,' Marian said. 'Surely he has some say in this, he's older than Barry, anyway.'

Charlotte looked at Alex enquiringly. 'Would you like to live in this house, Alex, is that why you're objecting?'

'I would hate to live in this house, Granny, and I'm not actually objecting, merely wondering how you'd get along living in the same house as Julie.'

'Do you think like a lot of people that the house is too big for me, that I'm an old woman living in a mansion believing in a world that no longer exists? You've often said you worry about me in this big place, Glenda, would you have been interested in moving in with me?'

'No, Mother, I like my home, it's small compared to this. I just often wished you would exchange this for something more like mine.'

'Actually it was Julie who thought I should look for something smaller.'

'And doesn't that tell you something, Granny?'

'Like what?'

'Oh, I rather think Julie fancied herself living here, with Steven of course when she thought he was affluent, living here with you might not be how she envisaged things, but we'll soon know. When are you thinking of telling her?'

'The sooner the better I think?'

'Well, I for one think it's wrong. Did Gloria put you up to it, Mother?' Georgia said adamantly.

'That's what I meant when I talked about resentment and jealousy. After all these years you can still be resentful about Gloria. I know she hasn't always been easy but she is one person who assures me she wants nothing from me, either now or in the future.'

'I know you've asked us all to come here, Mother, but you've already made up your mind. Isn't there an alternative or does it have to be this?'

'If I give her money I'm depriving all of you, but if I offer them a home she'll have the money from the sale of her house, and I can reassure myself that I've done my best.'

'It still isn't fair, Mother. After you've gone she'll have the house, which would normally have been sold and the money divided between us, now it will be Julie's house to do what she likes with.'

'It will be Barry's house. It will be up to him how he resolves things with his mother.'

'She'll still be doing very well, the house and her share of the money.'

'Not the money, Georgia. Steven has already had his share.'

'What do you mean by that?'

She had not meant to tell them. If he'd paid her back as he'd promised there need not have been any mention of it. She looked at Alex helplessly, and with a wry smile he said, 'I know about the loan, Granny. Uncle Steven was good at talking about money, where it came from, but not where it went. Granny lent him money because he was in debt. He's dead so we have to forget it, no amount of arguing among ourselves is going to bring him or the money back.'

Charlotte looked at Alex gratefully before she said, 'We have to talk some more, Alex. I was hoping you'd drive me there tomorrow evening if that's convenient.'

'Of course, Granny, I'll stay on for a while, perhaps you'll drive Marian home, Kate.'

'I thought we were all gathered so that we could all talk,' Georgia said.

'Mother's made up her mind,' Glenda said. 'I'm tired, it's time I went home.'

Alex smiled. 'Good idea, Aunt Glenda. Granny keeps a good cellar, would any of you like a drink before you leave, or shall we talk, Granny, and then enjoy a tipple on our own?'

'Oh, you make light of everything,' his mother said feelingly. 'I sometimes wonder how you put up with him, Marian.'

'Most of the time he exasperates me,' Marian said. 'I'll probably be in bed when you get home, don't forget to lock up.'

Looking at Charlotte, Alex smiled. 'The story of my life,' he said, and while the rest of them left the room she felt a tinge of sadness that all was not well in her grandson's marriage.

'I think we'll have that drink now,' she said with a smile.

'Yes, what'll it be? Sherry for you I think, G and T for me.'

As he poured the drinks Charlotte said, 'I know you're not happy with all this, Alex, but I have to do something, you do see that don't you.'

'Of course, I'm only concerned about how you're going to live with Julie.'

'Don't you like her?'

'I don't really know her. We've met at Christmas, weddings and funerals, birthday parties like yours, but although we chat I never really knew her. She talked about where they'd been, who'd they'd been with, where they were going next. It was all rather boring, Granny.'

'Then perhaps I must be prepared to be bored.'

'I rather think so.'

'I take it you don't want me to contribute anything to your meeting with Julie, simply to be there for you in case things take a turn for the worse.'

'Something like that, Alex.'

'Then I'll call for you around seven thirty and I'll inform them that we intend to visit. Another drink, Granny?'

'No thank you, Alex. I worry about you sometimes, you don't seem as close as you should be to Marian.'

'We soldier on.'

'But that's not how it should be. What's wrong with your marriage? It always seems so empty.'

'That's what it is: empty. We were young, we were told we

were right for each other, right background, a bit like the Bannisters really. It hasn't worked for us, I doubt if it's worked for them.'

'But Joyce always seems so happy.'

'That's Joyce, Granny. If the world fell apart there'd be a corner in it where Joyce could find her Utopia.'

'But not Marian.'

'I doubt it.'

'Surely you loved her once.'

'Maybe I never really knew what love was about. I'll see you tomorrow, Granny.'

'You haven't exactly stayed very long.'

'No, but I want to see Harrison in the Bull's Head. Perhaps he might be able to elaborate a little on his life. He was pretty entangled with my little sister you know, or maybe you don't.'

'I don't listen to gossip.'

'Good for you, Granny. It's never very reliable.'

Alex was witty and audacious, but she was glad of his company the next evening. Alex could be relied on to make light conversation even though she regarded Julie's melancholy as being a little too dramatic.

She had provided refreshments but said she didn't want anything – hadn't eaten in fact for several days, she was far too upset – to which Barry said, 'Oh, come on, Mother, it's sad for all of us but how long are you going to keep this up?'

She dissolved into tears and then Charlotte said firmly, 'We have to talk about a good many things, Julie. I thought your father might have been here.'

'I spoke to Grandfather this afternoon,' Barry said. 'He said he had the utmost respect for you, Granny, he felt sure you didn't need him.'

'Then perhaps I should tell you what I know, and what I can do to help resolve it. You're very short of money, Julie, as my son was in debt to a great many people and a lot of his money problems now rest on your shoulders.

'You know that I lent him money he didn't pay back, and I cannot dole out any more. I have other members of my family to think about, and after a great deal of reflection I really think the best thing I can offer is that you and Barry come to live with me at the manor.

'You can sell this house, the money you get for it will go some way to settling your debts, and it will be considerably more than if you were to purchase a smaller house.

'I know you may not like the idea, feel that living together would be foolish in case we didn't get on, but the manor is a very large house, you could have your own rooms, make some alterations and I'll be quite happy for you to do that. I don't want your answers today, just think about it and then tell me if you think it would work. You'll have the money for this house, you wouldn't be asked to contribute a great deal to live with me, and it's the only way I can think of to solve many of your problems.'

Julie was staring at her in some amazement while Barry stared at his mother curious as to how she would respond.

Julie had already forgotten some of her earlier dramatics as she said, 'But whenever something happens to you would the house have to be sold so that the money from it could be divided between the family?'

'The family will have my money, the house will be in Barry's name and matters to do with the house will be dealt with in my will.'

'In Barry's name!' Julie cried.

'Barry is my grandson, the only one to bear the Chaytor name. I don't know how long I'm going to live, none of us do, what I want to know now is whether you think this will work or not. Not today but when you've had time to think about it and possibly discuss it with your father and talk it over with Barry. Perhaps we should go now, Alex has a meeting to go to.'

As they drove away Alex said, 'Where is this meeting I'm supposed to be going to, Granny?'

'I thought we'd been there long enough, Alex. Julie seemed a bit stunned and they really do need to discuss it on their own.'

'And what do you think the outcome will be?'

'Alex, I don't know, she's possibly too upset to think straight at the moment and it's quite a big decision. Her father's a very astute man, and I'm sure he and Barry will be able to talk it through with her.'

They would both have been surprised if they could have heard Julie's words at that moment.

'Barry, it's the house, we're actually going to live at the house, what I've always wanted.'

'Mother, it's not our house.'

'It's as good as. It'll be yours one day, your name on the deeds, and the rest of them can do nothing about it.'

'How are you going to get along with Granny, why don't you think about that? Until she dies we'll be lodgers, or like she says we can make alterations, cut the house in half or have a flat there.'

She stared at him furiously. She'd do none of those things, she'd wanted that house for too long to even think of turning it into flats.

Nothing would be changed, none of the furniture, none of the ornaments and nothing in the gardens. She'd be Mrs Julie Chaytor living at the Chaytor manor house and she'd hold dinner parties and garden parties and the rest of the family could say what they liked.

She was remembering the look in Alex's eyes, cynical, as if he already knew how she would react, but she'd keep them waiting, make it seem as if she was unsure.

She wasn't very sure about Barry, he was a lot like Alex, and what would her father think about it all?

Her father knew that whatever he had to say wouldn't matter in the slightest; his daughter had made up her mind. They had discussed it most of the following morning and he had tried to advise her about the pros and cons. She would have none of it.

In her mercurial little mind she was already planning which bedroom she would have. Not Charlotte's of course, but one equally as grand, and they'd need more staff, surely Charlotte would see that.

After she had left him he thought about their conversation with a wry smile. He liked Mrs Chaytor, she was a charming, intelligent woman, and whatever Julie's plans were she would find herself facing a wily opponent.

Julie strolled through the city streets with her head in the clouds. She'd need some clothes for the week in France. She'd changed her mind about going and too much black could be quite demoralizing.

Twenty

Her mother had been so insistent that she should come up to London for several days and had seemed reluctant to offer a good reason.

'Oh, darling, we really don't see very much of each other and it does seem rather silly that we don't meet.'

'But you came to London three times last year and we didn't meet. Why is this time so different?'

'Because it is. Ludvig wants to see you: he's always saying we don't see nearly enough of you. You like him, don't you?'

'Very much.'

'Then humour me, darling.'

So this was it, afternoon tea at the Savoy and the place was crowded, although she did manage to find a table opposite the door so that she could see her mother when she chose to arrive.

She came at last, followed by a waiter carrying an array of parcels, smiling, apologizing for being late, and then charmingly thanking the waiter for his kindness.

'Isn't Ludvig with you?' Elvira asked.

'He's coming, darling. He had an appointment but he'll be here.'

'How was granny when you left her?'

'Much better. I think she's sorted things out with Julie. I just hope it works, that's all.'

'Why, what are they going to do?'

'Julie and the boy are hopefully going to live with her. There didn't seem any other solution.'

'Julie and Granny. Can you really see it working?'

'Julie's father has asked Mother if she can help. After all, it's my brother who's landed them in this mess: gambling, stupidity. The woman's no money except for what her father gives her and the boy has his education to think of. Julie's always had a hankering after the Manor. She'll love queening it there.'

'What did the others have to say?'

'I stayed well out of it, darling. They won't think Julie's Manor material. My sister Georgia was always a terrible snob.'

'What about Alex and the younger element?'

'Alex saw the logic of it. You know I rather like Alex. Did you never fancy him?'

'No. He always had the big brother element.'

'He was your cousin.'

'I know, but he used to call me "that cheeky kid" and I used to think he was insufferable. I like him now though. I thought he was the best of the bunch.'

'What sort of luggage have you brought?'

'Very little. How long have you booked me in for?'

'Ludvig made the arrangements. Three nights, I think.'

'It's really very generous of him, Mother.'

'Yes, dear, that's what I most like about him, his generosity, and so many other things I can't remember them all.'

'You never change, Mother.'

'Do you want me to change?'

'Why wish for something that isn't going to happen. Ah, here comes Ludvig now. Mother, you didn't tell me Max would be with him.'

'I wanted to surprise you, darling.'

Elvira rose to her feet to greet Ludvig and, after kissing her on both cheeks, he said, 'I've brought Max to meet you, Elvira. Didn't your mother tell you we were here to hear him play?'

'No, she didn't. That's wonderful, Max, I only ever heard you play in Vienna at Christmas time. You played the Max Bruche Violin Concerto. It's my favourite.'

'Then you will be happy to hear me play it tonight.'

The two men took their seats at the table and Elvira said, 'You've been so kind about Charlie, Max, she was so keen to get into the Conservatoire. I don't suppose you ever hear how she's progressing.'

'On the contrary, I hear excellent reports from Professor Steinberg. One day I hope she too will be entertaining vast audiences here and elsewhere.'

'Well, she really is the first musician we've had in the family,' Gloria said. 'I was taught to play the piano but I was never much good, and Elvira loves music but never wanted to play anything.'

'Then it must have been Max,' Elvira said, 'listening to him playing the violin. She would sit for hours outside the music room with a dreamy expression in her eyes. I never even thought that one day it would be something she wanted to do.'

She looked into her mother's eyes and saw the cynicism in them. Charlie had never inherited music from her mother's family. Did Charlie really owe something to the father she would never know?

Quickly, to ease the tension, Gloria said, 'As you can see, darling, I've been shopping. When I'm in Vienna I rave about the shops in London, and when I'm here I tell everybody how much I adore the shops in Vienna. When you've had tea I really think I should take these parcels upstairs and sort things out.'

'Here's your room key,' she said to Elvira. 'You're just along the corridor. You're not staying here, Max?'

'Actually, no. I'm staying at a smaller hotel. I prefer it.'

'But we shall see you after the concert and during the next few days?'

'Yes, I hope so, and then I must leave for America. I have concerts in New York and Boston.'

'What a busy man you are.'

'Oh, well, we'll leave these two to chat, Ludvig. I'm sure they have plenty to talk about.'

For a brief moment she read the panic in her daughter's eyes. What had they to talk about, two people who had seldom met over the years since her mother had married Max's uncle, and in the initial stages they had hardly been compatible.

Almost before Ludvig and Gloria had left the table there were people greeting Max, shaking his hand, telling him how much they were looking forward to hearing him play and he was introducing her as a friend rather than a relative.

Why had her mother put her in this impossible position? Throwing them together in the hope of better things, but Max was no fool, he would know what she was about and, making up her mind quickly, she consulted her watch saying, 'Please excuse me. I only arrived this morning and I do need to take things up to my room.'

The woman sitting next to her said gushingly, 'Oh, have we interrupted things? I'm so sorry, but whenever Max plays we have to come to hear him, we've met so often all over the world. Isn't that so, Max?'

Max smiled and agreed that it was, and Elvira said, 'That's perfectly all right. Do please sit here and carry on with your conversation.' But it was Max who said, 'Before you go, Elvira, I do need to talk to you about something. Would you excuse us? It's so long since we've met and we really haven't much time.'

The man standing with the woman said quickly, 'Oh, we're so sorry, we have hogged the limelight but we just felt we had to speak to you. Please forgive us.' He smiled down at Elvira and, taking his wife's arm in a firm grip, pulled her away.

Max smiled. 'I'm sorry about that, Elvira. It does happen, I'm afraid.'

'Well, of course, they are your loyal admirers after all.'

'A funny way to describe them, Elvira. They just love my music, they enjoy hearing me play.'

He was looking at her with a whimsical smile on his face and she was feeling immeasurably stupid, so stupid that even the most banal thoughts were coming out wrong.

'Your mother told me you've been to your grandmother's birthday party. Did it go well?'

'Oh, yes, Max. The party went well, but we had a death in the family and there were other things we hadn't bargained on.'

'And you, Elvira, did your past catch up with you, or didn't you care anymore?'

'I've run away too long, Max. I had to face it, however dangerous it might have been.'

'And was it? Was there anything left?'

'At first I wasn't sure. All at once I was surrounded by people I had known then, emotions I'd been trying to forget, and when I saw him again I was afraid.'

'That there might be something left?'

'Yes . . . and then there was nothing. It was as though a cloud that had been there so long had been suddenly blown away. No, there was nothing.'

In his smile all the memories came rushing back and she was a young girl again, just sixteen and the mother of a new baby, when Ludvig's nephew had visited them on his way back from China.

He was already an acclaimed violinist, he'd been charming but distant, uninterested in a young unmarried mother even if she was the daughter of his uncle's new wife. Over the years they had met frequently and she'd heard him play. Then her daughter had developed her love for music and the violin in particular and it had been Max who had coaxed her and eventually obtained her place at the conservatoire.

Two years ago she had spent two months with her mother in Austria and Max had been there recovering from a virus he had picked up on his travels. For the first time they had really got to know each other and she realized he was important in her life.

She'd known a few men who had shown an interest in her but always she'd measured them beside the boy she'd loved before when she'd been too young to understand love, a boy who had been meant for somebody else and what they had had together was simply a foolish experiment with sex.

She'd been aware Max had cared for her, but he had gone away on a round of concerts and except for a reserved, tender embrace she'd felt unsure, like that other time, disbelieving.

Now faced with his grave smile she said, 'But you're happy with your full life, Max?'

'To some extent but not enough, Elvira. Is it really enough to travel the world, play my music to ecstatic audiences who acclaim me, and return to my empty hotel bedroom and something incredibly lonely?'

He was looking at her so intensely that they could have been alone on a desert island instead of being surrounded by people chatting across their tables, with the laughter of children and background music. He reached out for her hand. 'We have to talk, Elvira, but not here, not now. I knew how I felt about you two years ago but it was too soon to convince you that the past was dead, that you could love and be loved.'

'I did love you, Max. In my cautious, troubled world I had to be sure that nothing of the past remained.'

'And are you sure?'

'Very sure.'

'Then I suggest we tell your mother and Ludvig. I suspect Ludvig might feel a little unsure but your mother has been expecting it.'

Elvira laughed. 'You know, Max, Granny used to say Mother would face a revolution and it wouldn't affect her, she'd return from Armageddon sublimely triumphant.'

To people watching them leave the hotel lounge they seemed like two people who had discovered Utopia, a beautiful girl, a handsome man, and not a care in the world.

Charlotte found it hard to believe that she was actually sitting in a beautiful room overlooking the Vienna Woods just before Christmas. Outside the windows the fields and trees were covered with snow and she could hear the sound of bells round the necks of horses bringing guests to join in the celebrations.

Her invitation had arrived with pleas for her to attend, but she'd really thought it impossible. Long telephone calls, utter disbelief from both Glenda and Georgia.

'Has Gloria forgotten how old you are, Mother?' Glenda had said, and Georgia had been even more scathing.

'Think about the weather, Mother, in December,' Georgia had said, 'and who is this man she's marrying, you've never even met Gloria's husband and now Elvira's marrying a foreigner.'

'Then perhaps I should make the effort to meet both of them,' she'd replied. But Georgia would have none of it.

'Really, Mother, I do think you shouldn't even entertain the idea. Send her a present, and your excuses, but think a little bit about yourself and us too. We shall have to look after you if you're ill after the journey and who would go with you? You certainly couldn't travel on your own.'

'Perhaps Uncle Nigel and Isabel would go with me.'

'And Uncle Nigel's only six years younger than you are. It's all quite ridiculous.'

Charlotte saw the logic of their arguments. She had told them nothing about Charlie and she was reluctant to do so now. In the end it was Alex who said, 'Do you really want to go to this wedding, Granny, because if you do I'll go with you.'

She'd stared at him in dismay before asking, 'But what about Marian, would she want to come, Alex? I'm sure if she would they'd make her very welcome.'

'No, Granny, she wouldn't. She'd find a thousand and one

excuses not to come, all of them good ones. The children, Christmas coming up, you name it, she'd find it.'

'Then really, Alex, I can't expect you to leave them at a time like this.'

'Granny, this is a one-off and I'm not exactly noted for being around all the time. Have you mentioned it to Julie?'

'No, not yet.'

'Then perhaps you should. I can see this wedding's very important to you, perhaps Julie should go – and Barry.'

'I'll think about it.'

He stared at her doubtfully before saying, 'You know, Granny, I have the feeling that you're troubled about something to do with this wedding; to be perfectly honest you've been troubled about something ever since Elvira and Gloria went back.'

'You were always too astute for your age, Alex.'

'I know, but I would like to know what's troubling you. Aren't you happy with this marriage, would you have preferred she'd married somebody from this country?'

'It has nothing to do with that.'

'Then enlighten me, Granny, I swear I'll not tell a soul if you don't want me to.'

She didn't answer immediately. She wanted to tell Alex but to tell him and not her daughters somehow seemed wrong. But he was looking at her so intensely she looked away, suddenly afraid and he said, 'Come on, Granny, if we're going to Vienna together shouldn't I know if there's cause for doubt?'

'Alex, I'm going to meet the one great-granddaughter I've never seen; she's called Charlotte after me but prefers to be called Charlie. Elvira's her mother.'

He stared at her in amazement before saying, 'So they're tying the knot later rather than earlier.'

'He's not the girl's father, Alex. I don't know who the father is. Elvira hasn't told anybody, not even her mother.'

'How old is the girl?'

'Nine.'

'So she had her after leaving here.'

'Yes. Alex, who do you think could be the girl's father – who was Elvira particularly with most of the time that last summer she was here?'

'Well, Elvira was a very popular girl, Granny, particularly with the boys. She rode well, she was fun, I'd say she was a man's girl.'

'If you had any idea you wouldn't tell me, Alex?'

'I couldn't tell you.'

'But you know now why I want to go to this wedding. I want to meet Charlie. She's a musician by the way, a violinist.'

'Gracious, we haven't had one of those in the family before.'

'No. Alex, promise me you won't say a word to anybody, not even to your mother.'

'Particularly to my mother.'

She smiled. 'I know she means well, but she can be a little overpowering.'

As Alex drove home that evening his thoughts were busy trying to remember that long-lost summer. He ate his meal with the family and decided not to tell Marian about his idea to accompany his grandmother to Vienna, perhaps later when the children had gone to bed and even then it wouldn't be easy.

Around nine o'clock he said, 'I think I'll go down to the Bull, Marian, there's somebody I need to see down there.'

She offered no objections and asked no questions so he decided to telephone Roland feeling pretty sure that he would be at home. Surprised, Roland said, 'Is it something important, Alex?'

'I just thought you might be interested that's all.'

'Very well, I'll stroll down there. Joyce is at her mother's, her mother isn't well.'

He couldn't really say why he thought it necessary to see Roland, after all it had always been Joyce and Roland, and yet during Elvira's visit in the summer he'd seen them chatting together, and he'd felt there was something, something irretrievably potent but regrettably lost.

Several men greeted him at the bar but after a few words he made his way to a corner table where Roland joined him minutes later.

They talked about work, some court case they were both involved with and, judging the moment right, Alex said lightly, 'I may be going to Vienna just before Christmas, Roland, a wedding, and I've half promised to escort my grandmother.'

'Really, whose wedding might that be?'

'Elvira's, to some Austrian, a quite famous violinist she's known for some time.'

He was watching Roland's expression and trying not to seem too curious. In that first moment there had been something, a sudden tightening of his hand on the glass he was holding, a momentary flicker in his eyes, and then the calm, steady Roland he knew best was back saying, 'Did none of you know in the summer that marriage was imminent?'

'No.'

'So you're going. Marian too?'

'You know Marian, she'll not want to go, and I don't think she'd be happy going. For one thing she hates flying and it's Christmas with school concerts and the like.'

'Of course.'

He knew that Roland was uneasy. He watched him consulting his watch and in the next moment he said, 'I rather think I'd better be getting off now, Alex. I promised to pick Joyce up at her mother's.'

Alex somehow knew that Joyce's mother wasn't the reason for him leaving. He didn't want to hear any more about the wedding, something painful that belonged to another time and place had sent him hurrying away.

He wouldn't tell Roland about her daughter, perhaps some day he might find out from another source, but if Elvira's daughter was indeed Roland's, the pain for that one brief moment was enough.

As he had thought, Marian raised every objection she could think of why he shouldn't even think of accompanying his grand-mother to Vienna.

'What about the school concerts, what about the children and your mother's Christmas party? Why doesn't she ask Julie and Barry to go with her, they live in the same house, so why you?'

He'd listened without saying very much; at the same time he was very certain that he would go to Vienna, Marian or no Marian.

Twenty-One

It was early on Christmas morning and Charlotte was already dressed and sitting at her dressing table when Milly arrived with her early cup of tea. The maid looked at her surprised and Charlotte said, 'Good morning, Milly, I decided to get up and dress. A merry Christmas to you, my dear.'

'Oh, thank you, ma'am, and to you too. Cook said if you were awake I should ask you how many there'd be for lunch?'

'I think there'll be twelve, Milly. One of my great-granddaughters has a very bad cold and won't be able to come, that means her mother won't be here either. I decided on a buffet lunch so no doubt the younger ones will be leaving before it gets dark.'

Lunch on Christmas Day had been held at the manor always, even when her children had their own homes. It was a tradition Charlotte had often wished they could alter, but somehow or other nobody had had the courage to suggest it.

Of course the children would want to go home to look at their Christmas presents, and even the older ones would have things to do in their own homes.

Barry was leaving early in the morning to go skiing in France, and she wouldn't mind in the least if Julie decided to visit her father. It would be nice to spend the evening alone, to relive six months of what had surely been the strangest year of her life. A great-granddaughter she had not known existed, the death of her only son, the marriage of her granddaughter and the arrival of Julie and Barry to live with her.

She couldn't believe that she had actually spent two weeks in Austria to witness the marriage of Elvira to a young man she hadn't even known existed.

How beautiful that house in the countryside had been with its views over snow-covered meadows and its backdrop of mountains. There had been music and sleigh bells, laughter and feasting in front of roaring wood fires, and she'd sat listening to Charlie talking about her violin, her ambition, and all the time thinking how beautiful she was, and how much she reminded her of Gloria, the daughter she had somehow never really known.

Elvira and Max had departed early for America where Max had concerts to perform, and Charlie had said wistfully that one day she wanted to play for vast audiences and would great-grandmother be able to be there.

She had looked round that beautiful room warm with fire-light and seen Alex surrounded by a bevy of pretty girls, laughing, flattering and enjoying every moment of it, along with Barry who had danced with the same beautiful girl all evening.

How mundane it would all seem when they returned to reality and how Julie had loved being there at a function she would probably dine out on for some considerable time.

As she had sat watching the dancers, a tall white-haired man had stood before her, smiling gently and asking her to dance.

Surprised, she had said, 'Gracious, I must have forgotten how to dance, it's been so long. Will you forgive me if I don't?'

Softly, he said, 'It is a long time since I danced also Mrs Chaytor, shall we share our insecurities together?'

So they had danced together, and people cheered as they circled the room and she remembered how to dance.

He was charming and he danced well, saying with a smile, 'I am Ludvig's father, it is so right that we dance together.'

Charlotte was sure that Alex would never let her forget those few moments when she'd been young again.

And now it was Christmas Day and those two weeks of fairy tale were a memory.

Julie and Barry had erected a large Christmas tree in the hall and arranged around it were a great many gaily wrapped parcels for both the family and the servants. After lunch there would be the usual ceremony of handing the gifts round. The house-keeper and the rest of them would be there, all smiles and gratification and then they would be thinking of what to talk about and it would be the children who broached the question of going home.

Julie was still intent on arranging the parcels, greeting Charlotte with a smile and a kiss on her cheek before saying, 'I hope they all get here on time, fortunately it's a buffet so there's nothing to spoil.'

'Have you decided to see your father, Julie?'

'It will depend on the weather. I don't want to drive if it's icy.'

'Of course not.'

'Barry's off in the morning. I really don't see why he has to go quite so soon, it would have been better if he'd left it until the New Year.'

'I suppose it's something they're all agreed on.'

'Oh yes, it is, but I can't think that their families are all happy about it.'

Charlotte left her to go into the dining room where the buffet meal was set out on the huge dining table. It looked festive and most professional, and Charlotte wondered why she hadn't had it like this for her birthday instead of all the fuss, but she knew she wouldn't say anything to Glenda.

Joining her Julie said, 'I hope the children don't run riot all over the place, that little girl of Alex's is such a bossy child – she lords it over the others.'

Charlotte decided to say nothing and after a while Julie said, 'Are the Bannisters coming today?'

'No. Don't they always go to Joyce's parents for Christmas, why would they come here?'

'Oh, it was just a thought.'

Charlotte was remembering Roland at her birthday party, his conversations with Elvira, how they had looked together, the way he had smiled. Oh but no, of course it had never been Roland. Roland had always been with Joyce, they'd been destined for each other. He was naturally kind, charming, not the sort of boy Elvira with her frivolous sense of humour would ever have looked at.

She really had to stop thinking which young man in the vicinity could be Charlie's father. When she'd mentioned Roland to Alex he'd laughed saying, 'Granny, you're surely not going to spend the rest of your life dreaming up a father for Charlie.'

'No, I'm simply asking if you think Roland could be the one.'

'Never in a thousand years, Granny. He's far too staid and circumspect ever to have fancied Elvira or she him.'

'Even as a boy?'

'I sometimes wonder if Roland's ever been a boy. Joyce is a lot like Marian. She has kept Roland pristine and perfect; I was too far gone for Marian to have had that effect on me.'

'Sometimes opposites attract, Alex.'

'That's true, but look at the man she's married: Austrian, a musician, completely different from any lad she'd have known around here.'

'I don't think it's any use talking to you.'

'No, it isn't, Granny, not about something as incongruous as Elvira and Roland Bannister.'

She smiled. 'Perhaps in a way I wanted it to be him, not one of the other boys she went around with.'

'The boys she went around with were rather like me, mad on horses, not opposed to gambling and too much money in their pockets, usually with the added appendage of some girl or other their families wanted for them. Like Marian and me.'

'You have a successful career, Alex. I worry when you talk about you and Marian, surely it hasn't all been wasted.'

'No, Marian got what she largely expected. A husband with a lucrative career, money, a nice home and a certain prestige. Maybe she wasn't interested in anything beyond that.'

'They'll be asking a lot of questions about our time in Austria, Alex, though nothing about Charlie yet.'

'But what about Julie, is she likely to say anything?'

'No, because she doesn't know anything.'

'Gracious, how ever have you managed to keep that under wraps.'

'It wasn't too difficult. Julie was having a wonderful time dancing with . . . those all-too-charming Austrians and Barry seemed entirely taken with that girl.'

He laughed. 'It sounds as though they're beginning to arrive. I expect Aunt Glenda and her tribe will be the first.' There seemed to be a procession of them all bearing gifts of chocolates and biscuits, warm winter gloves and neckwear and, to Charlotte's dismay, a collection of Christmas fare.

The fact that the table was already piled high with food

failed to discourage them and it was Julie who said, 'Whatever shall we do with all this food, there's enough to feed a regiment.'

'I've told the servants to take whatever they want home to their families after they've looked after themselves.'

'We never used to have buffets, we always had the family sitting round the table.'

Julie was right. Charlotte had memories of Christmas Day lunches when the table was weighed down with crystal and silver, when the attire they had worn had been formal and when staff and family alike had gathered together in the hall to receive their Christmas presents.

Now the children were running around the room screaming with laughter and in the morning they would sigh over the state of the room and wish the old days were back.

'Whoever suggested a buffet meal?' Glenda asked plaintively.

'I rather think it was Marian, and your girls said the children would prefer it and that the other one was too formal.'

'Your servants will be left with all the mess. We all normally leave around three thirty.'

Glenda didn't know that her mother was looking forward to that. They would go to relatives, to Marian's parents and Glenda's daughters' in-laws'. It was then that Charlotte would find time to sit in front of her fire to watch television or read some book or other. Time too to remember all those other times, and probably resurrect others better forgotten.

She shivered a little in spite of the heat in the room and Julie said, 'Are you cold, Mother? If you are I'll go upstairs and get your shawl.'

Georgia was quick to say, 'I'll get it, I do know this house you know, I lived here until I married.'

Julie stared at her angrily but it was Barry who said, 'You don't live in it now, Aunt Georgia.'

They were constant these little reminders that Julie was there by invitation, not by birth, and while Georgia stalked across the room Charlotte said to Julie, 'Try not to mind, Julie. If it's not you she's getting at its probably Gloria or somebody else. She can't help it.'

'She's always like that, I can't really stand her.'

'I know. She does have some good points, I'm just trying to think what they are, dear.'

Julie and Barry laughed, and somehow the tension was relieved until Georgia came back with the shawl. She placed it round her mother's shoulders and said, 'You've changed the furniture around in your bedroom, Mother, I can't think why.'

'I asked Barry to move one or two things. The lighting was better and my eyes aren't what they were.'

'Any more alterations?'

'Possibly. Does Kate never advise you on things you could do to your property – I'm sure she does.'

'Well, Kate won't be here much longer, she's going to work in London, a very prestigious move for her.'

'So you'll be on your own.'

'Of course, but unlike some people I shall survive on my own without needing to move into somebody else's house.'

Quietly Charlotte said, 'Georgia, this is Christmas Day. I was hoping we could get through it without these silly resentments cropping up all the time, and largely I might add from you.'

'I feel I have a lot of resentments to think about at the moment, Mother. Kate is leaving to live in London so I'll be on my own, I'm not exactly looking forward to that.'

'But would you have been happy to move in with me, Georgia? I think not.'

'I don't know. I'm all at sixes and sevens at the moment, Mother.'

Charlotte looked towards the window where Kate had joined Alex. He was looking down at her with quiet amusement and Kate said, 'You heard mother saying I was moving to London, Alex. I don't suppose it was any surprise to you.'

'No, talk's been going around the circuit. I think you're sensible to move on.'

'Sensible?'

'Why yes, you were sailing very close to the wind and now Dora's back, but hardly likely to forget why she went away.'

'It was never serious.'

'From your point of view no, from his I rather think it was.'

'You think you know everything, don't you, Alex?'

'Not everything, Kate, but you were asking for trouble, both of you.'

She favoured him with a long, slow look before walking away and Marian joined him saying, 'What time are we leaving? Mother'll be expecting us around five and I need to call home.'

'Can you really face another meal, Marian?'

'Well, we'll have to show some enthusiasm, you know what a lot of trouble she goes to. What had Kate to say?'

'Very little actually, just her move to London.'

'I'm glad she's going actually, it was all getting rather embarrassing.'

'Not for you surely?'

'Well, she is your sister.'

'I'll just have a word with Granny, then we'll make our departure, it might conceivably start the ball rolling.'

'We're thinking of leaving soon, Granny, then perhaps the others will get the incentive. The buffet was super, I really don't think we should be going on to another banquet.'

'I hope everybody has enjoyed it, the servants went to a lot of trouble.'

'What will you do with all the food that's left?'

'The staff will have it, and take some to their families. I've told them to take everything they want.'

'Didn't we used to meet for the exchange of Christmas presents?'

'They're all around that tree in the hall . . . no more old-time memories, Alex, something far less formal suits me now.'

He bent down to embrace her. 'You'll enjoy the rest of the evening, Granny, you've a lot to think about, a lot to remember and a lot to grieve about.'

'Yes. Poor Steven, I do remember that he was a nice boy, full of high spirits and I loved him very much. You're right, Alex, I shall have a lot to remember after you've all gone.'

'I don't suppose you've heard from Gloria.'

'I have. She telephoned me early this morning from Vienna. They're going to the mountains – skiing. Elvira is with Max in America where he has concerts to perform and Charlie is going with her grandmother to the mountains.'

'It would seem Gloria is being a better grandmother than she ever was a mother.'

Charlotte smiled. 'Time alters many things, Alex, and sometimes for the better.'

'I'm sure you're right.'

'I can't help it, Alex, but when I go to church, when I go
anywhere I look around for some young man who might be
Charlie's father. I don't care that she hasn't married him, I'd
just like to know who he is, whether he's kind and gentle,
considerate and a good husband and father to whoever he
married.'

'Maybe he isn't married.'

'But did they meet when she came here, did he remember,
was there anything left of that other time?'

'I think you should forget it, Granny, it's all over and done
with, hopefully for both of them.'

'And will it be any better for you and Marian? Think of the
children, Alex.'

She looked up into his face, a remote, handsome face and eyes
that were filled with the usual cynicism. Suddenly she reached
out for his hand saying breathlessly, 'Alex, it wasn't you with
Elvira?'

He threw back his head and laughed so that those around
them turned to stare at them, then he said, 'Granny, you're clutching
at straws and I can assure you in all honesty that I never even
thought that Elvira would fancy me or I fancy her. Before you
drift into any more realms of fantasy I'm going to find my wife
and children and get out of here.'

He was gripping her hands, looking at her sternly, and at last
she said, 'I'm sorry, Alex, I'm a silly, foolish old woman. Please
forget I ever said something so foolish.'

He bent to kiss her cheek, and then the others were gathering
round to say their farewells.

Glenda looked at her uncertainly before she said, 'Mother, it's
Boxing Day tomorrow. I think you should come with me to the
girls' party – you mustn't be on your own.'

'Darling, I need to be on my own. I have letters to write,
books to read, and I've already eaten far more than is good for
me this festive season. I'll see you before New Year but please
don't even think you're neglecting me. I need to be on my own
these next few days.'

She wasn't sure how much Glenda believed her, but then Kate was saying, 'I'll see you before I go to London, Granny, we're going to Alex's tomorrow, I believe you're invited.'

'I was, and I declined, dear. Alex will tell you why.'

'Oh well, I'll be sure to see you before I leave.'

'Your mother will be very lonely without you.'

'Mother will never be lonely, Granny. She's got a multitude of things to keep her happy.'

'I'm sure she has.'

Their cars formed quite a procession down the long drive and Alex's car was the last to leave.

As she went back into the hall she heard the telephone ringing from the library and she went to answer it, not surprised to hear her brother's voice saying, 'We just want to wish you all the best Charlie. Is the tribe still there?'

'No, they've just left.'

'So you're on your own.'

'Yes, Nigel, and I really don't mind. It's been pretty hectic and now I can relax, read the book Isabel sent me for Christmas.'

The servants were busy clearing away the remains of the buffet and after congratulating them on their efforts she invited them to take their presents from under the tree, then she escaped into her favourite sitting room where the fire glowed halfway up the chimney and the lamps had already been turned on.

She stood looking out of the window for a while at the red sky and the light flurry of snow that swept across the grass. There would be so much pleasure in remembering days that had fled tinged too with sadness and the emptiness of regret.

Annie O'Connor stood in her garden searching for her cat. Well wrapped up against the raw wind she could see the line of cars sweeping towards the gate and she waited until they had all driven past. She had received a smile and wave from the driver of the last car and a cheerful wave from the two children sitting in the back seat. Master Alex, she thought, he'd always been the handsome cheerful one.

As she looked up the road she saw that a small brown dog was bounding towards her – Molly Woods' Border Terrier – and she gave a smug little smile of satisfaction.

There was something to be said for living in the last cottage nearest to the manor gates. Never mind 'my sister Rose', she was the one to see who came and who went.

She held open the gate for her visitor, and with a smile more welcoming than usual said, 'I'll put the kettle on, Molly, it's a cold afternoon.'